THE SLEEPING AND THE DEAD

Further Titles by Ann Quinton from Severn House

A LITTLE GRAVE

THE SLEEPING AND THE DEAD

Ann Quinton

This first world edition published in Great Britain 1994 by
SEVERN HOUSE PUBLISHERS LTD of
9–15 High Street, Sutton, Surrey SM1 1DF.
First published in the USA 1994 by
SEVERN HOUSE PUBLISHERS INC., of
425 Park Avenue, New York, NY 10022.

British Library Cataloguing in Publication Data
Quinton, Ann
  Sleeping and the Dead
  I. Title
  823.914 [F]

  ISBN 0-7278-4668-X

For Janet and Andrew with my love

Typeset by Hewer Text Composition Services, Edinburgh.
Printed and bound in Great Britain by
Hartnolls Ltd, Bodmin, Cornwall.

Infirm of purpose!
Give me the daggers. The sleeping and the dead
Are but as pictures; 'tis the eye of childhood
That fears a painted devil.

Macbeth Act 2 scene 2

I should like to thank the many people who helped me with research for this book, in particular Jenny Cryer, Simon Grew, John Pardy and Jeremy Trowell.

CHAPTER 1

The body was gracefully disposed on the grassy bank beneath a canopy of trees. It was the body of a woman, a young woman. She lay on her back, one knee drawn up exposing a gold embroidered slipper, her arms spread out in gentle abandonment. Her long, straight, silky blonde hair was spread out like a fan over its green pillow. There were no visible marks of violence; no blood or wounds or contusions. She could have been asleep except that her eyes, deep blue and fringed by curving chestnut lashes, stared sightlessly up at the branches overhead.

She was dressed in a velvet and brocade gown, low-cut in the bodice, long tight sleeves ending in a point over the backs of her hands, full flowing skirts and a jewelled belt slung low around her hips. It was a gown such as Arthur's Guinevere might have worn, or the Lady of Shallot. It could have been a scene from a medieval tapestry. There should be stylised flowers crouching in the mossy grass; golden fleur-de-lys perhaps and the red and white roses of Lancaster and York amongst the daisy stars. One expected to see a lion couchant in homage at her feet and a milky-white unicorn emerging from the trees.

However, it was not a unicorn that burst through the foliage scattering leaves and twigs, but a young, excited fox-terrier. He pulled up sharply, haunches quivering, when he was confronted by the body; then he pounced and started to worry the swathe of golden hair. A voice calling his name came faintly through the trees and he paused and listened; then, as the voice came again more insistently, he snatched at the hair and trotted off, the wig trailing like yellow seaweed from his mouth. Behind him,

1

the skull gleamed like a monstrous egg fallen from its nest, ivory white and naked.

The call came through to Felstone Police Headquarters as Detective Inspector James Roland was preparing to shut up shop and take an unscheduled lunchbreak at home with his family. Instead, he made a hasty phonecall to his wife and collected his sergeant, Patrick Mansfield, from the CID general room.

"Something's come up. A body has been found in Holgate Wood over at Saxton."

"Murder?"

"Sounds very much like it. The chap who found it was exercising his dog and apparently the dog turned it up. He rang the Station and Simpson, who took the call, said he was in a fair old taking and not making much sense. All he got out of him was the fact that it was a young woman and she was lying on a bank beneath trees on the southern edge of the wood. Simpson told him to wait for us by the old lichgate which is in that area not far from the phone-box he was calling from."

"I thought it was too good to be true" said Mansfield as they went out to Roland's car. "I actually told Jean I would be home early today. We're supposed to be going to a 'do' at one of the neighbours; a barbecue."

"I wouldn't have thought that was quite your scene."

"You're right, but Jean was looking forward to it and she twisted my arm."

Patrick Mansfield was a tall, burly man in his forties with close-cropped grizzled hair and deep-set dark eyes. Even in plain clothes he looked a typical policeman of the old school; solid, reliable, an excellent back-up to his more volatile colleague who had a reputation for unorthodox methods. The fact that Mansfield was nearly thirteen years older than his superior bothered neither man. The detective sergeant was content with his rank and station and although James Roland, tall, dark and handsome as a romantic hero, made no secret of his ambitions he intended climbing the ladder with Mansfield at his side. The two men made

2

a good team and had solved several tricky cases in recent years.

As he manoeuvred through the lunchtime traffic and headed out towards the open countryside Roland wondered just what was waiting for them at Saxton. On the face of it, it was not the sort of place where one expected to encounter a murder or any sort of violence. Whereas he and Mansfield lived in a village to the north of the busy port of Felstone which had witnessed its share of crime, Saxton was situated on the western side of the narrow peninsular wedged between the two rivers and was a throwback to an earlier, feudal age. Until well into this century the entire village had been owned by the Cardwell family, lock, stock and barrel. The Cardwells had lived at Holgate House and the whole population had been employed on the vast estate that had encompassed some of the richest farming land in Suffolk as well as Holgate Woods and extended river frontage. After the death of the last surviving Cardwell, Lady Eugenie, the estate had been sold up and the hall was now home to a minor boys' public school.

There was very little sign nowadays of the labouring classes that had served the Cardwells. The old houses had either been demolished to make way for luxury, executive-type properties or been "improved" and upgraded as holiday cottages and second homes. Wealthy people with wealthy belongings now predominated in Saxton and the re-distribution of this wealth was a more likely crime than violent death.

Mansfield echoed these thoughts as they drove past landscaped gardens resplendent with flowers and shrubs and statuary.

"If it *is* murder it will upset a lot of the locals; really lower the value of their properties."

"Do I detect a touch of sour grapes?"

"No way. I prefer Wallingford, at least it's a proper village, not . . ." Mansfield groped for words.

"Stuck in a time warp?" suggested Roland. "I know what you mean. It's a throw-back to feudal days when the squire ruled the roost."

"Is there a local big-wig these days?"

"I believe there's a retired naval chap who fancies himself in the role. It's the next turning on the right, isn't it?"

"Yes, past that antiques place."

An elderly man was waiting by the lichgate, a dog at his side. He was holding what looked like a length of cream-coloured material. As they got closer this material resolved itself into a hank of hair and for a few horrid seconds Roland wondered if the victim had been scalped. He pulled off the road and killed the engine and the man moved towards them as they got out of the car, a look of relief settling on his worried, pinched face.

"Detective Inspector Roland and Detective Sergeant Mansfield. Are you the man who phoned the Station? Who found a body?"

"Yes. At least it was Trixie here who found her." The dog wagged its tail on hearing its name and jumped up at Roland.

"Down, Trixie, there's a good girl" said her master.

"Your name?

"Stewart Carson. It's . . . it's horrible! I just can't believe it . . ." The man was twisting the hair round and round in his hands and as it rippled from his bony wrists Roland could see that it was a wig.

"It must have been a terrible shock finding a body. Just tell us in your own time exactly how it came about and take us to the place."

"I was walking Trixie through the woods and she ran off." The man gestured to the backdrop of trees and started to walk towards them with a stumbling gait, Roland and Mansfield at his heels. "I called and whistled and then she came bounding back to me with this in her mouth." He held out the wig. "I couldn't think how she'd got hold of it and I scolded her and wondered how on earth I was going to give it back without causing the owner terrible embarrassment. I followed Trixie into the wood and then I saw her and knew something awful had happened. She was lying there . . . the way she was lying there . . . I knew she was dead!" He turned back to the

4

two detectives. "I mean Why? We all knew she was desperately ill but why did someone have to kill her!"

"Wait a moment, Mr Carson, are you saying you Know the victim?"

"That's what I've been telling you, isn't it? It's Alison Barnard!" Seeing the blank look on the detectives faces he paused and rubbed his hand across his brow. "I'm sorry, I'm not making much sense, am I? It's the shock."

"Take it easy. Who is Alison Barnard?"

"She's one of the Barnard twins, they live in the village. She's got leukaemia . . . that's why she wears a wig. The chemotherapy made her hair fall out . . .

Comprehension began to dawn as Roland exchanged glances with his sergeant. Perhaps the woman was in a coma or had died from natural causes and not been murdered after all.

"Are you sure she's dead?" enquired Mansfield, ducking as a branch whipped back in his face. "Did you touch her?"

"Only her hand. It was cold and stiff and her eyes were staring horribly . . ." The man gulped.

"Right. How much further is it?"

"Just through there." He gestured to the right where the trees thinned out and the ground sloped away to an unseen stream. "Do you need me?" He hung back reluctant to go any further.

"Stay with us please but put your dog on a lead."
Stewart Carson produced a lead from his pocket, snapped it on Trixie's collar and followed the two detectives unwillingly.

At first sight of the body Roland experienced a sense of déjà-vu. There was something theatrical and contrived about the scene, it could have been a tableau from a play; Shakespeare perhaps, except that the leading lady had managed to lose her hairpiece. His eyes travelled over the shining white skull and the glassy blue eyes. Well, she certainly wasn't asleep. He dropped down beside the body and scrutinized it carefully, looking for signs of violence before reaching out for the pulse.

Stewart Carson looked wildly about him, willing to concentrate on anything rather than the still figure stretched out on the bank. He didn't see the extraordinary expression on Roland's face as he straightened up and beckoned to his sergeant and at first he didn't take in what the detective was saying.

"Alison Barnard isn't dead."

"What do you mean?"

"This isn't Alison Barnard."

"I don't understand . . .?"

"Come closer Mr Carson and take a proper look. This isn't a real body, it's a model, a waxwork."

"Oh my God! Thank the Lord for that! I really thought she was dead!"

Roland tapped his fingers against the pale, curved cheek. "Why did you think it was this Alison Barnard? It's a dummy out of a shop window in some sort of period costume."

"Not a shop." The man was recovering his aplomb. "It's from Holgate Lodge. She worked there when she wasn't painting. Do you know the place? It's run as a sort of museum dedicated to the Pre-Raphaelites. I thought she was wearing one of the costumes . . ."

Then Roland realized why he had felt something familiar tugging at his memory when he had first viewed the body. He did know Holgate Lodge, he had been there with Ginny, his wife. Holman Hunt, one of the leading Pre-Raphaelite painters, had owned Holgate Lodge at one point in his life and he and other members of the Brotherhood had gathered there from time to time. In recent years, the property had been acquired by a trust and set up as a shrine to the Pre-Raphaelite movement. He remembered that in many of the rooms tableaux had been set up depicting some of the more famous paintings. This waxwork effigy came from one of these.

"Yes, I do" he answered Carson, "and that would account for the costume, but I still don't understand why you thought this was Alison Barnard; granted it's very lifelike."

"I'm sure this is her wig" said the man stubbornly, "and

6

it's been put there to make it look like Alison. You don't know what a turn it's given me!"

"You mean as some sort of malicious joke? But why should anyone do that?"

"I don't know. It's grotesque . . . horrible." The man shuddered. "Look, I'm sorry I bothered the police, but I really thought it was her and she was dead . . ."

"Don't worry, Mr Carson, I'm only too glad you were mistaken. Tell us about this young woman; I take it she lives in Saxton?"

"Yes, in the Old Bake-house. She and her sister Lindsey have converted it into a studio. Lindsey is a potter and Alison dabbles in painting when she's not helping out at Holgate Lodge. I mean, she used to. Some months ago she was diagnosed as having leukaemia. Quite upset the local community it did, she's well liked. Anyway, she's on a course of chemotherapy which seems to be holding the disease at bay . . . but of course she lost her hair."

"I see. Well, I'll take charge of that, shall I?" Roland took the wig from the man who looked doubtfully back at the dummy.

"What about that?"

"We'll sort it out. You can carry on with your walk, but give my sergeant your address in case we need to get in touch with you again."

After he had gone Mansfield turned to Roland. "What an extraordinary thing, what do you make of it?"

"If it is this Alison Barnard's wig and it's been used to perpetuate a rather nasty practical joke it leaves a bad taste in my mouth. It sounds as if someone has got it in for her."

"So what do we do? It's hardly a case for the police."

"I think we'll go and see her and return her property. Put the dummy in the back of the car."

They found the Old Bake-house easily. It was in the main street and there was a sign above the door announcing it was the Saxton Pottery. One of the front bays had been converted into a shop window and contained a display of grey and blue pottery and in the background a couple

7

of paintings were propped up on easels. Roland parked the car a little further down the road and the two men walked back to the house. The doorbell was answered by a well-built young woman with dark curly hair who bore no resemblance to the model languishing in the back of Roland's car. She looked at them enquiringly and then caught sight of the wig.

"Oh, you've found it – thank goodness! But where was it? And who are you?"

"We're police officers. Are you Miss Lindsay Barnard?"

"Yes, but . . ."

"This wig belongs to your sister?"

"Yes, it went missing earlier. But I don't understand . . .?"

"Perhaps we could come in?"

"Yes, I think you had better." She took them into a room that led off the front hall. It was on the opposite side of the front door to the one that displayed her craft, but although it was obviously a sitting room it contained an inordinate amount of bowls and plates and dishes, all in the same blue and grey pottery. Roland wondered how successful a potter she was and if she sold much of her work.

"Is your sister in?"

"She's upstairs resting, she's not very well."

"So I understand. Let me explain why we're here."

Roland told her briefly what had happened and she gaped in astonishment.

"But how extraordinary! Why should anyone do that?"

"How did your sister come to lose her wig – does she usually wear it most of the time?"

"Yes, she's embarrassed to let people see her without hair though it is starting to grow back again. But it has been so hot this last week that when we're here on our own she takes it off. She left it draped over a chair near the kitchen window. We thought at first that the wind had snatched it, but there IS no wind today."

"It would have been easy for someone to have reached inside the window and taken it?"

"Yes, I suppose so." The girl looked at them doubtfully. "Did you really think that waxwork was Alison?"

8

"Mr Carson, who found it, certainly thought so."

"That old busybody! He used to teach us you know."

"Who used to teach us?"

The young woman who drifted into the room was as unlike her twin as it was possible to be. She was slim and pale, waif-like, and her eyes were the same cornflower blue as the glass versions that had stared up at Roland a short while ago in Holgate Wood. A blue and white scarf was knotted round her head, Mammy fashion.

"Stewart Carson. Look, your wig has been found." A light blush flooded Alison Barnard's face and quickly receded leaving it chalky white. Roland wondered how to explain their presence without upsetting her but her sister had no such qualms.

"These are policemen, Allie. Your wig was found in the wood on the head of one of the models from Holgate Lodge. Stewart Carson saw it lying there and thought it was you and you'd been killed and he called the police."

"Killed? But . . . but why should he think that? I don't understand . . ."

Roland explained the situation for the second time and she echoed her sister.

"Why should anyone do that?"

"I have no idea, Miss Barnard. It looks as if you're the victim of a bizarre joke. It IS your wig?" In reply, she untied the scarf and eyed the two men defiantly as she slipped it off her head. Roland saw that what at first seemed to be a bald head was actually covered in a fine blonde down that put him in mind of day-old chicks. Beside him, his sergeant shuffled in embarrassment. She picked up the wig, moved over to the mirror hanging above the mantelpiece and adjusted it carefully over her head. When she turned back to them her likeness to the dummy corpse now tucked away in Roland's car boot was startling.

"I can understand why Mr Carson thought it was you. I believe you work at Holgate Lodge where the model comes from?"

"I help out on a part-time basis when I'm not painting. I haven't been in much over the last few months . . ." she made a little droll moue with her mouth. ". . . but I'm much better now and I intend buckling down and relieving Anthea again."

"Anthea being?"

"Anthea Campbell-Haigh. She's the widow of Professor Campbell-Haigh. He was an expert on the Pre-Raphaelites and after he died she took over the task of completing the book he had been writing on them. She combines that with being the curator of the Lodge."

"I see. Well, perhaps she can throw some light on it. I'm sorry we've disturbed you but thankful it's not a police affair. I wish all my cases were as easily solved."

"Please, will you stay and have some tea?" asked Lindsay Barnard, "I was just about to put the kettle on."

Aware that Mansfield was willing him to say yes and feeling hot and thirsty himself, Roland accepted the invitation. They sat down on the chairs offered and Lindsay went through to the kitchen. Left on her own with the two men, Alison seemed to wilt and retreat into her own world. She leaned back on the sofa and tapped her fingers listlessly on the arm, gazing fixedly through the open french doors onto the stone terrace that shimmered in the heat. Roland wondered how ill she really was. It was tragic for someone of that age to be struck down with a potentially mortal illness and it must be almost equally distressing for her twin sister. He sought to engage her attention.

"May I see some of your paintings?"

"You may," she drew her gaze back to him, "but I doubt if you'll appreciate them." She pointed to the alcove set in the wall overlooking the garden and he saw a small pile of canvases stacked against the window seat. He went over and looked through them and his sergeant peered over his shoulder.

At first sight they appeared to be traditional landscapes; local scenes painted in a competent, detailed manner, but when he looked closely at what seemed to be bland, pleasant compositions, they took on sinister depths. The trees and houses acquired a life of their own. It was not quite Arthur Rackham; there were no actual twisted, macabre faces peeping out of the knotted bark and gnarled beams, but it was hinted at, and the painted shadows encroached black and curdled on the painted landscapes like malevolent beings. Roland found himself at a loss for words and wondered if his sergeant had noticed anything odd about the paintings. Mansfield had, and remarked later that he wondered if she had always painted like that or whether the morbid effect was a result of her illness.

"Are you interested in art?" Her faint yet precise voice challenged him.

"My wife used to be Head of Art at Felstone High School so some of it brushed off on me. I can see you've been trained, your technique is superb."

"But you don't like them?"

"I'm not sure I'd like to live with them" admitted Roland. She gave an ironic little smile as she turned the canvases to the wall and went off to help her sister in the kitchen.

Eileen Dexter looked out of the window onto the deserted street and sighed. It was pointless really, staying open on Thursday afternoons. It was early closing day in nearby Felstone so why bother to keep her antiques shop in Saxton open? Besides, business had dropped off considerably in the last few months. Not that that worried her; she had made her penny and could retire comfortably, a prospect that she was viewing with increasing enthusiasm.

She got up from behind her desk and strolled through to the back of the shop to where the showroom opened out into a spacious conservatory which, in turn, led to a small walled garden complete with pool and fountain. A quaint two-storey building at the bottom, that had been the original stable block was now converted to house the collection of old books and first editions she had accumulated. The conservatory and garden were crammed with flowers and foliage and climbing shrubs and amongst this floral jungle were the Victorian garden ornaments she specialized in.

11

Shy cherubs and tactfully draped stone maidens peeped out from behind fern and flower and wrought-iron seats and urns and troughs fought for space. There was even a little gazebo in the far corner complete with hanging baskets housing a jardinière of quite awful Victorian floridness and vulgarity. Her assistant, Mark Copley, was at that moment in the process of watering these hanging baskets and the bright green plastic watering-can he was wielding struck an incongruous note amongst his surroundings.

If Mark had his way this part of the premises would be used to display arts and crafts. He had long been urging her to diversify and combine a craft gallery with the antiques but she disliked the idea, seeing in her mind's eye the rows of pottery and china and bowls of over-perfumed pot-pourri where her beloved Victoriana now lurked. If she retired and passed on the goodwill of the business to him she knew what alterations he would make but maybe she would sell out completely and move away from the district. There were offers pending and Mark was quite capable now of standing on his own two feet and making his own way. She had given him a good start, taking him on as her assistant and apprentice in memory of his grandmother, who had brought him up and had been one of her oldest friends. He had shown an aptitude for the business, learning quickly and assimilating her knowledge of the trade and was particularly interested in the second-hand book trade. He spent hours browsing amongst the collection and although they maintained the fiction that he was engaged in repairing and cleaning the tatty, dog-eared volumes she knew that much of the time he spent in the old stables was involved in reading and devouring the contents. Well, good luck to him. It didn't hurt to specialize and maybe he would end up as an antiquarian bookseller; better that than pushing craft kitsch.

She watched him as he put down the watering-can and started to dead-head some of the overblown geraniums and smiled. With his dark olive skin and long black hair tied back in a ponytail he was quite a shock to some of her more conservative customers, and the single gold earring and the purple shirt and black cords that he wore added to his gipsy image; but his looks belied his character. He was quiet and introspective and when you delved below the surface you realized how shy and serious he really was. She reckoned he was trying to boost his ego by hiding behind the somewhat flamboyant appearance and it didn't bother her. She looked at her watch and called out to him:

"You may as well go home, Mark, I doubt we'll get any more customers today."

"Are you sure? What about locking up?"

"I can do it later. I've got those auction catalogues to check so I'll be here for the rest of the afternoon but there's no need for both of us to stay around."

"Well, if you're sure." He swept the dead flower heads into a neat pile and flicked brown, dessicated petals from his fingers. "I want to call round and see Alison."

"How is she?"

"She seems to be holding her own but it's difficult to tell. She starts the next course of chemotherapy soon."

"Mark . . ." Eileen Dexter hesitated and searched for the right words. ". . . don't get too involved. I know you're fond of her but her long-term prospects aren't good . . ."

"Fond of her!" he exploded in a flash of anger. "She's my fiancée for God's sake! I'm more than fond of her – I love her!"

"Yes, I know, I'm sorry. I didn't put that very well, but I don't want you to get hurt. I'm fond of you, you know, and I can see only heartbreak ahead."

"She's a fighter, she's going to pull through."

"Yes, I'm sure she is. Well, give her my regards. You can take the car, I shan't be using it this evening."

When did she ever use it, he thought with a grin as he washed his hands in the little cloakroom at the back of the shop and let himself out of the side door. The car in question was an ancient Volvo estate, large and cumbersome and ideal for the amount of stuff that was carted around in it. Although it was officially Eileen's car

13

– she had bought it originally and she paid the insurance and road tax – he was the one who maintained it and drove it around, humping furniture and sundry antiques in and out of the back, and he looked on it as his own. Yet she always persisted in this fiction that she used it perpetually for her almost non-existent social life, relinquishing it only on the odd occasion, and he was happy to go along with it. He wound the window down and drove along with his elbow propped outside the car, the turgid wind lifting his ponytail limply.

Lindsay was filling the kettle at the sink as he stepped through the back door and crept up on her and nuzzled the back of her neck. She squealed in surprise, nearly dropping the kettle and water splashed over the floor and worktop.

"Mark! You startled me – what are you doing here?"

"That's not a very nice welcome. Who are your visitors?" He was aware of the rumble of male voices in the other room. "Is this what you two get up to when I'm not here – entertaining strange men?" Then, as she didn't reply: "I know, don't tell me, it's the Inland Revenue, they've caught up with you at last."

"Don't be ridiculous. But I suppose you're not so far out. It's the police."

"You're kidding!"

"That I'm not. It's two CID officers."

"Why, what's happened? You haven't been burgled?"

She told him what had happened and his astonishment turned slowly to anger as he heard her out.

"But this is unbelievable, who could do this to her? How is she taking it?"

"You know Allie, she doesn't show her feelings, but she could do without something like this."

"God, yes. What are the police going to do about it?"

"Why don't you go and ask them?"

"I shall do just that, especially as you obviously can't wait to get rid of me."

"I thought you'd come to see Alison. After all, you're her fiancée, not mine."

For a few seconds a strange tension hung between them and he made as if to speak, then he changed his mind and with a shrug, went through to the sitting room.

Alison looked up from the sofa and a smile lit up her delicate features.

"Mark – I thought you were at work."

"We've shut up shop for the day and I thought I'd call in and see if you'd already left for the lodge. I was going to offer you a lift if you were still here or pick you up and drive you back if you were gone."

"I shan't be going this afternoon now. Has Lindsay told you what's happened?"

"Yes." He looked enquiringly at the two policemen and she made introductions.

"Well, we'll be on our way, Miss Barnard" said Roland getting to his feet after they had exchanged a few words.

"Are you sure you won't stay for another cup? The kettle will soon boil."

"No thank you, you've done us proud. Don't brood over what's happened. I can't explain it but try and put it out of your mind. We'll see ourselves out."

They let themselves out of the front door but as they walked down the road back to Roland's car, Mark Copley ran after them.

"I didn't want to say too much in front of Alison but it's a rotten thing to have happened. Have you any idea who could have done it?"

"I could ask you the same question, Mr Copley. You know her better than I – can you think of anyone who would play this sort of sick joke on her?"

"It's . . . it's just unthinkable. You do realize, don't you, that she was meant to see it."

"What do you mean?"

"She was meant to be going over to Holgate Lodge this afternoon. She would have taken the short cut through the woods and walked right past it."

"I see" said Roland who was thinking that a nasty joke had taken on an even nastier aspect, "fortunately someone else saw it first and reported it."

"What are you going to do about it?"

15

"There has been no crime committed so there will be no official action on behalf of the police."

"But this is preposterous!"

"But it WILL go down on record and please keep me informed if anything else similar should happen."

"What can I do?"

"I suggest you go back to your fiancée, Mr Copley, she will be glad of your support."

A very dissatisfied young man turned on his heel and went back to the cottage and the two detectives got into the car.

"It's a rum old do" said Mansfield, fastening his seatbelt, "what now?"

"I think we'll just pop over to Holgate Lodge ourselves and return the waxwork."

"Wasting police resources?"

"Luckily we're not overstretched at the moment. I must admit I'm curious about the whole business, aren't you?"

Holgate Lodge was an example of Victorian High Gothic at its very best – or worst, according to one's viewpoint. It was a tall, ill-proportioned building fashioned from some unidentifiable dark stone and it bristled with turrets, towers and crenellations; a cross between Walt Disney fantasy and a Scottish pele tower with overtones of Dracula and Transylvania. On a grey winter day it would look sinister and brooding; in the middle of a summer heatwave it looked out of place and faintly absurd, standing starkly amongst the green and gold trees and parkland.

The two detectives drove past the reed fringed lake that flanked the left-hand side of the drive, past the notice board stating the times of opening and drew up in front of the imposing porch that housed a massive, iron-studded oak door.

"It's closed this afternoon" said Mansfield, "there may be no-one here."

"There's one way of finding out." Roland left his companion to retrieve the model from the back of the car and walked over to the porch and pounded on the door. After a long pause and just as Roland was about to abandon the

16

venture and return to the car, the door opened, revealing a woman in her early forties with a mass of grey streaked black hair swept back and tied with an orange scarf. She was wearing orange patterned leggings and a loose black top and yellow plastic flip-flops on her feet.

"I'm afraid we're closed this afternoon." She blinked short-sightedly at Roland and her gaze drifted beyond him to Mansfield. "Oh, you've found my Lizzie Siddal!"

"This is yours?"

"She's one of my exhibits. Where did you find her and who are you?"

Roland introduced himself and Mansfield and explained their presence.

"You'd better come in. I'm Anthea Campbell-Haigh, the curator and general dogsbody of this place." She stepped back and ushered them in through the door which opened onto a large manorial hall, dark and sombre with heavily panelled walls covered with paintings and tapestries.

"When did you discover this model had gone missing Mrs Campbell-Haigh?"

"Not till after lunch. I had a couple of coach parties round this morning – one of them was a party of school children – and I didn't get around to checking everything and locking up until about two o'clock. I thought at first that one of the school kids had taken it for a joke, they were fifth and sixth formers and most of them were bored out of their tiny minds."

"A macabre joke, as it turned out, and not one likely to have been carried out by school kids."

"No. Poor Alison." She gave a little shudder. "That's why whoever did it left the wig behind I suppose. Come and see."

She led the way up the staircase which curved upwards from the far end of the hall and through an archway into a room that looked like a set from Camelot. A group of medieval figures were seated round a table set with pewter plates and heavy flagons. One of the heavy carved chairs was empty apart from a wig of gleaming red hair draped over its back.

17

"Is this where she belongs, Ma'am?" asked Mansfield and the woman nodded and helped him to prop the model up on the seat. She then carefully placed the wig back on the bare skull and patted it into place.

"There we are – Elizabeth Siddal restored."

"Elizabeth Siddal? asked Roland.

"She was Rossetti's model, mistress and eventual wife. She was painted over and over again by him in various guises and Holman Hunt and Millais also used her as a model. Came to a tragic end though."

"Oh?"

"Committed suicide by taking laudanum. The Victorian version of a heroin overdose."

"What did you do when you discovered her missing?" Roland found that he too was referring to the life-like waxwork as if it were a real person.

"I had a quick scout round to see if she had somehow got mixed up with one of the tableaux in another room. I tell you, I thought it was a joke and she would turn up again later, I wasn't really worried. I was anxious to get on with my research this afternoon as the Lodge is closed to the public. I'm completing a book on the Pre-Raphaelites that my late husband was working on at the time of his death. You've probably heard of him: Professor John Campbell-Haigh; he was an expert on the Brotherhood."

Roland managed to indicate that he had without giving away the fact that he had come across the name for the first time only that afternoon.

"Anyway, I intended putting in two or three hours work at my desk, then, if Lizzie was still missing I'd have done a more thorough search and if I still hadn't found her I'd have reported it to the police I suppose."

"Did you know that Alison Barnard meant to come here this afternoon?"

"She comes over when she feels like it" said Anthea Campbell-Haigh vaguely. "She likes to feel she's keeping in touch but whether she'll ever come back to work properly, I don't know. I encourage her to keep an interest in things, but . . ." she shrugged her shoulders.

18

"So, as far as this theft is concerned, it could have been removed any time between late morning and say, two o'clock?"

"Yes. Everything was present and correct when I took the two parties round between eleven and twelve; I didn't check after that until around two o'clock as I've said."

"What about security? Surely you have an alarm system and secure locks with all these valuable pictures around?"

"You don't think they're the real thing, inspector? Would that they were! They're all copies, alas, and though they have some value they're certainly not heirlooms." She gestured to the paintings lining the walls as she led them back to the entrance hall. Some of them looked vaguely familiar to Roland. Surely the original of "The Light of the World" was in St Paul's Cathedral? And he'd certainly seen that painting of Ophelia before, which, as he looked closely, was another version of Elizabeth Siddal; pale face and long red hair drifting in her watery grave.

"Do you live on the premises?" asked Mansfield.

"Good God no! I'm not such a martyr to the cause! I like my mod cons. No, I live in the old gate-house over on the other side of the park. It's been thoroughly modernized and is just the right size for me."

"You live on your own? You have no family?"

"No, my wax family are children enough for me."

"Well, what did you make of all that?" asked Roland as they drove back to Felstone HQ.

"It's certainly made a change from writing reports and investigating real crime."

"Let's hope it doesn't develop into something more serious."

"How do you mean?"

"I hope it's not the start of an epidemic of unpleasant practical jokes; these things can escalate into something much nastier."

CHAPTER 2

On the Saturday following the incident at Saxton, James Roland and his wife Ginny were enjoying a night out at the Felstone Maritime Festival. In recent years the dock complex at Felstone had been modernized and enlarged to such an extent that it was now one of the busiest container ports in the country. However, the original harbour, which had been by-passed by the dredging of the new dock, had been left virtually untouched and was being returned to its former glory as a tourist venue and attraction. The Wherry Quay, as it was known, was now home to several Thames barges and old sailing ships which were open to the public, and a long redundant warehouse, fronting the water, had been turned into a maritime museum.

A visit to this museum was proving fascinating to the Rolands as they wandered round the old two-storied brick building. A large part of the ground floor had been turned into a re-construction of the malting business that had flourished in a bygone Felstone and on the upper floor was an exhibition showing what conditions had been like below deck in a square-rigger. It was very lifelike, from the stuffed rat scuttling across the floorboards to the flickering horn lantern illuminating the figure of the old salt asleep in his hammock, his straw hat tipped over his face. In another part of the building there was a display of model ships and maritime artefacts and a section devoted to rope-making,

When they had seen enough they walked along the quay to The Jolly Sailor, where the local Morris Men were performing in the courtyard in front of the pub and Ginny sat down at one of the outside tables and watched them whilst her husband went inside to get their drinks.

"We are getting a dose of 'Merrie England' this evening" he remarked after he had fought his way back through the crowd with their drinks. At the end of the display, as the dancers reeled off to the strains of Bonny Green Garters, the Rolands' attention was attracted by the Hobby Horse who was leaping amongst the spectators collecting donations.

"Why, that's Mervyn Souster" declared Ginny, watching the comic figure of the capering man hung about with his puppet horse, "he teaches at Felstone High." The man had seem them and made his way circuitously towards them with little forays into the crowd, butting the squealing children with the head of the horse and inviting the young women to stroke his steed. He was a tall man with an impish smile and a shock of dark red hair escaping from under his straw, be-ribboned hat. The framework of the horse was slung around his waist and his lower legs were visible below the caprisoned skirts of his charger. It had a very life-like head with gleaming eyes and a shaggy mane and tail.

"So this is what you get up to in your spare time" said Ginny as the man pranced up to them.

"Ginny, my dear, how are you?" He nodded to Roland and grinned at her. "Give my Dobbin a pat and he'll reward you."

"Why, what is he supposed to do?"

"He's a fertility symbol. Touch him and you'll be pregnant within the year."

Ginny's hand, which had moved towards the hobby horse, froze and dropped back to her side. The gesture was not lost on her husband and as she chatted to her ex-colleague his thoughts echoed her involuntary rejection of the idea. God no! they didn't want any more children – yet, if ever. Ginny was still recovering from a severe case of post-natal depression following the birth of their daughter Katherine who was nearly one year old. Looking at the animated woman sitting opposite him with her tumbling strawberry blonde hair and odd-coloured eyes, one blue, one hazel, now both crinkled in amusement, it was difficult to reconcile her with the disturbed, despondent woman of a few months ago.

She had been a young widow with a teenage son when Roland had first met her during a murder case in which, at one point, she had figured as the chief suspect. After a chequered courtship, not helped by the fact that he himself was a divorced man who had gained a bad reputation with women after his wife's desertion, they had married and Katherine had been born a year later. They had been thrilled with her and Simon, his step-son, who regarded Roland with very mixed feelings, had fortunately also been besotted with his little half-sister and become her willing acolyte. Another baby at this point would be a disaster in more ways than one, though why in God's name was he, a practical, clear-thinking police officer even considering such a superstitious bit of mumbo-jumbo? He joined in the conversation.

"Have you finished your display for the evening?"

"We're now coming to the serious part." Mervyn Souster lifted his elbow in a time-honoured gesture and left them to join his companions inside the pub.

As the sun dropped lower in the sky and the shadows crept across the cobbles Ginny brought up the subject of Simon.

"I wish he could find a job. I don't like him at a loose end."

Simon had recently completed his GSCE's. He was going up into the sixth form to study for his A levels in September but in the meantime he was idle at home, the school apparently not requiring his presence any more that term.

"It's early days yet, he may still be lucky. He seems to be occupying himself anyway, he's never at home."

"That's just what I mean. I don't know which is worse; having him at home all day under my feet or disappearing with his friends and I don't know where he is or what he's getting up to."

"You worry too much. A boy that age needs to feel a little independent. I can remember when I was his age I couldn't bear having to account to my parents for every movement; not that I was getting into any mischief. More a case of kicking my heels and feeling thoroughly bored and fantasising about the local girls."

"Things are different now, there's so much more temptation, drugs and the like."

"Drugs?" He was startled.

"Oh, I don't mean Simon would dabble in anything like that. We'd know, wouldn't we? Or you certainly would."

"I should hope so." But would he? A colleague who actually worked in the drug squad had been devastated last year to discover that his own daughter was involved in a drug ring, and that had been the hard stuff, not soft drugs which was presumably what Ginny meant. He had overlooked the tell-tale signs which he would have noted in someone with whom he was less emotionally involved; the irritability, mood swings, lack of appetite and money. Do we ever really know our own children? he thought.

"The staff at school are sure that drugs are available and changing hands. But I surely don't have to tell you that."

"No, we're aware of it and trying to crack down on the suppliers, but I'm sure Simon wouldn't get involved in anything like that, he's too sensible to experiment."

Yet not so long ago he might have done just that to shame and embarrass me, thought Roland. At least they were on better terms these days and he knew where Simon was that evening, having been pressed into babysitting for Katherine.

The sound of sea shanties played on the squeeze-box wafted out of The Jolly Sailor and as it was now quite dark and getting chilly the Rolands went inside the pub and found seats in a corner not far from the community singing that was taking place near the bar. Although they had now discarded their straw hats and bells, the Morris men were easy to pick out with their blue embroidered jackets and cross garters as they mingled with the crowd and added their voices to the refrains. Some time later a bellow from the door silenced the chorus and the squeeze-box petered out in a discordant squeal.

"Who the hell's been messing about with my Dobbin?" Mervyn Souster stood framed in the doorway. There was an expression of anger and shock on his face. His hands were covered with blood.

"James, look!" hissed Ginny in apprehension.

There was a babble of voices as people moved towards him but the Bagman's powerful tones could be heard above the startled exclamations.

"What's the matter, Mervyn?"

"Is this someone's idea of a joke?" demanded the Morris man. "Look!" He disappeared momentarily from the doorway and re-appeared carrying his hobby-horse. A wooden-handled sword protruded from its flanks and blood cascaded down the heraldic blanket that covered its framework and dripped onto the floor.

"Wait here" said Roland, and started to push his way through the crowds. Ginny ignored him and followed at a discreet distance. There was uproar surrounding Mervyn Souster and Roland had to shout to make himself heard.

"Let me see." He reached out to take the hobby horse and the Morris man swung away from him.

"What the . . . oh, you're a policeman, aren't you?"

"When did this happen?"

"Sometime after I came in here."

"You left it outside?"

"Yes, in the old stables round the side. We left all our gear in there."

Roland examined the hobby-horse. Sawdust was now leaking from the gash and mingling with the blood.

"But James, it can't be real blood" whispered Ginny at his elbow, "it's stuffed."

"Don't worry, this isn't real blood." Roland straightened up and spoke to Souster. "Someone is playing tricks on you. I think this is stage blood; the stuff you get from theatrical suppliers for use in the theatre. Any idea who the culprit can be?"

"No." Mervyn Souster glared round at the crowd who had been momentarily silenced. "But that muck is going to be a devil to remove and my wife spent hours embroidering that covering."

Roland pulled out the sword and more sticky sawdust oozed from the hole.

"It's one of the swords we use for our sword dancing!" exclaimed one of the other Morris men.

The sword in question was about one metre long with a wooden handle and a metal, square-ended lathe-like blade. It was blunt and could never have been used to inflict a real wound.

"Does it belong to one of you?" Roland asked. There was a murmur of dissent from the Morris men.

"They were left in a bundle in the stables," said Souster, "we don't own them individually; they're just props that belong to the group. Anyone could have got at them."

"Have you got across any of your companions?"

"You think it was one of the lads? No I'm sure it wasn't."

"Well, I should just ignore it."

But Roland brought it up again as he and Ginny drove home.

"You don't happen to know where Souster lives, do you?"

"In Saxton."

"Saxton?" Roland felt a flicker of unease.

"Yes, I always thought it was strange that he should go and live there after all the bad feeling between him and Stewart Carson."

"Stewart Carson?" Her husband drew into the curb and gave her his full attention.

"They both taught history. When the two sixth-forms at Felstone and Woodford amalgamated Mervyn Souster was made Head of History and Stewart Carson was eased out. He was very bitter about it and everyone was surprised when Mervyn chose to go and live in the same village."

"This is the second such incident in a few days involving a Saxton resident. I don't like it."

"You don't think they're meant as death threats, do you?"

"That's what I'm afraid of."

*　　*　　*

25

Roland was busy on routine work the next week, preparing evidence for an embezzlement case due to come up in court and investigating a series of break-ins and criminal damage at local video shops, and he was unaware at first that another macabre incident had taken place, this time involving the Maritime Museum he had recently visited. It was brought to his notice by William Evans, the young detective constable who formed part of his team. William Evans was a garrulous celt from Swansea who, although now permanently settled in East Anglia, had lost none of his Welsh rhetoric and still regarded rural life, as lived in the wilds of Suffolk, with suspicion and distaste. He had recently split up with his girl-friend and was making his colleagues' lives a misery, bemoaning the fickleness of women in general and his ex-girlfriend's in particular. He had taken to drowning his sorrows in off-duty hours at one of the locals and he, in turn, had learnt about the episode when drinking with a friend one evening in the Jolly Sailor.

The friend was Michael Parker, a law student in his final year at university, who was supplementing his grant by helping out at the Maritime Museum during his holidays. That evening William Evans had been in a particularly trying mood, hunched over his beer and eyeing the local talent with a jaundiced eye and his friend sought to distract him.

"I know you're so wrapped up in your own misery that my conversation is boring you to tears," said Parker sarcastically, "but as a policeman you may be interested to hear what happened the other morning in the museum."

"You're going to tell me anyway, aren't you."

"For God's sake, William, you're becoming a bore. You're not the first man who's been stood up, and from what you've told me you screwed it up yourself. Either make it up with Theresa or find someone else, soonest preferably."

"I've finished with women, full stop." The Welshman ran a freckled hand through his mop of bright ginger hair and stared defiantly at his companion, then shrugged his shoulders.

26

"Sorry, I know you're getting fed up with my harping on about my love life. What were you saying?"

"You've been round the museum, haven't you?"

"Yes."

"You know the section that's rigged out to look like the interior of an old sailing ship?"

"Uh ha."

"Well, it was most odd, more than odd. It scared the shit out of me at first."

"What did?"

"Do you remember the figure of the sailor asleep in his hammock?"

Evans searched his memory. "Yes, I think so. It was slung between two of the beams, wasn't it? And he was wearing old-fashioned gear?"

"Yes. Well you see I was the first person in that morning and before we open up to the public we have to check everything's okay. I was just having a quick dekko round the place when I realized he wasn't there."

"The sailor in his hammock?"

"Yes."

"So someone had nicked him in the night?"

"That's what I thought at first, but he was there all right, hanging from a beam."

"How do you mean?"

"He was slung up with a rope round his neck as if he had hung himself. It looked just like a real body and I can tell you it gave me a shock."

"Any idea who had done it and why?"

"Wait a minute, there's more to come. The figure in the bunk had been wearing a straw sailor hat over his face. Well, that hat was lying on the floor and the strung-up figure was wearing a panama hat, the sort of thing elderly men wear. It really did look as if he had a broken neck. The head had been wrenched and tilted to one side and this hat was perched over one ear."

"Nasty. So what did you do?"

"By that time I could hear movement downstairs and I knew Charlie Todd had turned up."

"Who's he?"

27

"Retired naval chap, lives out at Saxton. God help me if he heard me calling him Charlie. He is CAPTAIN Charles Todd, with the emphasis on the rank. He helped set up the exhibition in an advisory capacity, though if you ask me he was more of a hindrance than a help, throwing his weight about and getting up everyone's nose. Anyway, he also helps out manning the place on a voluntary basis and he was on duty with me that morning. I called him up to come and have a look and he nearly blew a gasket."

"Didn't like his precious exhibition being mucked about?"

"The hat was his panama."

"Really." The policeman took over and Evans began to show more interest.

"Yes, it really was, his name was inside. He reckoned it had gone missing last weekend and he thought at first it was MY doing; that I'd set it up to make fun of him."

"What did you do about it?"

"We got the figure down – I think originally it had been a shop window dummy – straightened up the neck and popped it back in the hammock with the correct hat. Charlie wanted to call in the police but I managed to calm him down. Said I knew someone in the Force and would have a word with him, so there you are."

"We're into real crime, mate, not practical jokes. Sounds as if someone was getting his own back on your Captain Todd." But although William Evans made light of it to his friend he remembered the other similar incident that Roland had reported and the next morning he told the detective inspector about it.

"I don't like it," said Roland, when Evans had relayed the tale, "that's three particularly vicious hoaxes that could be construed as death threats involving Saxton residents. On the face of it, that's the only thing they have in common – the victims all live in Saxton – but otherwise I can't see how they can be connected. I don't see what we can do apart from keeping our eyes and ears open."

"We're not taking any action?"

"Officially no, but I think you'd better pay this Captain Todd a visit. Now he's had a chance to calm down he may have more idea who the culprit could be. Find out how and where he lost his hat and how it was possible for someone to get into the museum – presumably it was set up during the night before it was discovered. But keep it low key. We don't want the Press getting to hear of it or the inhabitants of Saxton getting into a panic about a practical joker in their midst."

Superintendent Lacey, Roland's immediate boss, put it more strongly when Roland reported to him.

". . . mass hysteria stalking the streets of Saxton if this gets about." He glared at his inspector as if he held him personally responsible for the macabre happenings. He was a lumbering, overweight man whose hectoring, belligerent manner hid a razor-sharp brain. Nothing escaped his notice, as his subordinates knew to their cost, and one of his delights was to cut James Roland down to size. Whilst he was fair enough to admit that his inspector frequently achieved results with his somewhat unorthodox methods of policing, yet he resented Roland's background and university education. He had got where he was the hard way, as he was fond of stressing, and he had no time for people who took short cuts with fancy degrees.

His speech was littered with clichés. No matter what the situation, Lacey was never at a loss for a well-worn aphorism; they rumbled from his massive frame and tripped from his fleshy lips as if original offerings. Roland had once bet a colleague that it was impossible for Lacey to utter a sentence that did not include at least one cliché, and he had almost won the wager.

"Some joker with a warped sense of humour must be at the bottom of it" continued Bob Lacey, tapping his ballpoint against the report in front of him, "got a grudge against some of his neighbours."

"Who could harbour a grudge against a leukaemia victim?"

"There's nowt so queer as folks. How did the victims react? Have they any idea who could have staged the little dramas?"

"To a certain extent they misfired. In two of the three cases the victim was not the first on the scene;

29

in fact, Alison Barnard never did see the little tableau set up for her, but the instigator must have thought he'd arranged things so that his victims were on the spot before anyone else."

"Well, as I said, we don't want any publicity about it. The local Press would have a field day if they got their teeth into it – there's not much news about at the moment, even the Royal Family are keeping their noses clean, must be the heat."

"So we sit on it and hope it dies a natural death?"

"What else do you suggest – a twenty-four guard on the people concerned?" growled Lacey sarcastically.

"No, sir, I agree there's no case for the police but there's a nasty feel about the whole affair, it worries me."

"When the murders start happening for real, that's when you want to get worried." Lacey dismissed his inspector with a wave of a podgy fist.

"It will be too late then" muttered Roland, sotte voce, as he took his leave.

Tina Fairbrother inched round the window display she was setting up and stuck out her tongue at the pimply youth who was leering in through the plate glass. It was great fun to observe the male reaction to her occupation but this one was far too young and callow to be interesting. She propped another pile of CDs in front of the pop poster and smoothed her leather mini skirt over her hips. The effect she was aiming for was somewhat spoilt by the thick black tights she was wearing. Damn that old busybody from her village who had complained to her boss that she was corrupting the morals of the male population of Felstone, bobbing about in the window of the record shop in what he had called "a bit of fringing that exposed more than it concealed." Dirty old man! He must have had a good eyeful himself before accusing her of flaunting herself and Steven, for once, had taken his point. Steven encouraged his young assistants to dress fashionably but this time he had acted the big boss and insisted that mini skirts, with the resulting bared flesh, did not go with window-dressing, so she had compromised. She still wore the mini-skirt but underneath it her thighs were clad in opaque tights and with the temperature in the eighties she was decidedly uncomfortable.

She crawled round to the front of the window and propped up the poster, dislodging the fan of LPs she had already spread out in the front of the display. Muttering under her breath she re-positioned them. Most people in the business reckoned vinyls were out, practically pre-historic, but not Steven. He insisted that many of them were collectors' pieces and he did a roaring trade in second-hand recordings. There was currently a revival of The Beatles music. She wasn't into this sort of music at all, it was childish, outmoded; she eyed some of the titles – "Eleanor Rigby" and "A Hard Day's Night" and snorted. The Beatles were making a comeback along with all the 60's gear; the platform shoes and flares and long pointed collars, but you wouldn't see her jumping on the bandwagon, nothing would part her from her Doc Martens. She glanced complacently down at the clompy boots encasing her feet and then became aware that someone was trying to attract her attention from outside in the street.

It was her friend Karen Green. She was gesticulating and pointing to her wristwatch. Tina had arranged to meet her during her lunch break. She glanced down at her own watch; five minutes to one; Tina was early. She mouthed through the window that she would join her friend in five minutes and held up her hand with digits extended to back this up, and as Karen nodded and moved on she hurriedly piled up the rest of the records and discs that were to complete her display and went in search of her boss.

"I'm just going for my lunch, Steven" she called to the man who was pouring over a catalogue at the main counter.

"Have you done the display?"

"Nearly. I'll finish it when I get back."

"I don't like a half-finished window, it's bad for business. Can't you finish it first?"

"I've arranged to meet a friend, she'll be waiting for me."

"Alright, but don't be long. No hour and a half like it was yesterday."

"Ooh it wasn't, there was a queue at the bank . . ." Steven's attention had reverted to his catalogue so she waggled her fingers at the other two assistants, grabbed her satchel-bag from the cloakroom and slipped out of the shop.

Karen was waiting for her in the pizza house. She gave her order and joined her friend at the table near the window.

"You look pleased with yourself." Karen looked at her friend hopefully, "have you had any luck?"

"Yes, you can tell Rod his troubles are over, it's definitely on."

"You've found a place?"

"Yep, it's just perfect. I can't think why I didn't think of it before when we were looking for a venue."

"So where's it to be?"

"In Saxton."

"Saxton? You're joking!"

"I'm not. You know Holgate Hall?"

"The boys' school? Where the little blue bloods go? You can't mean there!"

"Just shut up and listen! I don't mean in the school itself, though they'll all be on holiday. Over on the other side of the grounds, furthest from the village, there's the remains of a farm. The house has gone and most of the land was sold off to the school and incorporated in the playing fields, but there's a huge derelict barn still standing. It's ideal. It's enormous and there's a big yard outside so we can spread."

"But there'll be someone still living at the school surely?"

"Only the caretaker and he's as deaf as a post. He won't hear anything across acres and acres of rugger and cricket pitches and there's a belt of trees in front so he won't see the lights either if he happens to look that way. There are no other houses anywhere near and the river's just down from there. In fact, if the tide is right some people can get there by boat, it will be great!"

"Right, I'll pass the word."

Tina attacked her pizza – tomato, mozzarella and pepperoni – and eyed her friend.

"So how's things?"

"I saw an old friend of yours this morning." Then, as Tina paused with fork halfway to her mouth and raised her eyebrows enquiringly, "Mark Copley."

"Oh."

"I don't know why you gave him the push. I think he's rather dishy, he looks like a Latin."

"He didn't behave like one, no passion or fire I can tell you. He was a sad disappointment. Still, he's got himself another girlfriend now I've heard, one of the Barnard twins – the ill one."

"I wonder what he sees in her, after you. Perhaps he's into blondes." Tina patted her platinum crop smugly. "There are blondes and blondes. I'm sure she's more his type – a real milk-sop. Not like her sister."

"They're not a bit alike are they? For twins I mean."

"She's a pain in the neck, it doesn't do to get across her."

"How do you mean?"

"You know that cat I ran over – I told you about it, remember? It was theirs."

"Oh God, was it really?"

"I couldn't help it, the damn thing ran out right in front of me and there's no way I could have avoided it but she said I was speeding. Kicked up a hell of a fuss and reported me to the police.

"Were you?" Karen looked at her friend shrewdly.

"Was I what?"

"Speeding."

"Of course not. Well, only slightly. Anyway, she really got her knickers in a twist and then I made matters worse."

"How?"

"Well, I went into the house to tell them what had happened. I suppose I was feeling upset – well, wouldn't you be – and I tripped and knocked all her sister's painting gear over. There were paints and brushes and crayons

33

rolling all over the place and I went and trod on something – a damn big charcoal stick – and got bits of it stuck to my feet and tramped it all over their precious fawn carpet."

"You must have been popular."

"Too true. Anyway, he's welcome to Miss Namby-Pamby and her sister."

"How about asking him to the Rave. Do you think he'd come?"

"You bet, if I wanted him to. I haven't lost my touch yet."

The two girls giggled and moved on to other topics.

"Mark, have you seen my brooch?" Eileen Dexter popped her head out of the door as she heard her assistant draw up and slam the car door.

"Your Mourning Brooch? You haven't lost it!"

"I think it's been taken. It's my own stupid fault!" She clutched the neck of her dress in distress.

The brooch in question was a Victorian Mourning Brooch fashioned out of Whitby jet and set with amethysts and seed pearls. There was a receptacle in the back covered with glass in which a lock of hair was displayed. Mark was convinced that this was not the hair of some long dead Victorian but had belonged to Eileen Dexter's fiancée who had been killed in the Korean war. No matter what outfit she was wearing, she always wore the brooch, pinned at her throat or fastened on a lapel.

"The safety catch was bent, I've been meaning to have it repaired. I was afraid I'd lose it so I took it off yesterday afternoon and laid it down on the desk."

"Come and sit down and tell me all about it." Mark put an arm round the elderly woman and propelled her back into the tiny office which led off the front shop.

"Now, when did you see it last?"

"I told you, yesterday afternoon. I put it down, meaning to wrap it up and put it in a box but I got side-tracked and forgot about it – we had a lot of customers in and it slipped my mind when I closed shop yes-terday afternoon. You didn't happen to see it before you left?"

"I certainly didn't notice it. You think one of the customers took it?"

"Anyone wandering round the shop can see in here easily, the doors were open. Oh, how could I have been so careless!"

"Has anything else been taken?"

"I don't think so, I suppose we'd better check."

They went through into the shop and Eileen Dexter's gaze roved round the tightly packed shelves and tables.

"Charlotte Rose has gone!" She blundered towards the display of Victorian and Edwardian toys that occupied the space to the right of the window, looking frantically for the doll that should have been propped up in the doll's cradle.

"She has too, how odd!" A quick search found no trace of the doll. "Why on earth should anyone want to take Charlotte Rose?" continued Mark, "she's not all that valuable, is she?"

"No, the rocking horse is worth far more, and even poor old Not Quite."

Not Quite was a bear. He had all the looks and characteristics of a Stieff bear but was not tagged with the all important Stieff button, hence his name of Not Quite.

"Nothing else seems to be missing."

"Not as far as I can see." Although to an outsider the contents of the shop appeared as one glorious jumble, Eileen Dexter knew, down to the last thimble, where everything was positioned.

"I'd rather have lost anything than my brooch, it's the sentimental value . . ."

"You'd better report it to the police. Shall I ring them?"

"No, I don't want them round here poking into everything. I'll call in at the Police House. I promised Constable Porter some of my geranium cuttings; I'll take them round now and kill two birds with one stone. You stay in the shop and keep an eye on things, you can unload the car later."

Eileen Dexter let herself out of the back door, her basket over her arm, and walked down the street. The

Police House was at the other end of the village and as she crossed the village green she saw a group of people gathered round the pond which was in the far corner where the ground dipped down to a copse of trees. Something in the pond was exciting interest; she could see people gesticulating and heard the sound of raised voices. She changed direction and walked towards them quickening her pace. As she drew near, she saw their attention was fixed on a little island in the middle crowned by a stunted weeping willow tree. This willow thrust knotted roots into the murky depths of the pool and floating in front of these she could see a white shape. As she peered closer this shape resolved itself into the body of a young child. Its garments were trapped in the gnarled roots and as she stared horrified a small head and a chubby fist bobbed into view.

CHAPTER 3

Eileen Dexter felt a sick horror enveloping her. This was terrible! How on earth had a child fallen into the pond?

"I'm going in," said Eric Land, who combined a milk-round with a window cleaning business, "I reckon I can wade across to there, the water level's gone down in this drought."

That was true, thought Eileen Dexter, watching him take off his shoes and socks and roll up his trousers. The contours of the pond had shrunk, leaving a wide rim of hardened, milk chocolate-coloured mud round the edges. If not exactly stagnant, it wasn't far off this state. Green scum floated on the surface and as Eric Land paddled towards the centre, a rotten stench rose up from the murky depths. He stumbled and swore as the water slopped up round his waist.

"This pond is just a tip! God knows what's been dumped in here!"

He'll probably catch typhoid, thought Eileen Dexter, and what about the poor child? It couldn't still be alive surely? Lack of oxygen, irreversible brain damage . . . a cabbage for the rest of its days . . . unthinkable . . .

A thread of excitement ran through the onlookers as the milkman reached the island and grabbed at the white bundle trapped in the willow roots. Water streamed from the clothing as he lifted it out and darkened Titian red hair clung to the little white face. He lurched round and there was an expression of stupefaction on his face as he held it up for all to see.

"It's a doll! A bloody, large doll! Not a child!" There was a chorus of relief as he waded back and eager hands helped him out of the water and up the bank. The suspicion that had been lurking at the back of Eileen Dexter's mind since his triumphant shout blossomed and flooded her with a new horror. The doll was Charlotte Rose. Green-streaked finery clung to the jointed limbs and the bisque head was smeared with mud but her eyes were drawn to the brooch pinned at the doll's throat – it was her mourning brooch! She felt reality slipping away. The voices became a distant babble as the roaring in her ears crescendoed and she drowned in the blackness spinning round her.

"Miss Dexter, are you alright?"

She opened her eyes to see PC Porter looming over her. She was lying on the village seat and his face hovered a few inches above her. What a stupid question to ask, of course she was not alright! She struggled to a sitting position.

"That's my doll! It's Charlotte Rose – from my shop! And she's wearing my brooch – the one that went missing!"

"You mean this?"

He laid a fleshy finger against the ornament pinned at the doll's neck.

"Yes. I always wear it but it needs a repair and I took it off and left it lying on my desk . . ."

"When would this have been?"

"Sometime yesterday afternoon. I've only recently discovered it was gone and then I realized that the doll was missing as well."

"So you think someone helped themselves to the brooch and the doll. Have you reported it?"

"I was just coming to the Police House to tell you when . . . when this happened . . . I don't understand. Why should someone take just those two things from the shop? There are far more valuable things lying around . . . and then to pin the brooch to the doll and throw it in the pond . . . it doesn't make sense . . ."

"Perhaps whoever took it thought they'd stolen something really valuable and when they realized their mistake they threw it away, or maybe they had acted on impulse and thought better of it later and dumped it. Can you clean them up or are they ruined?" He handed over the doll and she ran distracted fingers over the limp lacework.

"I expect I can restore them but I don't think this was an ordinary theft."

"Oh?"

"No." Eileen Dexter's brain was now in overdrive. "I think it was meant to be *me*. It's another one of those horrid practical jokes like the one that was played on Alison Barnard – did you hear about that?"

"Yes. Well maybe it is the work of some nutter playing stupid jokes but I shouldn't worry about it, Miss Dexter. You've got your doll and brooch back and no real harm has been done, though I don't know if Eric Land would agree with me. He's threatening to sue the parish council for not cleaning out the pond!"

"But why me?" She was not to be distracted.

"Who knows, but I should try and forget about it. Do you want a lift home or are you going back to your shop?"

"I must go back to the shop."

"Will you be alright? I'm sure someone will walk back with you."

"I'll be alright on my own, silly of me to faint – it must have been the heat."

She didn't want company, she was starting to feel faintly ridiculous. All she wanted was to regain the sanctuary and coolness of her shop and to tell Mark what had happened. She got to her feet and started to walk back unsteadily the way she had come.

Bob Porter watched her go and wondered if he should have hung on to the doll and brooch. He was very much aware of the memo that was lying on the desk back in his office. It was from the CID and asked to be kept informed of any incidents such as sick practical jokes that came to light in Saxton or the neighbouring area.

James Roland had finished cutting his front lawn and was debating whether to run over the back one whilst he still had the mower out. The sight of his stepson sprawled beside the pond, his belongings strewn across the grass, decided him against it. Ginny was out with Katherine, this might be a good opportunity to have a word with Simon, whose behaviour was causing her some concern. He put the mower back in the shed and walked over to Simon who was engrossed in the torrent of music pouring through his earphones.

Simon became aware of his presence and reluctantly removed them. He eyed Roland warily.

"Hi James, did you want me?"

"I wondered if you would like a beer. I've been cutting the front grass and it's thirsty work."

"Yes *please*. Shall I get them?"

"Okay. *Half* a can for you, understand?"

"Will do. I think there's some crisps in the pantry."

He bounded indoors and Roland dragged the garden seat under the shade of an apple tree and sat down, stretching his legs out on the bleached grass. It really was exceptionally hot. If they didn't have some rain soon there would be no fruit to speak of. Already the wizened, insect-pitted apples were falling; a June drop which was extending to a false autumn crop. He should really do some watering, the tomatoes were visibly wilting . . .

"Here we are." Simon dumped a tray bearing glasses, two cans of beer and some packets of crisps on the other end of the seat.

"I'm surprised at you, encouraging one of my tender years to drink" he joked as he attacked the ring-pulls.

"The occasional beer won't do you any harm. There are other more addictive habits."

"You mean smoking?"

"Actually I was thinking of drugs: pot, acid, speed . . ."

Roland spoke casually but he was watching carefully to see how Simon would react. The boy carried on pouring out the beer without a pause but the wary look was back in his eyes.

"What's that to do with me? You surely don't think I'VE had anything to do with drugs?" He was indignant but guarded.

"I hope you've got more sense than to experiment. But it does go on, you know that."

"Yes."

"In your school."

"Yes." It was dragged from him reluctantly.

"Your classmates and friends – some of them are involved."

"Oh God, James, don't come the heavy on me!"

"I suppose I'm speaking as a policeman as well as a parent," admitted Roland, "but I know how easy it is to try out something for fun and how easy it is to get hooked. Once on the slippery slope . . ."

"I don't know why you're telling me this."

"These young people need help, before it becomes a habit."

"You're asking me to grass! To become a police informer!"

"Don't be melodramatic! I'm not asking you to squeal on your mates. I'm more interested in finding the source of the drugs. Someone supplies them. The very fact that Felstone is a port means that it is that much easier to smuggle drugs into the area. These pushers need to be stopped."

"Don't preach at me James."

"I'm only saying that if you know anything, anything at all, don't hold out on me from a misguided sense of loyalty."

"Since when have you been working for the Drugs Squad?"

"Simon!"

"I don't know what you're talking about!"

Christ, I've made a pig's ear of that, thought Roland facing the boy's mutinous glare; all I wanted was to sound him out and give him a friendly warning and we end up shouting at each other. He heard the sound of the patio doors being opened and held up a warning hand.

"That's your mother back. We don't want to drag her into this. Remember, Simon, I'm not getting at you."

"You could have fooled me" he muttered, but he shrugged and picked up the glasses with better grace.

"James, you're wanted on the phone – didn't you hear it ringing?"

41

Ginny appeared in the doorway with Katherine clinging to her skirts. Roland got to his feet with a sigh.

"Who is it?"

"Who do you think."

He gave her a quick kiss as he stepped into the sitting room and ruffled Katherine's fiery mop of curls. She gurgled with delight and sat down abruptly as she lost her balance.

As he had feared, the call was from the Station. He listened grimly, barked a few questions into the phone and put the receiver down.

"I've got to go."

"Oh James, I was going to suggest we went to the beach this afternoon. Why do things always happen on a Saturday? Why don't the criminal fraternity take the weekend off like everyone else? Is it serious?"

"Someone's been killed over at Woodford."

"You mean murdered?"

"It sounds like a pub brawl."

"But why do you have to go? Surely it's not a matter for the CID?"

"Apparently it's not as straightforward as it appears. I'll try and get back later on."

He sorted out his car-keys and made for the door. "Try and persuade Simon to cut the back lawn. The exercise will do him good!"

"Which pub?"

"The Queen's Head."

"The Queen's Head?" Patrick Mansfield looked dubious as he slammed the door and fastened his seat belt. "Not the place where you'd expect a fight to break out. They always pride themselves on their upmarket clientele – it's in the guide books. Now, if it had been the Benson Arms down by the river I wouldn't be surprised. It's the meeting place of a lot of the local yobbos and it's often a rough house."

Roland had collected his sergeant and was now heading for the small market town of Woodford, which lay ten miles north of Felstone, on the banks of the river which snaked inland through the coastal marshes and widened into a respectable waterway brimful of yacht moorings and marinas.

"What happened?"

"A man has been knifed."

"Do we know who he is?"

"No," Roland squinted sideways at his sergeant, "but apparently the Morris Men are involved."

"The Morris Men? You don't think . . .?"

"I don't know but we'll soon find out."

There was a large yard at the back of the Queen's Head and he arrived there to find it had been cordoned off. He rolled down the window and a harassed constable bent down.

"You can't come in – oh, it's you, sir, I didn't recognise the car."

"Where can I park?"

"Over behind the old stables in the far corner."

"Who's in charge?"

"Sergeant Burton. He's inside and the police surgeon's been and gone."

The inside of the Queen's Head was cool and dark, in startling contrast to the midday heat beating off the white-washed exterior walls. Sergeant Jim Burton detached himself from the knot of policemen and greeted Roland and Mansfield. He was a tall, gaunt man in his early forties whose poker face reflected his phlegmatic character. Roland knew him of old.

"What happened?"

"The Morris Men were performing out in the yard. There was a big audience, lunchtime drinkers, tourists, families with kids. After they'd finished they were knocking back a few and mixing with the crowd and this fight broke out. Apparently a few of them got into an argument with some of the bystanders and they were taunted with being Nancy Boys and the like. It didn't go down too well, they're big hefty chaps, most of them, and the punches started flying. It was quite a harmless scrap to start with but then someone pulled a knife and one of them bought it."

"Who?"

"His name is Mervyn Souster. He was the Hobby Horse."

Roland and Mansfield exchanged glances and Roland said sharply:

"You say it happened out in the yard – has the body been moved?"

"He didn't die straight away, sir. They brought him inside – to the landlord's private sitting room – but he was a goner before they could get any medical help."

"Did he know his assailant?"

"I don't know sir, but we do. He's an old friend of ours – Mickey O'Rourke."

"Mickey O'Rourke? A nasty bit of work and plenty of form but I wouldn't have called him a killer."

"He's been down for GBH, hasn't he?" put in Mansfield.

"True. Mostly petty thieving and thuggery but he's a gutter rat. Turns vicious when cornered."

"Which he was in this case" said Burton. "He was getting thumped and he retaliated. Says it was self defence."

"You got him?"

"Oh yes, sir. He's safely under lock and key."

"There's no doubt he was the culprit?"

"No doubt at all. He admits it and there are plenty of witnesses."

"Let me see the body."

Mervyn Souster had been laid on the sofa. He was dressed in the same costume that he had been wearing the evening that Roland and Ginny had met him in Felstone but the white shirt and blue jacket were soaked in blood. He had been stabbed in the lower chest; there was a ragged entry wound and a pile of blood-stained towels nearby. His face was drained and waxen, utterly unlike the merry, genial man Roland remembered but there was a faint, twisted smile on the lips as if he were amused at the irony of his own death.

"Have his wife and family been told?"

"Not yet sir. The leader of the Morris Men, the Squire I think he's called, has offered to do it, but I thought you'd want to speak with him first. He and the other men are upstairs. We've hung on to all those involved in the fight and the immediate onlookers but dispersed the rest of the crowd."

"I'm surprised the Press aren't beating a path to the door. Well, let's see this Squire. I'll interview him first before I question our Mickey."

Andrew Parfitt, the Squire, was in a state of shock. He was a tall man with a full, greying beard and looked older than most of his fellow Morris dancers.

"I can't believe it! One minute we were downing a pint and engaging in some good natured banter, then it started getting nasty and Mervyn ended up dead!"

"Tell me exactly what happened – you saw it all?"

"I wasn't involved in the fight myself but I was right amongst them when the fracas started so I reckon I saw what happened. Well, there was this little whipper-snapper of a chap who kept needling Mervyn and some of the younger lads. We're used to it, look on it as one of the pitfalls of the game, but he was very persistent and his mates were egging him on. Before you knew where you were a fight had started and it snowballed from there."

"Your little whipper-snapper is one Mickey O'Rourke, known to us. Could he have been known to Mervyn Souster?"

"I wouldn't have thought so." Andrew Parfitt looked speculatively at the two policemen. "You mean this . . . this Mickey O'Rourke might have deliberately picked a quarrel?"

"I have to investigate all possibilities."

The Morris Squire was quick on the uptake. "You're thinking about that incident at the Jolly Sailor last week? You think there may be a connection?"

"I can't ignore it. Mervyn Souster was the victim of a sick practical joke that could be construed as a death threat; a week later he ends up stabbed to death."

Both men were silent for a moment, remembering the prancing hobby-horse limp in Souster's furious grip, dripping blood and sawdust onto the floor of the quayside pub. That had been stage blood but now Souster's own blood had been spilled and Andrew Parfitt relived with sickening clarity the terrible moment when his fellow dancer had sunk to the ground and a scarlet rivulet had trickled across the white sunlit paving slabs of the courtyard outside.

"Look, as far as I can tell they'd never met before. It was a pub brawl that got out of hand and went wrong . . . horribly wrong. I'm pretty sure Mervyn didn't know this chap but I suppose he could have known Mervyn."

"We'll have to look into it but it will probably turn out to be just a coincidence. We'll keep it under wraps anyhow, I don't want wild conjectures about death threats doing the rounds."

"I won't say anything but of course all of them are remembering what happened and wondering . . ." He looked at Roland in entreaty. "What the hell do I tell Denise, his wife?"

"I'll send a constable with you. Are there children?"

"Three. All still at school, poor little devils."

"Are there any other relatives around?"

"Her mother lives nearby. Mervyn used to moan about his mother-in-law living on the doorstep but it will be a comfort to Denise now."

Roland had a quick word with the other witnesses but learnt nothing new. Everyone thought it had been an unpremeditated scuffle that had turned nasty. He made arrangements for the body to be taken to the mortuary and left to question the man in custody.

Mickey O'Rourke was an unprepossessing looking individual and as he faced Roland across the table in the interview room he looked decidedly the worse for wear. His weasel-like features were battered, he had a black eye and a gashed lip and although he was obviously very frightened he tried to cover it up with a belligerent manner.

"It weren't my fault! He attacked me! I was just defending myself!"

"That's not what I was told, Mickey."

"You can't pin it on me."

"Are you denying you killed him when there are at least a dozen witnesses who saw it happen?"

"I tell you, it was self-defence. Look at me!" He fingered his stubble-pricked face. "He HURT me!"

"You don't look your usual beautiful self but I have it on good authority that you provoked him, that you started the affair."

"It was only a bit of fun, I didn't know he was going to turn nasty!"

"I don't think a jury will have any trouble in deciding that YOU were the one who turned nasty."

"I tell you, I thought he was going to kill me. I had to defend myself."

"And you just happened to have about you a lethal knife in the event of being attacked. Don't waste my time, Mickey, I've examined it – as nasty a little weapon as I've seen in a long time."

"I carry it in self-defence – in case I'm attacked."

"It's an indictable offence to carry a weapon as you well know."

"You're not safe on the streets these days" he whined, "you coppers aren't doing your job properly."

Roland tried another tack.

"Who put you up to it?"

"What do you mean?" O'Rourke blinked at Roland suspiciously.

"Who hired you to kill him?"

"I don't know what you mean! He attacked me – he HIT me and I had to defend myself!"

"Supposing I were to tell you there was a contract on him."

"I don't believe it!"

"Been receiving death threats, Mickey," Mansfield joined in the questioning, "we were almost expecting something like this to happen."

"No." O'Rourke was very alarmed. "I don't know nuffink about it. I'm not a hitman – you know that."

"Granted, you haven't got the guts or the cunning, but I reckon someone was desperate. We all know you'd sell your mother for a handful of the ready."

"No, it wasn't like that – it was an *accident!*"

"How much did they pay you?"

47

"No, you've got it wrong. You've *got* to believe me!"

By now Mickey O'Rourke was in such a state that he would have implicated the entire local underworld if he had thought it would help his cause, but he stuck to his story and after a further lengthy session of questioning, which got them nowhere, Roland called a temporary halt.

"Do you reckon he's telling the truth?" asked Mansfield as they went back to Roland's office.

"Yes I do. He hasn't got the bottle to carry out a deliberate murder and no-one in their senses would hire him as a killer. Much as I hate to admit it, I think it happened just as he said. He got scared and pulled a knife and within a few minutes three kids are orphaned and there's a grieving widow."

"You reckon he'll get off with manslaughter?"

"I can't see a jury convicting him of anything else."

"So that trick that was played on Souster had nothing to do with his death?"

"If Mickey's telling the truth, I can't see how there can be a connection."

"Just a coincidence."

"Yes, and you know how I hate coincidences! Let's hope the Press don't get hold of it."

But it was a forlorn hope. The local paper the next morning carried banner headlines: MAN DIES AFTER BIZARRE DEATH THREAT. It went on to describe in detail the incident in the Jolly Sailor alongside an account of Mervyn Souster's killing. This was followed by a long obituary mourning the loss of the well-loved local teacher. The final paragraph was devoted to a sensational statement that several Saxton inhabitants had been the victims of similar macabre jokes that could be taken as death threats. It ended with the rider: WHO WILL BE NEXT? WILL THE JOKER STRIKE AGAIN?

"I don't believe it!" Roland flung the paper down on his desk in disgust and appealed to Mansfield. "Who's been feeding them this? how did they get to know about it?"

"There were plenty of witnesses around to the incidents involving Souster and Eileen Dexter."

"But not the other two. How did they get to hear about them?"

"Someone's talked."

"Hmmm. This is sensational journalism at its worst. Lacey's going to blow a gasket when he reads this."

Alison Barnard leaned back amongst the pillows and let the sheet of newsprint slip from her fingers. Why had this come through the post for her? What did it mean? Who was it from? She struggled up the bed and searched through the rumpled bedclothes for the envelope. It was a white foolscap one and her address was typed; the postmark was blurred, she couldn't tell where it had been posted or the date of posting. She slowly read through the cutting again. It had been taken from the front page of the local gazette and it was the self same article that had infuriated James Roland a few days earlier.

She had heard about the murder of Mervyn Souster over the local radio and there had been coverage on TV's Look East. She had been horrified and distressed because he had taught her for a time and she had liked and admired him. What she hadn't known was that before his death he had been the victim of a death hoax. Like her . . . the thought flashed unbidden into her head and she tried to thrust it away. There was no similarity, no connection . . . there couldn't be, could there? But somebody thought there was – the person who had sent the cutting to her. And was it meant as a warning or a threat? Oh, this was ridiculous, she was letting her imagination run away with her, but *why* had it been sent? It surely couldn't be the action of a friend; but who . . . who in God's name could ill-wish her at a time like this. If it really had been a death threat why bother? She was likely to die without any help.

No, she mustn't think like that. She had promised herself she would think positively, would fight this beastly disease and get the better of it. She wasn't going to die. She'd had three courses of chemotherapy spread over the last few months and she was shortly to start the final one. She hated the thought of all that again, the sickness and all the side effects it engendered, but she knew it was vital to her chances of survival. She had gone through the stage of "why me?" That had belonged to the terrible period when her illness had first been diagnosed; those long weeks of feeling ill and lethargic before the blood test that had led to the horrible fear and outrage that had overwhelmed her. Well, she still felt weak and lethargic but that was par for the course. She was recovering, getting stronger every day, and lolling in bed at nine-thirty in the morning was no way to behave.

As she picked up her dressing gown she heard Lindsey coming up the stairs. Was it her imagination or was Lindsey possessed of a super abundance of energy these days? It was almost as if the strength that had ebbed from her had been added to her sister's normal robust vigour. Still, she had need of it. Poor Lindsey had to cope with everything, they had no relatives to fall back on.

"I've brought you a coffee." Lindsey pushed open the door with an elbow, her hands being fully occupied with the tray she was carrying, and shut it behind her with a well-angled foot.

"You spoil me. I was just about to get up."

"There's no hurry and I'm ready for a coffee break anyway." She put the tray down on the bedside table. "Anything interesting in your post?"

In reply, Alison handed her the cutting. As soon as her sister saw it a flush ran up under her skin.

"Where did this come from?"

"In the post. In an envelope addressed to me."

"But who . . . ?"

"Quite. I can't understand why I didn't see the original paper, after all, we HAVE the Felstone Gazette."

"That must have been the one I accidently wrapped the kitchen refuse in."

"That's not true." Alison had been eyeing her twin closely. "You didn't want me to see it, did you? You deliberately hid it from me."

"I didn't want you to get upset." Lindsey looked uncomfortable.

"Why should it upset me? It seems to have upset you though. Is it because you think it's true?"

"What's true?"

"This business about these stupid jokes being death threats?"

"No, of course not. That article's really gone over the top. Since they've had that new editor the paper has gone downhill – it's worse than the gutter tabloids."

"Eileen Dexter had one played on her, didn't she?"

"Yes. I can't think why Mark had to tell you about it."

"Who do you think is doing it?"

"Someone who is trying to put the fear of God into people and getting a sick satisfaction out of it."

"They're sick all right." Alison made a face. "Well, I'm not letting it bother me. I thought I'd go over to Holgate Lodge today."

"Are you sure you feel well enough?"

"Yes, and I know Anthea could do with a helping hand."

She didn't tell Lindsey that she also had a compulsion to view the tableaux again; to see the waxwork effigy of Elizabeth Siddal that had been taken to the wood and arrayed with her wig.

She put down her coffee mug and reached out for the wig that was draped over the stand beside her bed.

CHAPTER 4

"A straight forward stabbing in front of witnesses and we've got the culprit under lock and key plus a confession. All neatly tied up, so what's bugging you James?" Superintendent Bob Lacey shifted his bulk on his office chair, which creaked ominously under his weight, and looked shrewdly at his inspector through his piggy eyes.

"It all appears straight forward," admitted Roland, "it's just this business of these death threats that's bothering me."

"And so it bloody well should. Who fed all those details to the Press – that's what I want to know."

"It certainly didn't come from us, but the speculation should die down now we've made an arrest and there's obviously no tie-up between Mickey O'Rourke and the other incidents."

"You're not harbouring any doubts about O'Rourke's guilt?"

"No, he did it all right and I'm convinced it happened as he said. It's just a bit out of his class. Wife-bashing is more in his line, not taking on someone bigger than himself."

"Bit off more than he could chew, didn't he? And when he got backed into a corner he got shit-scared and pulled a knife."

"Well, this should put him away for a few years and the said wife won't be shedding any tears, you can take it from me."

"Nor his other victims – that caretaker he thumped when he did over the British Legion Hall and that shopkeeper who got in his way when he was helping himself to goodies off the shelf. It's a wonder no-one's croaked before; it was only a matter of time before he did for someone permanently. No-one's going to shed any tears for Mickey O'Rourke."

"True, Sir."

"Well, I'm glad we haven't got a murder hunt on our hands. We've had a tip-off that there's one of these Rave Parties being organised locally."

"Here in Felstone?" Roland was openly sceptical.

"Not necessarily in Felstone but somewhere in the area. One of the local hustlers is climbing on the bandwagon."

"I don't see how that involves me."

"Don't be too sure, a lot of manpower is needed to deal with this sort of gig. If there are hard drugs involved I'll be drafting in men from all over, the CID may not escape."

I wonder where that tip-off came from and whether there's any truth in it, thought Roland back in his office. He certainly couldn't see any large-scale Rave or Acid Party being co-ordinated in Suffolk. The county was too isolated and cut-off from the rest of the country. What Lacey had got hold of was probably a teenage rave-up in a private home whilst the parents were on holiday.

It was soon brought home to him how wrong he was in this supposition.

It was a still sultry night. The wafer of moon lying on its back shed no light on the world below. The car parked beneath the trees not far from the river bank was a darker mass amidst the dark surroundings. The river was discernible by scent rather than sound; a faintly rotten-sweet combination of salt and marsh and seaweed as the water slid silently away, uncovering shoals of oozing mud. The courting couple in the car were oblivious of their surroundings until the woman, coming up for air from the back seat, looked out of the window and tried to distract her companion.

"What are those lights over there?"

"Mmm. Come here."

A few minutes later the woman broke away again. "Look, Steve, those lights are still flashing."

"It's Felstone Docks. It's always as bright as daylight there even in the middle of the night. It's the floodlights."

"No, not over there, behind us – look! You don't think it's a UFO, do you?"

"A space craft? Don't be ridiculous Angie!"

"It's just like ET . . . did you ever see it?"

"Ages ago, when I was a kid."

"Well, it reminds me of that."

"You'll be saying you can see flying saucers soon. I'm sure there's a perfectly logical explanation for it."

"What? It's coming from nowhere – there are only fields over there and it's such a strange colour, all sort of purple and flashing blue."

"I suppose it IS a bit odd. I wonder what it is?"

"I think we should report it."

"The little green men have landed," Constable Ryder, who took the call, grinned over at his colleague, "or so someone would have us believe."

"Well, I suppose anything is a diversion on a quiet night like this. Where are they supposed to be?"

"Somewhere over at Saxton. It sounds as if the callers are a courting couple whose heavy session was interrupted by flashing lights."

"We're not really expected to take this seriously, are we?"

"It will have to be investigated. Who is in the area?"

Before a squad car could be mobilized another call was received reporting noise and disturbance coming from the direction of Holgate Park School in Saxton. The caller had noticed it when taking his dog for a walk.

"Christ! Who walks a dog at two in the morning!"

"Someone sleepwalking and having strange dreams."

A further call complaining of noise and flashing lights in the same area triggered comprehension.

"Sounds like the Rave Party we had the tip-off about. So the action's out at Saxton. That's a turn-up for the books and bang goes our quiet night."

A short while later, two vans containing uniformed police, some members of the Drugs Squad and a couple of dogs with their handlers converged on Saxton. The village appeared deserted, the inhabitants asleep in their darkened houses. It wasn't until one of the vans turned down the steep rutted track towards the river that they knew they had found their quarry. A thick band of trees and scrub stood sentinel on the western perimeters of the grounds of Holgate Park School and, from behind this, a blue glow lacerated by flashing strobes betrayed the venue. As they drew nearer the noise reached them; the ear-splitting boom and throb of ghetto blasters whose decibel readings had soared off the scale.

Keeping under cover, the police presence discovered that there were about one hundred and fifty young people cavorting in the hijacked barn, small by Rave Party standards, where it was usual for the police to find themselves dealing with over 1000 young people in a very volatile state, who had been directed to the venue from all over the country by mobile phone. The organiser of this event was one Rod Lewis, a small-time drugs dealer with a finger in many entrepreneurial pies of dubious legality. Once it had been ascertained that heroin, crack and other hard drugs were unlikely to be changing hands, the police were content to bide their time and approach the problem from the Public Order and Noise Abatement angle.

An environmental health officer was winkled from his bed and in company with four of the police officers he entered the barn and served a notice on the organizer. The silence, as the stridor from the banks of amplifiers was suddenly cut off, was painful. Young people froze in their gyrations and disbelief settled on their faces, then panic broke out. There was mass rush for the exits which went unhindered; check points had already been set up on all access roads and the ravers would be intercepted and searched for drugs as they left the village. Rod Lewis was found in possession of ten Ecstasy tablets and was arrested together with two of his henchmen, also involved in supplying the partygoers.

Unbeknown to the police, some of the revellers had reached the barn via the river. A large, unwieldy clinker-built dinghy of venerable age, fitted with an outboard in addition to the oars, had been "borrowed" and used to convey a dozen young people upriver. The tide had been full when they had arrived and they had stepped ashore onto hard shingle and the boat had been tied carelessly to a convenient stake. None of the twelve had any experience in seamanship. After the police infiltration of the party they had scrambled down to the shore to find themselves confronted by a vast sea of mud and no boat. No-one had thought of tides.

It was not as dark as it had been. There was a pre-dawn lightning of the sky behind them to the east and ahead of them the floodlights of Felstone Docks glowed whitely above the stretch of mud they faced with horrified eyes. The boat had slipped its mooring and lay beached on a gleaming shoal a tantalizing few yards away from the river. Runnels of water laced the turgid mudflats that sucked and slurped at rocks and reed clumps.

"Hell! What do we do now?!

"Who tied it up?"

"Wouldn't make any difference, it would still be high and dry!"

Some of the girls in the group began to whimper, the drug-induced warmth and euphoria dissipating rapidly in the early morning chill.

"We'll have to leave it and get home somehow else."

"And get picked up by the police? Are you clean?" In reply, the youth tugged at an inner pocket and produced a tablet which he tossed away into the mud.

"Twelve bleeding quid down the drain!"

"Ssh, keep your voice down. Look, I'm sure we could wade out to the boat, it's only a bit of mud. Once we get to it we can use the oars to push it back into the water."

"It's dirty and it stinks!" The speaker shivered and brushed the hair out of her eyes.

"Well, have you a better idea? Even if you avoid the police it's a good six mile walk."

"It's worth a try" said another youth, already starting to remove his shoes and socks. "Come on."

In a straggling line, they floundered through the mud and heaved themselves aboard. The girls shivered in the bottom of the boat whilst the boys battled with the oars.

"How long will it take to row back?" asked one of the girls, fingering her reeking finery.

"We're not rowing anywhere, we're still stuck in this shitty mud!"

"You're not trying. Where's Jason?" The boys paused in their endeavour as a head count was taken. "He's not here!"

"Don't be daft, he *must* be!"

"Jason, Jason, where are you?" carolled the girl, making an exaggerated pantomime of looking out to sea. "Oh my God! Look!" The others followed her gesture. A black hump lay wedged in the mud a few yards away. Under the whitening sky they could just make out the blonde hair plastered to the back of the head.

The girl started to scream.

The body of Jason Ball was recovered from its muddy grave by the team of policemen fortunately at hand. Desperate attempts were made to resuscitate him but it was too late. What had started as a spree had ended in tragedy and his companions huddled on the shore in a little knot awaiting further police action, some frozen in misery, others openly weeping.

James Roland was the CID officer on call that night and he was alerted at five am. He managed to grab the receiver at the first ring without awakening Ginny and he snatched up his clothes and crept downstairs to dress. As he backed the car out of the drive the sun burst over the horizon, igniting the scene in molten gold. Already it was hot; each bush and tree was enveloped in a golden haze, an early morning mist that would soon burn off under the powerful rays of the sun and the grass shimmered with a myriad of dewdrops. It was going to be another perfect summer day, he thought, as he drove through the sleeping village, or, as Lacey would put it, the sort of day when you were glad to be alive, and he was going to deal with death. And worst of all, the death of a young person.

He had only been given the bare details over the phone but it sounded like an accidental death. Why, he mused as he crossed the A45 and headed west, was everything happening at Saxton? This could have nothing to do with The Joker but why had Saxton been chosen as the venue for a Rave Party? He was becoming haunted by the damn place. At the approach to the village he was directed by the policeman on duty to the area behind Holgate Park School where the Rave had taken place. He jolted down the track and parked beside the other police vehicles. The barn was to his left and ahead of him lay the river, but as he moved towards it a police officer appeared from behind the barn and intercepted him. It was a uniformed sergeant from Felstone HQ whom Roland knew well.

"What is it, Fielding?"

"Could you come over here, sir?"

"Where? I thought the accident had happened in the river?"

"Yes, sir, but before you go down there, there's something else."

"Well, what is it man?"

"We've got a van load of youngsters over there. I think they're all under age so we're taking them back to the Station. The parents will have to be contacted before we can search them."

"Fielding, why are you wasting my time? I'm here to investigate a suspicious death; rounding up the ravers is your job."

"Yes, sir, but there's something I think you should know."

"Don't tell me, you've found the person who is behind these malicious jokes and he's below the age of criminal responsibility."

Roland walked towards the van and Fielding swallowed what he had been going to say and moved after him. The back doors of the van were open and inside were about fifteen young people of both sexes looking flushed and unhappy. In the middle of the group sat Simon.

For a few long seconds step-father and step-son stared at each other, Roland deadpan and Simon half-apprehensive, half-defiant. Then the boy croaked:

"James . . .?"

Roland ignored him and snapped at Fielding: "Drugs?"

"Ecstasy and possibly LSD we think."

"Presumably these aren't the only ones you've netted?"

"No, sir, another van load has already been taken to the Station. We picked these up cycling along the Woodford Road and turned back to take on board another group that were intercepted near the school."

"You're going to have a busy morning, rounding up all the parents and guardians."

"Yes. What about your . . . er . . . son? You can't be involved – do you want me to get Ginny?"

"No," said Roland sharply, "I don't want her bothered. Get a social worker." He turned on his heel and walked away without a backward glance but, inwardly, he was seething with mixed emotions, anger foremost amongst them. Bloody little fool! How had he come to be involved in this? He was supposed to be spending the night with his friend Mark – had he often deceived them like this? How *could* he? Christ! thought Roland furiously, it was only the other day we had that little talk, and all the while he must have already had his ticket for this Rave. Well, if he thought he was going to get preferential treatment he could think again! He would be treated just the same as all the others who had been rounded up, which meant at best, a caution and his name going officially on record. And wouldn't that make some people happy! Colleagues whose toes he had stepped on would be highly amused to see him embarrassed in this way. Lacey too would get plenty of mileage out of it.

The body was lying on a tarpaulin just above the high tide line and Roland was surprised to see that George Brasnett, the pathologist, was already in attendance. He had been crouched over the body but he got to his feet as Roland approached and looked at him over the top of his glasses.

"Stupid young fool, what a waste."

"What happened?"

The young uniformed constable in attendance answered.

"A party of them came up the river by boat. They forgot about the little question of tides. When they arrived back

59

the boat was stuck out in the mud. They tried wading out to it and he must have slipped and got sucked under."

"Any witnesses?"

"His companions didn't actually see it happen. One moment they were all traipsing through the mud with him up in front, the next, they'd clambered into the boat and were trying to get it afloat and someone noticed he was missing. He wasn't far away – only a couple of yards – but nobody saw him go under and they couldn't have done anything if they had."

Roland bent over the body. It was heavily encased in black mud and slime but the face had been wiped clean when the kiss of life had been tried in vain and a wedge of blond hair was plastered over the forehead. He didn't look much older than Simon, thought Roland. It could have been Simon, for God's sake!

"Who is he?"

"Jason Bolt. According to his friends he's nineteen and lives in Felstone."

"We have no reason to suppose his friends are lying? He did slip and wasn't pushed?"

"No, I think it happened just as they said; they're all in a state of shock now."

"What had they taken? I presume they've been searched?"

"Ecstasy. They insist they only had one tablet each, which was consumed early in the proceedings, so the effects should have worn off by the time they left. There was nothing on them when they were searched."

"Hhmm. Well, Doc, is that consistent with your observations? It was accidental?"

"That's your department, not mine, James. I'm just a mere medic, but he certainly wasn't bashed over the head first."

The moment someone treated Brasnett as a mere medic he'd be heading for trouble, thought Roland. The man was pompous and full of his own self-importance, but he was good at his job and the two men had a healthy respect for each other. Although he had also been called from his bed, Brasnett looked as if he had spent some while achieving his appearance of sartorial elegance. His trousers had an immaculate crease and his silk tussore jacket fitted his portly body like a second skin. He flicked a speck of mud off this jacket now and shook his head.

"I'm never sure which is worse. A body that has been violently done to death at the hands of its fellow men or one like this, who has been cut off in his prime by some freak, senseless accident. He had all his life before him. It's obscene."

"I know," said Roland harshly, "why do the young think they are omnipotent and it can never happen to them? When you do the PM I want a drugs check. Whatever he took probably made him happy and careless."

"Have the parents been informed?"

"At least that's something you don't have to cope with. I'll arrange for the body to be taken to the mortuary. Did you come in your . . . yes, what is it now, Fielding?"

Sergeant Fielding hurried down the track towards them, his hand upraised.

"Don't go yet, sir!"

"I'm not going anywhere," snapped Roland, "what's the matter now?"

"I mean the doctor. We've found another body!"

"What!" Roland's immediate thought was that it would certainly be a drug overdose this time and why the hell hadn't the police moved in earlier? "Another kid?"

"No, an elderly man. We were searching through the rest of the outbuildings and we found him swinging from a beam. It looks as if he's hung himself!"

It was dark inside the shed and James Roland had difficulty at first in adjusting his eyes to the dimness of the interior. The body was hanging from a beam about equi-distant from the door and the dirt-encrusted window. The feet were suspended about a foot from the floor and were encased in highly polished brogues. Old man's shoes, thought Roland as his gaze travelled upwards and he saw what he had feared and half-expected to see: a panama hat tipped forward over the head, partially obscuring the face and resting on one shoulder.

"We didn't cut him down because he's obviously been

61

dead for some time and as you and the Doc were here we thought you would want to see him first" said sergeant Fielding.

"I don't want him cut down yet" said Roland sharply, "I want the SOCO's and the photographer here immediately."

"You don't think it's a suicide?"

"I'm pretty certain it's not. Get me a torch and something to stand on, I want to get a closer look at that hat."

A packing case was found and Roland climbed on to it and accepted the torch Findlay held up to him. Very carefully he put a finger under the brim of the panama and eased it forward so that he could see the band inside. A name tag was sewn over the label and he flashed the torch on to it and could just make out the name. The face was congested with bloodshot eyes and he thought he could see another ligature mark round the neck below the rope. He grunted and stretched up to examine the rope and beam. The rope looked slightly frayed where it had come into contact with the wood and he could just make out filaments of fibre clinging to the beam itself. He jumped down.

"Get DS Mansfield and DC Evans here. We've definitely got a murder enquiry on our hands this time." He turned to George Brasnett, who was staring at the body with an inscrutable look on his face. "Well, Doc, what do you say? You're being remarkably quiet."

"I'm not usually on the scene when the body is first discovered; I'm fascinated to see you in action, James. I take it you think he was strung up after he was killed?"

"Yes. A suicide would sling the rope over the beam first before putting the noose round his neck. In this case I think the rope was put round his neck and then the end was thrown over the beam and the body hauled up; you can see the results of the strain and friction on the rope.

"Can I touch him yet?"

"Just wait until the photographers have had a go at him then we'll get him down."

George Brasnett adjusted his silk, polka tie and looked shrewdly at Roland through his bi-focals.

"You know who the victim is, don't you? You've been expecting it?"

"His name, unless we're being deliberately misled, is Charles Todd and he was on the receiving end of one of the malicious jokes."

Roland told the tale, as it had been related to him by William Evans, of the episode in the Maritime Museum and when he had finished the doctor whistled.

"It's like something out of an Agatha Christie – did you ever read 'A Murder is Announced'? The details of a forthcoming murder were set out in the local rag."

"Well, we were given the MO but not the time or the venue."

"What do you know about him?"

"Very little so far. He was a retired naval officer living here in Saxton and apparently not very popular with his neighbours. Tried to pull rank and got up everyone's nose."

"So maybe someone with a grudge against him topped him and set it up to look as if it were the work of The Joker?"

"That's one of the angles I'm going to have to check. If only the Press hadn't got hold of it. Everyone in Suffolk now knows every detail of each nasty little spoof. I still don't know how they found out about this one – it certainly didn't come from us."

"Perhaps The Joker is feeding them the information himself, trying to get maximum footage out of each incident."

"You may have a point there, Doc, and it will be followed up. Perhaps you should join the team, you seem to be more on the ball than I am at the moment."

"You're certain that your Morris dancer wasn't a victim of The Joker?"

"As certain as it's possible to be at this stage. I've no doubts myself but that it was manslaughter."

Roland squinted up at the body of Charles Todd again.

"How soon can you do the autopsy?"

"Today is Sunday."

"And this is a murder investigation."

"Okay, okay, as soon as I possibly can but don't forget

63

I've already got another one – that poor young fool out there." Yes, thought Roland, and I've got Simon to deal with. But not now, not yet. He had more important things to cope with at the moment, Simon would have to wait.

"I think I can hear the reinforcements arriving. Stay around, Doc, he'll soon be all yours."

Tina Fairbrother crept up the stairs and flung herself down on her bed. She'd been lucky, very lucky, as she was only now beginning to realise. Who had tipped the police off about the Rave? All those weeks of scheming and planning down the drain – but no, they'd had a great time and the Old Bill hadn't appeared until it was nearly over. She could only feel relief that she had got away without being picked up.

As soon as she had realized what was happening she had bolted out of the barn and run back towards the school grounds. She had dropped down into the ha-ha that separated the gardens from the playing fields and crawled along on her belly until she had reached the perimeter wall. Near this was a fallen oak and she had stuffed the four Ecstasy tablets into a hollow in the trunk of this oak. If she had been caught with those on her she might have been done for dealing. She wasn't a dealer, she had got them off Rod for her friends' use. Poor Rod; he'd been arrested and would probably face a prison sentence. They'd be no more Raves for a while.

She sat up and examined her arms and legs. Having discarded the Ecstasy tablets she had reached home by a tortuous route that involved creeping along ditches and across a field of wheat and pushing through hedgerows and thickets. Luckily she knew the area well and had been able to avoid the road blocks but she was covered with grazes and scratches and her limbs throbbed. Hell, she was thirsty but she daren't go down to the kitchen in case she woke her father.

She knew nothing of the tragedy that had befallen one of her fellow Ravers.

Over on the other side of the village Mark Copley let himself into his flat and stumbled into the bedroom. He leaned against the bed and struggled to get his breath back. His brush with the police had rattled him badly. He'd been intercepted before he'd got back to where he'd left the car and searched and questioned. Bloody police! Just because he wore his hair long and had pierced ears they seemed to think he was a prime candidate as a junkie.

He went over to the dressing table and looked in the mirror, Bloodshot eyes stared back at him out of a face that was sallow with fatigue. His mane of hair was lank with sweat and he released the leather band that held it back and ran a comb through it. Well, they hadn't found anything, had they? He didn't need drugs to psyche himself up, he got his kicks in other ways. All those ravers, high on "E", hugging and embracing each other had turned him off completely. And made him feel guilty. Why had he gone?

Because Tina Fairbrother had taunted him about being tied to the Barnard twins' apron strings and he had wanted to prove to her that he was still his own man. And also, he supposed, if he were truthful, she had seemed to be making a play for him again and he had been flattered. His pride had been badly dented when she had dropped him before and he had had some idea of leading her on that night and then being the one to ditch her and get his own back. He needn't have bothered, she'd been as high as the others and had hardly noticed him apart from throwing her arms around him early in the proceedings and mumbling something about loving everybody. Supposing Alison got to hear about it? Or, even worse, Lindsey? He had cheated on Alison but Lindsey wouldn't cheat on her own sister . . .

He had a shower and drank a glass of milk before drawing the curtains to shut out the strengthening daylight and took to his bed for a few hours sleep.

Simon Dalton sat hunched on the bench staring at the floor, which was covered by golden-brown vinyl tiles with a grained pattern intended to make them look like real parquet; part of the recent revamp of the public section of Felstone Police HQ. They could have been gingerbread for all he knew or cared. Around him his friends whispered

65

amongst themselves and wondered what would happen to them. The numbers were going down as various parents arrived and were united with their offspring and taken off to another part of the building. Apparently it was all right to drag parents out of bed at the crack of dawn, social workers and the like were accorded a more civilized hour.

He was desperately thirsty and also feeling rather sick. The euphoria and warm glow of affection for his fellow men which he had experienced earlier in the night had dissipated; all he could remember were the screams of the girls down on the shore. They echoed round in his head still, the way they had rung out in the still grey light as he and his companions had been herded into the police van and they had learned that someone had died. It would be bad enough if it had been a stranger, thought Simon, but he knew Jason Ball. He had been a member of the Sixth Form last year and had been popular. There had been a time, before he grew out of such things, when Simon had hero-worshipped him. And now he was dead; drowned in the river or suffocated in the mud, he wasn't sure which but it was a nightmare. How could he be dead? How could such a thing have happened?

And how could he have been so stupid as to have gone to the bloody Rave in the first place? If only he could put back the clock so that none of it had happened: no partying, no being persuaded to part with his precious allowance for an Ecstasy tablet, no terrible accident, no police . . . He gulped. Soon, he would have to face Janes.

A short while later the scene inside the shed was transformed. Arc lights had been set up and the body had been photographed from every angle whilst the Scene of Crime Officers and fingerprint expert went about their business. Mansfield and Evans had arrived on their heels and the latter had confirmed Roland's suspicions.

"Crikey. It's just as Michael described it. This body strung up in the Maritime Museum wearing Captain Todd's hat."

"But this time it's a real body and almost certainly that of Charles Todd himself."

"The Joker strikes!"

"Stop talking like the gutter press and make yourself useful. I want a list of all the people who were at the Rave. Most of them were intercepted and searched as they left and they'll all have to be interviewed."

The body was cut down and immediately he had made a quick examination, George Brasnett drew Roland's attention to the victim's neck.

"It's as you thought. See – there are two ligatures. The lower one is thinner and has bitten deeper into the flesh; he was probably strangled with a cord – say something like a piece of flex – and later the rope noose was put round his neck. You can see the weave in the wider scarring and it's right under his chin and slopes slightly upwards to a suspension point at the back of the neck, which fits in with being strung up."

"Would he have struggled?"

"Very little if he was taken unawares from behind."

"He's a small man, probably not much more than ten stone in weight, so moving him afterwards wouldn't have presented a problem to a reasonably fit, healthy man."

"Or woman."

"You think a woman would have had the strength?"

"It's surprising the almost super-human strength a woman in a frenzy can command; but I don't have to tell you that."

"Except that this wasn't done in a frenzy. It was a cold, pre-meditated murder."

"There's rigor mortis present in the jaw, arms and legs. Can I remove some of his clothing now?" Brasnett delved into his bag and produced a rectal thermometer.

"Sure, go ahead, I'd like to have some idea as to when he died."

A short while later he got his answer as Brasnett got to his feet and squinted at his thermometer. "There's a rectal temperature of 25C. Allowing for this heatwave, I should say he's been dead approximately twelve hours, give or take three hours either way."

"Which means some time yesterday evening. I wonder if he was moved here before or during the Rave? There were

67

enough people milling about all night; our murderer took quite a risk."

"I don't know," said Mansfield, "once they were all at it in the barn a volcano could have erupted outside without anyone being any the wiser, what with the noise and one thing and another."

"You've got a point there but there was always the chance that someone would wander outside for a pee or a couple might come in here for a session in privacy. That's one of the things you must check, Evans, when you interview the Ravers."

After Brasnett had concluded his preliminary examination and the body had been taken away to await his attention in the morgue, Roland went into the barn to co-ordinate his team and issue instructions. By now the sun was beating relentlessly down on the parched countryside; it was no cooler inside. It was as if the heat that had been generated earlier by the pulsating bodies still lingered, tangible and feisty. There were crates of mineral water stacked against one wall and the floor was littered with empty bottles. Roland trod on one and the plastic crackled and split under his foot.

"Get this lot out of here" he snapped, kicking it aside.

"Your Gov's in a filthy mood," said the young uniformed constable who had been talking to William Evans, "is he always like this?"

"It's probably because of this." Evans tapped the list he had just been perusing. "His son's name is on it."

"I think you should tell the police."

Lindsey Barnard picked up the letter from the kitchen table and examined it again. It had arrived earlier by post addressed to Alison in an innocuous looking white envelope with a typed address. Inside had been a single sheet of paper bearing one line which consisted of letters and numerals cut out and stuck on. It read: MATT XIX 30. She had read it in puzzlement and held it out to her twin.

"What ever is this? Who is Matt?"

"How peculiar. It's almost like an anonymous letter."

"Who would want to send me an anonymous letter? And

I thought things like that were very crude and obvious. This is like a reference."

"Of course, that's just what it is – a reference! It's a Bible reference, Matt must mean Matthew."

They had searched through their bookshelves for the old copy of the Bible which they knew should be there somewhere and when they had found it Alison had flicked through the pages of the New Testament.

"Here we are: 'But many that are first shall be last; and the last shall be first.' What ever does that mean?"

"Search me! Can you read the postmark?"
Alison turned over the envelope. "Felstone I think, it's a bit blurred." She put it down on the table. "I don't understand what this is all about. It's crazy – why should someone send me an obscure Bible quote?"

"I don't know, but don't worry about it. Finish your breakfast, your coffee is getting cold."

Alison Barnard toyed with her piece of toast and made a pretence of sipping her coffee. Her sister eyed her anxiously.

"That damn letter has upset you, hasn't it?"

"No . . . yes . . . the envelope is the same, isn't it?"

"What do you mean?"

"It's the same sort of envelope, the same typed address, as the one that was sent before . . . the one that contained the newspaper cutting . . ."

"All typewritten stuff looks the same, only experts can tell the difference."

"I'm right thought, aren't I?"

"It could be, I suppose."

"Why? why is someone trying to frighten me? What have I done that someone should be so cruel?"

"Allie, don't upset yourself."

"Why are they bothering? Wasting their time? I shall be dead soon anyway!"

"DON'T talk like that! You're being ridiculous. You KNOW you're going to get well, you're just having a bad day."

"I don't know anything anymore. Sometimes I feel much better and I think I really am recovering, then I think –

don't kid yourself, those horrible little mutants are lurking in your blood and they're going to zap all the healthy cells . . ."

"Stop it, Allie, that's just defeatist talk. You *are* going to get better. You've got to for my sake, for Mark's sake – what would he do without you?"

"Find someone more suited to him." Alison turned a sudden accusing look on her twin and the colour flooded into Lindsey's face.

"Don't be ridiculous . . ."

"Am I?"

"I can't reason with you when you're in this mood. You're letting your imagination run away with you." She banged the coffee pot down on the table and picked up the letter. "Show this to the police. They'll know what to do."

"We can't waste their time over something unimportant like this."

"Look, it's not trivial to you, is it? And this is the second one if you count the newspaper cutting. I think they ought to be told and you know what that detective said – to get in touch if anything else untoward happened."

"Yes, but . . ."

"No buts. I'll ring up the Police Station and ask to speak to him; Detective Roland was his name wasn't it?"

"I don't remember."

"Well, I do. He was one of the handsomest men I've ever seen, don't say you didn't notice?"

"I found him rather threatening. He wouldn't suffer fools gladly."

"I'm sure he wouldn't think you were foolish to report something like this."

"Maybe not . . . Leave it for now. I'll think about it."

A mobile Incident Room was set up in the grounds of Holgate Park School. James Roland assembled his team and the murder enquiry got under way. The school caretaker had been one of the first people to be interviewed but could tell them little of use. He was way past retirement age and partially deaf and had heard nothing of the happenings of the past night, having slept like the proverbial log.

"Before we do anything else we had better visit Todd's cottage" said Roland. "I want to have a good look around before the SOCOs go in. Evans, you went there and interviewed him after the incident in the museum. Jog my memory."

"He lived on his own" said Evans, talking with his mouth full and hastily removing the ham roll from Roland's sight. "I gathered he'd been a widower for some years and he didn't take kindly to being interviewed by a mere constable. It was all in my report."

"Yes, but you're here and the report isn't. What was the place like?"

"Very neat, excessively so, almost as if he lined things up with a ruler, but he was slack about security, locking up door and windows etc."

"What impression did you get of him?"

"He was a snob. I was below his notice. I reckon he made a lot of enemies."

"Which doesn't make our task any easier. A lot of the Ravers on your list must live here in Saxton. When you're checking them out sound out them and their parents on Todd; you may pick up some interesting titbits."

"This is going to take forever" grumbled Evans.

"I've allocated four of you to the job so it shouldn't. Concentrate on the Saxton ones first, then you can move on to the others. I don't think you'll get any joy. Most of them were so spaced out they won't have noticed anything."

"Do you want every name on this list checked?"

"Haven't I just said so?"

"Every single name?" persisted Evans.

"Leave Simon to me. Now MOVE. Come on, Patrick, we'll have a poke around chez Todd."

"Did I hear correctly?" said Mansfield as they got into the car. "Simon . . .?"

"You did" replied Roland grimly. "Simon was here last night and as high as the rest of them I gather." Mansfield glanced at him and decided he would be pushing his luck to ask any more questions. He stared out of the windscreen as

Roland angled out of the school gates and drove the short distance to Charles Todd's cottage.

As soon as they walked through the gate the two men could see what Evans had meant. The garden was laid out with obsessional neatness, the plants in straight rows, the hedge clipped to within an inch of its life. The front and back doors were locked but the french doors, which opened out onto a concrete patio, were ajar. They pulled them open and went inside. The room was L-shaped and furnished in mock Regency style with a sofa and easy chairs upholstered in cream and green striped chintz and curtains of a similar design. There were several small occasional tables in rosewood with brass stringing dotted about and one of these was tumbled onto its side in front of a winged chair which faced inwards. A newspaper was scattered on the floor near this chair and Roland caught sight of something gleaming under a nearby bookcase. It was a cut glass whiskey tumbler lying on its side, where it had rolled.

"It's easy to see what happened. He was sitting here reading his newspaper with his back to the french doors. The murderer comes through these and creeps up on him unheard and unseen. He whips a cord round his neck and pulls it tight and hey presto. The paper shoots off Todd's lap and the table gets knocked over, sending his glass rolling across the floor until it fetches up under the bookcase."

"He wouldn't have stood a chance, would he?"

"No, it would have been all over before he knew what was happening to him."

"So, do you reckon his body was taken away immediately?"

"It would still have been daylight – there are no lights on in the place – it would have been very dicey for our murderer to have moved him straight away; he would have risked being seen by one of the neighbours or a passer-by. No, I reckon he was killed and left for a few hours and his murderer came back later, after it was dark, to carry out the next step in his plan."

"But Todd might have had a caller yesterday evening and have been found almost immediately."

"I don't suppose this was a spur of the moment thing. I reckon our killer had had Todd under close observation and knew that there was little chance of any visitors. He probably left him slumped in the chair and came back after dark with something to wrap the body in."

"There were no foreign fibres on his clothing, were there?"

"Not as far as I could see but Forensics may come up with something when they get his clothes in the laboratory. It was more likely to have been a length of plastic; every well-read murderer these days knows about fibres being traceable."

"He must have had a car."

"Yes. We'll have a good look around in here and then explore the garden."

Some time later when they had thoroughly searched the house Roland had to admit that they were no nearer to learning anything of significance about Charles Todd. The only personal touch they had found had been a photo of a woman who they had presumed to have been his wife. A check through the personal papers in his bureau revealed that he was comfortably off but they didn't find a will. In the garden they discovered a wheelbarrow lying on its side near the bottom hedge. This hedge had a gap in it and the grass beneath was flattened.

"What's the betting the murderer trundled the body down here in that wheelbarrow and hid it under the hedge – probably wrapped up in something – and came back later when it was dark and removed it" said Roland. "The farm track runs the other side of this hedge; he could get a car along it easily."

"He ran the risk of being seen by the neighbours" pointed out Mansfield. But when they went back to the road they saw that the house on one side was empty and up for sale, whilst the one on the other side looked shut-up, with tightly drawn curtains, as if the owners were on holiday.

"Come on, there's nothing more to be done here at the moment. Let's get back to the MIR and see if anything else has come up."

CHAPTER 5

Ginny Roland put down the receiver and stared at the phone in dismay. At first she hadn't understood what Penny Taplin had been trying to tell her; now that it had got through she felt anger and distress in equal proportions. How COULD Simon? Where had she gone wrong? What would James say? Where WAS James – she needed him to cope with this. She sat down on the bottom step of the stairs and Katherine crawled onto her lap and played with the gold chain she was wearing round her neck. She absentmindedly patted her daughter's carroty curls and went through the telephone conversation she had just had once again. Simon had been staying with his friend, Mark Taplin, and Mark's mother Penny had rung to ask if Simon had come back yet.

"No, isn't he still with you?"

"Why should he be here?" Penny had sounded hostile. "Mark was supposed to be staying with you."

"I don't understand, Simon was at yours last night."

"Oh no he wasn't. So that's how they worked it, little devils!"

"What do you mean? Is something wrong?"

"Wrong? I should say there is. Don't tell me you don't know?"

"Know what?" Ginny had asked, thoroughly alarmed.

"Our two teenage monsters were not tucked up safely in bed last night, they were at an all night party. One that was raided by the police and they were picked up."

"You mean an ACID party?"

"You're out of date, Ginny. It's Rave parties these days, as in Ecstasy!"

"Oh my God!"

"Quite. Do you mean to say you know nothing about it? Haven't you been sent for? We had to go to the Police Station whilst Mark was searched for drugs and questioned."

"No. No-one has contacted me."

"I suppose Simon gets preferential treatment just because James is a policeman," Penny had said aggressively.

"No, of course not. If they're under seventeen they have to have a parent or guardian present before they can be interviewed by the police. James is out on a case – he went off in the early hours, but he couldn't act for Simon anyway, it certainly wouldn't be allowed. Had . . . had they taken anything?"

"You bet they had. Do you know, Ginny, I go out to work so that we can have a better lifestyle; so that Mark can have his mountain bike and his state of the art trainers and a decent allowance – and what does he spend it on – drugs! Ecstasy!"

"You mean he was found in possession?"

"You've got all the jargon, haven't you? He – and I presume your Simon too – hadn't got any on them but they'd consumed an Ecstasy tablet at the start of the party."

"So what happened?"

"He was given a good talking to and a warning and he's now got an official police record!"

"They haven't kept him at the Station?"

"No, we were allowed to bring him home with us but he's in a terrible state."

"You mean because of the drugs?"

"Not just that. One of them died!"

"Died? How? Where WAS this party?"

"Over at Saxon."

At that point in the conversation Ginny had thought she was going to faint. James had left a note on the kitchen table saying he had been called out to Saxton . . . Simon had been there . . . Simon was now missing . . . Simon was dead or seriously injured . . .? Then common sense took over. Penny had already said that the two boys had been picked up and taken to the Station. This death couldn't involve Simon.

"What happened?"

"I can't get much sense out of him. Apparently some of them went up river by boat to the party and one of them fell in and was drowned."

"How awful!"

"And we know him, Ginny. His name is Jason Ball, he was that blonde, good looking boy who used to go to their school, very good at acting. Didn't he play Romeo to your Simon's Tybalt last year?"

"I used to teach him," she had said faintly, "he had a very good eye for line."

"Well now he's dead! It could be Mark or Simon . . ."

She had rung off shortly after this leaving Ginny's thoughts in a turmoil. Where was Simon now? Was he still at the Station? Why hadn't she been contacted? Did James know about what had happened? Had he been called out to this Rave party? She decided that she must try and contact him so she carried Katherine into the sitting room and deposited her in the playpen. Katherine started to cry in protest; she pulled herself up by the bars and howled at her mother, her face rapidly rivalling her hair in colour.

"Just be a good girl for a few minutes. I shan't be long and then I'll play with you." Ginny firmly shut the door on her and dialled the Station. She made herself known and asked for James.

"I'm afraid he's not here, Mrs Roland."

"Is Simon there?"

There was a pause and Ginny asked sharply: "Hello? Are you still there?"

"Yes, Ma'am."

"To whom am I speaking?"

"Sergeant Crowther."

"Oh Bob, I'm glad it's you" said Ginny, relieved it was someone she knew. "Is Simon at the Station?"

"He was here. I think he's just left, a social worker was taking him home."

"Oh. Do you know the whereabouts of my husband?"

"He's out on a case."

"Yes, I know. Look, you're in radio contact with him, aren't you? Can you ask him to phone me as soon as possible?"

"I'll see the message is passed on to him, Mrs Roland."

"Thanks, Bob. Are your wife and family well?"

"Yes, we're hoping to get away on holiday soon."

"Lucky you, I hope you make it."

Ginny put down the receiver and went to rescue her daughter who was working herself into a frenzy.

There was a clammy chill in the mortuary that brought Roland out in a cold sweat. Although it was late afternoon it was still in the eighties outside and the sudden contrast combined with the harsh fluorescent lights and the all pervasive smell of formalin and disinfectant wrenched at his guts. George Brasnett was just removing his rubber apron when Roland arrived and greeted him cheerfully.

"You're too late, I've finished. I thought you were going to be in on this."

"I've been too busy." Roland nodded at the Coroner's Officer, the mortuary attendant and Mansfield. The latter was looking somewhat pale and tight-lipped. Poor Patrick, he thought, after all his years in the Force he was still squeamish about what he called cadavers and cut opens. He'd learnt to control it though and not let it interfere with his police duties.

"What have you got for me?"

"Nothing new. He was definitely strangled and then strung up. He must have been taken completely unawares; no sign of him putting up a fight – no cuts or bruises on his hands but there is slight grooving across the thumbs as if he had tried to release the pressure of the ligature."

"Any nearer to the time of death?"

"Sometime yesterday evening, probably mid-evening but don't quote me on that. The stomach contained a little partly digested food and alcohol. He was in pretty good nick apart from an enlarged prostrate gland which is not unusual for some of his age. It will all be in my report."

Roland nodded and thrust his hands into his pockets. "What about the boy?"

77

Brasnett's eyes glinted at him over the top of his glasses. "How did you know I'd done him first?"

"I know how your mind works." As I well ought, he thought, we've known each other a long time. Brasnett liked to think he was in control at this stage and it was typical that he should carry out the autopsy on Jason Ball first although Roland had stressed the urgency of the other.

Brasnett smirked. "You'd better listen to my on-going commentary." He reached over and switched on the small pocket dictating machine which he used to record his findings as he was working. His voice sounded even more plummy and sonorous on the tape. Roland listened to the phrases rolling off his tongue: fluid in air passages . . . lungs have doughy consistency and exude fluid and air bubbles when sliced . . . stomach contains a little partly digested food and much water and mud . . . much mud also present in airways, mouth and oesophagus . . . At the end Brasnett flicked off the switch and cleared his throat.

"The toxicology results will take about three weeks to come through as you well know. I've asked them to check for 3,4-methylenedioxymethamphetamine."

"Why can't he just say Ecstasy like anyone else?" muttered Mansfield at Roland's elbow.

"Not that they will add much of significance to my report" continued Brasnett, "he died of too much river. What a waste."

And what a way to go, thought Roland. One minute full of the joys of life, the next struggling as the water and mud closed over his head. It was bad enough to drown in clear water but the mud added an extra dimension of horror to the situation. Mud: the stinking, black, viscous mud being sucked up his mouth and his nose as he writhed and wallowed in vain . . . It didn't bear thinking about . . . He pulled himself together.

"As you say, what a waste. The parents are nearly out of their minds."

Jason Ball's mother and father had identified his body and Roland had undergone a very bad twenty minutes when he had tried to cope with their grief and get across to them that no funeral arrangements could be made until after the inquest had taken place.

"Anyway, thanks Doc. Next time I'll try and make sure it doesn't happen on a Sunday."

"Is there going to be a next time?"

"Keep your fingers crossed."

"What's the next move?" asked Mansfield as they stepped out of the building into blinding sunshine.

"Back to the Station. Lacey wants an up-date on what's happening and rather in his office than the Incident Room at Saxton. I want to keep him out of the team's hair as long as possible."

". . . you've already issued a statement to the Press! Why wasn't I consulted first?"

Lacey glared at the two detectives and rapped his pen on his desk top. It was a little later in the Superintendent's office and Roland had already run through the salient progress of the day's investigation.

"There was no way of keeping it quiet and rather than have them print wild speculation I thought it was best to try and curb their sensational excesses."

"Then I hope your comment wasn't 'no comment?'"

"I told them that we were treating the death as suspicious and following up several lines of enquiry and we would keep them informed of any significant developments."

"And how they'll embroider that! You haven't made much progress yet, have you?"

"It's early days." Roland invariably found himself exchanging cliché for cliché when he was in Lacey's presence. "We still haven't contacted all the people who were at the Rave and there must be some who we didn't pick up originally and of whom we know nothing as yet. So far, nobody admits to seeing or hearing anything untoward last night. Whenever and however the body was removed to the barn at Holgates and strung up, it was done without anyone noticing."

"And Forensics have come up with nothing?"

"There were no fingerprints, apart from his own, in Todd's cottage and none on the door of the barn or shed apart from a smear. Our murderer wore gloves. We have found a sheet of polythene – of the sort people use in the garden for forcing early potatoes – it had been stuffed under some pallets in the barn and we think it was what was used to wrap the body in. Forensics have got it now for testing, and also the rope that was used to string him up, but it's my bet that although they'll find traces of Todd on it there'll be nothing of his killer. This was a carefully planned murder and he'd worked it all out; it was no spur of the moment killing."

"Yet he took an appalling chance of being caught in the act when he took the body to the barn. Why did he bother to do that?"

"Because he wanted to parrot the macabre little tableau that was set up in the Maritime Museum?"

"But why not string it up in Todd's garage or in the house itself – it would still look the same."

"Because he wanted the maximum publicity and coverage for his act?" said Roland slowly.

"He certainly got that but he didn't know that young fool was going to drown himself and there would be a heavy police presence."

"He must have known that the police would be called out to the Rave party anyway . . . but maybe not. Maybe our murderer had planned to leave the body in some out of the way spot and had lighted on the barn as a suitable location. He would have been horrified when he arrived there to find that half the youth of the area were having a thrash in the very place he had chosen. But then he decided to cash in on it and left the body in a nearby building knowing that whether we found it sooner or later the very fact that there had been a hundred and fifty or so people milling about in the place would obstruct our investigation considerably . . ."

"Thinking along those lines, you're saying that this killing had nothing to do with the death threat jokes – that it was totally unrelated?"

"I think someone was making use of it. Someone who had a grudge against Todd or wanted him out of the way for some reason, decided it would be the ideal cover-up for his crime. He could kill Todd and make it look as if it were the work of this Joker. God! How the Press latched on to that name. The original Joker was Batman's adversary, wasn't he?"

"I agree with you, James" said Lacey, ignoring his last remark, "these jokes, death threats or whatever you like to call them are the work of someone with a twisted mind and a warped sense of humour. Someone who's thought of a ghoulish way of putting the wind up the old biddies of Saxton. What you've got to concentrate on is finding out who had it in for Todd."

"A great many people, as I've already discovered. It would be far easier to find the few who hadn't crossed swords with him at some time or other."

"Maybe he was blackmailing somebody. You say he was into all the village organisations – he might have picked up all manner of juicy titbits about his neighbours and locals."

"Yes, sir. Can I have some more men to help me with the house-to-house enquiries?"

"That's quite out of the question, James. You know what it's like at this time of the year with holidays and such-like. You've got your full team plus two extra constables already." He turned to fix his basilisk stare on Mansfield. "Why aren't you out there doing your bit?"

"My sergeant has far more important things to do" said Roland crisply, "I can't spare him for routine work."

Lacey lumbered to his feet and swatted a fly that had been buzzing groggily at the window. "I want this case sewn up and put to bed. We've got to put a stop to all this Press speculation before it gets completely out of hand."

"Yes, sir."

With a wave of his hand Lacey dismissed them and the two men retreated to the canteen.

"What's this important job you've earmarked for me?" asked Mansfield, depositing two cups of tea on the table and subsiding onto a chair.

"You heard what the good superintendent said; we've got to deal with the Press. Aren't you friendly with one of the sub-editors on the Gazette?"

81

"I've had dealings with the business editor. I wouldn't call him a friend but we're acquainted. He owes me."

"Good. I want to know just how the Press have been so well-informed about the Joker's activities; who's been feeding them information. Go and lean on your friend and see if you can't persuade him to reveal their sources."

"Will do. What about you?"

"I just have to pop home . . ."

"To deal with young Simon?"

Roland raised an eyebrow frostily and Mansfield said sarcastically: "Sorry, SIR, if I spoke out of turn!" His superior took a swig of tea, grimaced and banged the cup down in the saucer.

"No, Pat, it's okay. The truth is I need some advice. What would YOU do?"

Mansfield took his time answering. He pulled his pipe out of his pocket and went through the elaborate process of lighting up. When he had got it going to his satisfaction and the two men were wreathed in smoke he leaned back in his chair, removed it from his mouth and squinted at Roland.

"I'd give him a rocketing. Maybe that's not the best way to cope with the situation but that's what I'd do if it were my Stephen."

"Yes, well, but it's different for you. You're Stephen's real father."

"I don't see what difference that makes."

"All the difference in the world. I'm just Simon's step-father, I haven't got the authority you've got behind you."

"That's nonsense. You may not have officially adopted him but you're his father figure. You support him financially, provide a stable background. You're married to his mother and you've given him a half-sister whom he adores. I'd say you had every right to give him a right rollicking when he goes temporarily off the rails."

"Maybe you're right. I've always felt I was treading on eggs when dealing with him. I've been so careful not to presume, so scrupulous in not upsetting his sensibilities . . ."

"You've pussyfooted around, I know. I've noticed it. I can't blame you but it's not the way to deal with a mixed-up teenager. Put your foot down and he'll respect you more. This may even be his way of getting . . ."

". . . his own back?" interrupted Roland.

"I was going to say, getting a committment out of you. A sort of cry for help. He's testing you to find out if you really care."

"And how long have you been writing an Agony Aunt column?"

"No, seriously, James, let him know you're not going to put up with this sort of thing. Come down on him hard and I think he'll be relieved and will co-operate with you. He's a good lad at heart – I'm very fond of young Simon – and I'm sure this is just a bit of teenage rebellion; he's been led astray, probably doesn't realize the seriousness of it."

"Well, I asked for your advice and I've got it, but whether I'll act on it . . . I don't want to upset Ginny."

Mansfield raised his eyebrows. "Do you think she'll not be upset already?"

As Roland was leaving the Station the message was passed on that Ginny was trying to contact him. He had already ascertained that Simon had been sent home some hours earlier so he got into his car and headed for Wallingford. The main road was busy with a stream of cars flowing inland from Felstone; the day trippers were going home. He was thankful to get onto the B road that ran through the village and leave the traffic behind. There was a sullenness about the heat now; the sun was a copper disk in the evening sky and the air blowing in through the windows was sultry and dust-laden. There would be a storm before long, but not yet; there were no clouds, only a pink haze settling over the parched fields and tired looking trees and hedgerows.

When she heard the car in the drive Ginny darted out of the door.

"James, I've been trying to get you . . ."

"Yes, I know. I've only just got the message and as I was on my way home I didn't bother to ring. Where is he?"

"Upstairs, in his room. He won't have anything to eat."

"You know what happened?"

"Yes, but not from him. Penny Taplin rang me earlier and then I spoke with the woman who brought him home – she was from the Social Services Department. Is it bad?"

"I just hope it was the first time and he hasn't been making a habit of it unbeknown to us."

"Where are you going?" Ginny laid a hand on his arm as he made for the stairs.

"To have it out with him."

"Won't you have something to eat and drink first, it won't take a minute?" she appealed to him, anxiety lurking in her odd-coloured eyes. She'd pinned her hair up in a knot on top of her head and her translucent skin smelled faintly of ripe peaches. She looked good enough to eat but Roland was not going to be diverted.

"I'll sort this out first. Is Katherine asleep?"

"She was a few minutes ago. James, wouldn't it be better if I dealt with this?"

"No." He started to climb the stairs.

"Are you very angry with him?"

"I could break his neck! But don't worry, I'll endeavour to behave in a civilized manner."

He paused outside the door of Simon's room and rapped on it sharply. Dead silence.

"Simon?"

What could only be called a grunt issued through the door and he pushed it open and went in to the room. Simon was sprawled on top of the bed dressed in filthy jeans and tee-shirt. His back was turned away and he did not look up as his step-father entered. Roland said nothing and eventually the boy twisted round and looked at him warily through his tangle of black hair.

"I suppose you've come to read the riot act?"

"You bloody little fool! Why did you do it?"

"I don't know what all the fuss is about – we weren't doing any harm. Just having a party and enjoying the music where it wouldn't disturb anybody else . . ."

"And providing rich pickings for the pushers!"

"No, it wasn't like that!"

"Wasn't it? How many Ecstasy tablets did you take?"

"Only one. I don't know why there's all this bother about

84

Ecstasy. It's not addictive . . . it just makes you feel warm and happy and . . . and sociable."

"It's a Class A drug – do you understand what that means? It's an amphetamine and God knows in what back street factory it was manufactured, or what unholy concoction went into its making! Do you know, only the other week a youth died after taking just one tablet? He literally burnt up inside . . ."

"Okay, you've made your point."

"Have I? I hope you weren't indulging in alcohol at the same time?"

"Oh no. They never have alcohol at Rave parties."

"You've been to others?" Roland asked ominously.

"No, this was the first one. I swear it, James! I've never been to one before – but I know you mustn't mix alcohol with Ecstasy."

"Well, I suppose we must be thankful for small mercies. It may interest you to know that Ecstasy was not the only drug circulating last night. We made quite a haul."

"I don't know why you were there . . ." muttered the boy scowling at the floor.

"A youth died last night – didn't you know?"

"Yes . . . yes, it was awful . . ." A spasm crossed Simon's face.

"Have you any idea how I felt when I saw you there?"

"Embarrassed? I suppose it really queered your patch!"

"For God's sake, Simon! I'm speaking as a parent, not a policeman. I'd just been dealing with the body of that young man and all I could think of was, it might have been you! Don't you understand – I'm bawling you out because I *care* for you – as much as if you were my own son!"

There was a dazed expression on Simon's face as looked at his step-father, then it crumpled and he started to sob.

"I'm sorry, James . . ." He balled his fists into his eyes. ". . . I . . . I can't believe Jason is dead . . . *why* did it have to happen . . .?"

"Why indeed." Roland put an arm round his shoulders. "Well, I've had my say, do you understand?"

"Yes. It won't happen again, I promise. Do you believe me?"

"Yes, and I trust you. Are you okay now?"

"Mmm. I'm sorry I blabbed just like a kid . . ."

"It's nothing to be ashamed of." Roland gave him a quick hug. "We must go down and pacify your mother, I think she's getting us a meal. But first . . . I have something else to discuss. I'm wearing my policeman's hat now . . . there was another death last night."

Roland quickly put him in the picture about the murder of Charles Todd and his body being found near the site of the Rave. Simon was horrified but could add nothing to what was already known; he had noticed nothing untoward during the course of the night. Roland had expected this and as he said later to Mansfield, a hundred and fifty youngsters zonked out of their minds with music, strobes and amphetamines were unlikely to come up with anything of significance and if anyone HAD noticed something, how much reliance could be put on information gathered from someone in that state?

As Lacey had predicted the morning papers carried graphic accounts of the murder heavily embellished with speculation about The Joker.

"Did you get any joy from your newspaper johnnie?" Roland asked Mansfield, slapping the Gazette down on his desk in disgust.

"He was away for the weekend but he's back today. I thought I'd nip over there first thing."

"Fine. We'll get the briefing over and then you can go. Oh, by the way, the report's come in from the Lab on the rope that was used to string up Todd's body." Roland sorted it out from the mass of papers on his desk. "Apparently it is quite distinctive, made of synthetic hemp and carries the maker's name and year of manufacture."

"Really?"

"Yes, they took it to bits for testing and there's a strip of clear plastic woven continuously through the rope. This has the initials BH stamped on it plus Din 3461 and the date 1984" read Roland. "The BH stands for Berkdale Holland, the name of the manufacturers and the Din number is the International Standard. According to the Lab boys it is a good quality rope."

"So it can be matched up?"

"Yes."

"Could be useful if we get a definite suspect. Now I suppose it's back to hard slog."

"Yes, we should have covered all the names on the list by the end of the day and there's something else you can do – ask the editor to publish a bit appealing to anyone who was at the Rave and has not been contacted already to come forward. Something along the lines of no repercussions if they own up. We may strike lucky and find a witness who did see something."

At that moment the internal phone buzzed and the WPC on the switchboard relayed the message she had just received.

"Did you get that?" asked Roland, putting down the receiver. "Alison Barnard has just phoned through and asked to see me. She rang off before she could be put through."

"I wonder what she wants. You don't think there's been another death threat made to her, do you?"

"Christ, I hope not! We'll have to see her."

"Do you want me to get someone over there?"

"I'll go. I want to deal with this myself. I'll take Evans with me whilst you tackle the Fourth Estate."

"Is she a cripple?" asked William Evans a little while later as they drove towards the Barnard's house. Always in robust health himself, he had a natural distaste for any form of illness.

"She's suffering from leukaemia not paralysis or congenital deformity."

"I mean, is she bed-ridden?"

"Not at the last count. She was up and about and leading as normal a life as possible under the circumstances, but I must admit she did have more than a passing resemblance to a consumptive Victorian heroine."

"Perhaps she's found out who played that dirty trick on her."

"We'll soon find out, that's her house – the second one along."

Roland parked the car and the two men walked up the path and rang the bell. The door was answered by Lindsey Barnard who seemed surprised to see them.

"Inspector Roland? I didn't expect you so soon."

"I received a message that your sister wanted to see me; is anything wrong?"

"I'm not sure" she said slowly, stepping aside so that they could enter.

"No more nasty jokes?"

"I'm not sure if you'd call them jokes . . . I thought you ought to be told about them and Alison didn't feel up to going to the Police Station."

"Stop talking about me behind my back."

Alison Barnard materialized out of another door. She was wearing a Laura Ashley style dress in blue sprigged cotton with puffed sleeves and a long, full skirt and looked even more ethereal than when Roland had seen her before. Beside him, Evans drew in his breath noisily and Roland introduced him to the two sisters.

"Please come into the sitting room, Lindsey will make us some coffee."

Lindsey looked as if she were going to object to these orders but then she shrugged and went through to the kitchen and Roland and Evans seated themselves on the chairs indicated. Alison leaned against the mantelpiece and fidgeted with a fold of her dress.

"She fusses so about me. She wanted me to tell you about this before but I didn't want to bother you. I know you're busy and I didn't think it was important, but now there's been another murder . . ."

"What's worrying you, Miss Barnard?"

"Sorry, you don't know what I'm talking about, do you? I'm not sure where to begin . . ."

"Just take your time and tell us what is bothering you."

"It's like this," she sat down opposite them, "I've had two communications sent me through the post."

"Anonymous letters?" asked Roland sharply.

"Not exactly . . . Look, I'll try and explain. After that

88

Morris dancer was killed there was a lot of speculation in the papers about his death and whether it tied in with . . . with the horrible jokes that had been played on people in the village. I didn't see it immediately – Lindsey was afraid I'd be upset and she hid the paper from me, but a little while later I received an envelope in the post and inside was the newspaper cutting. Nothing else, no indication whom it was from or anything, just the cutting sealed inside the envelope."

She went over to the bureau and opened the top drawer and took out a folded newspaper cutting which she held out to Roland.

"You say you had two?"

"The second one was even more . . . odd. It came a couple of weeks later . . . here . . ." she handed him the second piece of paper. "It's a Bible quotation, I've written the transcription underneath."

"'But many that are first shall be last; and the last shall be first'" Roland read out aloud. "Have you any idea who could have sent them?"

"No. What does it mean? I feel as if someone is making fun of me, having a joke at my expense."

"Have you got the envelopes?"

"The first one got thrown away but I kept the second one." She rummaged in the drawer and looked puzzled.

"How odd, it doesn't seem to be here."

Lindsey came into the room at that moment carrying a laden tray.

"Do you know what's happened to the envelope the second message came in?" Alison asked her.

"I thought you'd put it in that drawer, isn't it there?"

"Doesn't appear to be. I'm sure I put it there . . ."

"Let me have a look." Lindsey hunted through the contents of the drawer. "No, it's not here, it must have got thrown away after all."

"How were they addressed?" asked Roland, accepting a cup of coffee.

"To me. To Miss Alison Barnard."

"I meant, was the address handwritten or typed or made out of cut-out letters and words like the quotation."

"It was typed. They were white foolscap envelopes and I think the second one was posted in Felstone."

"It's a pity you haven't kept them, it might have been possible to have traced the typewriter they were typed on."

"Inspector, this murder of Captain Todd . . . it happened here in the village . . ." said Lindsey, offering a plate of biscuits, ". . . just like it said in the papers . . . like the trick that was played on him . . ." she stared at Roland intently. "Do you think these . . . these tricks ARE death threats and The Joker is now playing them for real?"

"I think someone wants us to think that but I'm keeping an open mind. Did you know Charles Todd?"

"I should think everyone knew *Captain* Todd" she said disparagingly and a moue of distaste flickered across her face.

"He doesn't appear to have been very popular?" Roland was fishing.

"No, well he wouldn't be, would he?" She refused to be drawn and wouldn't qualify her remark.

Roland didn't press her but decided to put into action the plan he had discussed with Evans on the way over. He wanted to get Lindsey on one side and ask her just how ill her sister was and what were her chances of recovery. He put down his coffee cup and changed the subject.

"Last time I was here I saw your sister's paintings" he said to Lindsey, "could I see some of your work?"

"It's all around you." She indicated the pottery displayed on the shelves and unit tops.

"I really meant your studio and some of your unfired work. I think I mentioned to you that my wife was an art teacher and she taught me to appreciate ceramics."

"Well, if you really want to . . . Actually, I was just about to start throwing. I suppose you can come through."

She got up and went out of the french doors and Roland followed her across the patio and into the detached brick building behind the rockery leaving his constable behind with Alison. For once, Evans was at a loss for words. Faced with the frail yet self-possessed young woman he felt over-large, gauche and tongue-tied. Roland had chosen

90

him today to be his sidekick instead of Mansfield and he had to prove himself. Whilst Roland was pumping the other sister he should be extracting some useful information from Alison, but all he could come up with was a trite remark about the weather.

"It's very hot today."

Yes, it is. You don't come from these parts, constable?"

"No, I was born in south Wales."

"You don't look old enough to be a detective."

Evans was affronted. "I've been in the CID several years and part of the DI's team."

"I suppose he doesn't look old enough either to have reached that level of responsibility."

"Don't be taken in by his looks. He's an old married man and having problems with a teenage son at the moment" said Evans crassly and felt himself flushing as she looked amused.

"Have there been any more jokes played on local people that the papers haven't got hold of?"

Not as far as we know. The person behind them must be somebody local, somebody who lives in Saxton and knows everyone – have you any ideas on who it could be?"

"You can't believe anyone you know could be so hateful."

"Someone with a warped sense of humour who could hold a grudge against people he imagines has slighted him."

"I've thought about it a lot and the silly thing is, the candidate who springs to mind most is Charlie Todd."

"Really?"

"Yes, crazy, isn't it? And I'm probably giving you the wrong impression. He wasn't liked in the village – he upset just about everyone he came into contact with, including Lindsey, but you couldn't actually imagine him getting at people in such an underhand way – he was far too bellicose and direct and he was quite elderly."

Her voice took on a bleak tinge and Evans was jolted into recalling her condition. She must be thinking that she might never grow old. He watched her playing with a lock of her long, golden hair. It was beautiful hair; and then he remembered that it was a wig. She was really bald, but her hair must have looked like that originally. How tragic. She was very attractive . . . it was a damn shame . . .

At that point he heard Roland's voice outside and the detective stepped through the french doors to collect his constable.

"May I take these with me?" he asked, picking up the letters.

"Yes, I suppose so."

"If you receive any other communication like these please contact me immediately and hang on to the envelope."

"Yes I will, I hope there are no more . . ."

"Don't worry about it. I know it was upsetting to be on the receiving end of these but don't read anything sinister into it, I don't think there is anything to get alarmed about."

"Did you mean that?" asked Evans as they were driving back, "about these letters being nothing to worry about?"

"No, I think they are very disturbing."

"First last and last first – whatever is it suppose to mean?"

"She was the first person to have a trick played on her."

"You mean she could be the last on The Joker's hit list, if . . ."

"We're not paid to speculate, Evans" said Roland crisply, "did you uncover anything useful?"

Evans told him what had transpired between him and Alison and asked how Roland had got on with Lindsey.

"She either doesn't know how ill her sister is or she's not saying. However, I've discovered that her GP is the local quack, Firbank."

"It's dreadful, isn't it – someone so young and lovely."

"I think she's made a conquest."

"Of course not. No woman will get her clutches into me again. Besides, she's engaged, did you know that?"

"Yes, I've met the fianceé. He's an antiques dealer, works for Eileen Dexter – the woman who had that trick with the doll played on her. He seems very devoted and it must help her to have reliable support like that even if he does look like the Pirate King. Mark Copley's his name."

"Mark Copley." Evans appeared deep in thought and then he snapped his fingers in excitement. "I've just remembered why his name seemed familiar, it was on the list."

"Are you sure?"

"Yes, he was at the Rave party."

"Has he been questioned?"

"No, he was one of the ones we couldn't contact. Wasn't at home yesterday when we called."

"He was probably at the Barnards. Now what was HE doing at the Rave?"

"So much for his support for Alison – it's a bit off, isn't it. His girl friend is dying of leukaemia and he takes himself off to a Rave party. I wonder if she knows?"

"It was sharp of you to pick up on the name, Evans. It escaped me when I ran through the list. Good work."

"I'll make him priority when we check out the rest of the ones we missed yesterday."

"No, leave him to me. I'll take this one – it will be interesting to hear what he has to say for himself."

CHAPTER 6

Patrick Mansfield arrived back from his visit to the Felstone Gazette offices shortly after Roland returned from questioning the Barnard twins and the two men pooled their findings.

"An anonymous tip-off" said Mansfield, collapsing on to a chair and fanning himself with his notebook.

"Don't give me that! You mean to say that on four separate occasions they had an anonymous tip-off and they didn't check it out?"

"Hang on, you're jumping the gun." Mansfield consulted his notes. "When Mervyn Souster was killed there was actually a reporter on the spot who, of course, immediately picked up on the hoax that had been played on him earlier, and that made headlines the next day."

"That was the article that was sent to Alison Barnard. It also stated that other people in Saxton had received threats. How did they know about those?"

"Just as the article about Souster was going to Press they received an anonymous call telling them that The Joker had already played death threat tricks on three other local people. The caller mentioned the Maritime Museum and Holgate Wood and said if they wanted more information to speak to Stewart Carson of Saxton."

"Stewart Carson?" Sorry, go on."

"A paragraph mentioning these episodes was hurriedly added to the article and then they set about following them up."

"This phone call – was it a man or woman?"

"An office junior took the call and she can't remember. When I pressed her she said she thought the voice had been heavily disguised to make it sound different but I shouldn't place too much reliance on that statement – I think she's been watching too much telly."

"So what happened next?"

"A reporter went to the Maritime Museum where the curator on duty told him about the business with the hanging body and Charlie Todd's hat. He then traced Stewart Carson and went to see him. Carson described in great detail the set-up in Holgate Wood which he'd stumbled on and also told the reporter about the episode with Miss Dexter and the doll from the antiques shop which was verified by the chap in the local post office."

Mansfield snapped shut his notebook. "So there you have it."

"Stewart Carson's name seems to be popping up all over the place."

"You think he could have been the anonymous caller?"

"I'm wondering if he could be The Joker himself. Somebody set them all up, why not him? Physically he could have carried out each hoax and according to the grape-vine he's a busybody with time on his hands.

"But you don't think he murdered Todd?"

"No. I feel pretty certain that The Joker is someone with a malicious, warped sense of humour who gets his kicks out of frightening his victims by sick jokes. He's not a killer, but the person who topped Todd wants us to think it is the work of The Joker."

"Wait a minute, I've just remembered something else. Those calls that were logged on the night of the Rave from people complaining about a disturbance – I'm sure one of them was from a Mr Carson."

"Check it out, Pat, this needs following up."

"Yes, I was right," said Mansfield a short while later, hurrying back to join Roland. "At 2 am on Sunday morning a call was received from a Mr Stewart Carson complaining of noise and flashing lights coming from behind Holgate Park School. He was walking his dog at the time."

"At two in the morning? Bloody hell!"

"Wouldn't you say that that in itself was suspicious?"

"I certainly would. I think a visit to Mr Carson is called for. Where does he live?"

"In the main street; number 45 – I think it's down past the Church."

"Right, we'll go straight there. We can walk, it's not far."

"It's not natural, this heat" grumbled Mansfield, mopping his brow as the two men crossed the village green and headed in the direction of the Church, "how long has it gone on?"

"Weeks. We haven't had any rain since early June."

"Everything's scorched up."

"Well at least you don't have to worry about gardening."

"True. I can't remember the last time I cut the lawn. It's completely brown and dead looking and Jean has given up on her bedding plants."

The lime trees that stood sentinel at the gate leading into the churchyard looked dessicated and tired. They drooped dusty leaves over the wall and leaves that had already fallen crunched under their feet on the tar-sticky road. From somewhere behind the Church came the distant roar of a combine harvester and a cloud of dust in the burning sky marked its progress across an unseen field. Stewart Carson lived in a detached bungalow surrounded by overgrown macrocarpa trees. A blue Escort stood in the driveway in front of closed garage doors.

Mansfield rang the doorbell. There was no reply and he tried again, keeping his finger on the bell and from the distance came an excited yapping.

"I reckon he's in the garden."

"Let's go and find out."

They followed the path that led round the side of the garage and as they turned the corner into the back garden the dog came bounding up to them, yelping in excitement and clamouring round their legs. Carson was reading in a deckchair and he dropped the book and got to his feet.

"Down, Trixie, that's a good girl!"

"Does she greet everyone like this?" asked Roland. "Not a very good watch dog."

"She's young and excitable and over-friendly. She'll calm

96

down with age, I hope. What can I do for you, Inspector, sergeant?"

"Answer some questions, Mr Carson."

"Er, yes. Shall we go inside?"

He took them into a room which overlooked the front garden. It was shabby but comfortable looking and the walls were lined with bookshelves that ran from floor to ceiling and were tightly packed with books. Mansfield moved over to look at these whilst Roland sank into the chair offered and wondered how he would get out of it without a struggle.

"How can I help? What do you want to know?"

Trixie had been shut outside in the hall and she whined and snuffled behind the door.

"We are investigating the events that took place in Saxton on Saturday night and Sunday morning."

"I'd heard the police were making door-to-door enquiries and I wondered when I'd get a visit, but I'm flattered that they've sent a detective inspector to question me."

"This is not a routine visit, Mr Carson. I'm here because I think YOU can assist us in our enquiries."

"Me? That sounds ominous inspector, but of course, anything I can do to help you in clearing up this terrible tragedy . . ."

"Which tragedy are you referring to?"

"Why, Charlie Todd's murder," he said in surprise, "and of course, these horrible threatening jokes."

"Yes, the threatening jokes. Shall we start with them? You seem very well-informed about every occurrence."

"Well, I should think everyone knows, it's been splashed all over the newspaper."

"Quite. And I understand it was YOU who informed the Gazette."

"What do you mean?"

"Are you denying that you gave them the details which they printed?"

"Look, I don't know what this is all about. *They* came to *me*. I presume my name had been mentioned as the person who had discovered the first one and they wanted to know exactly what had happened. Naturally I told them all I knew and I also mentioned Eileen Dexter and her mourning brooch and doll."

"And did you also phone the Gazette anonymously and drop hints about the other episodes?"

"Most certainly not! What are you getting at?"

"I find myself wondering, Mr Carson, if you are The Joker?"

"This is preposterous! Completely ridiculous!" He glanced at Mansfield as if expecting him to agree and Mansfield moved into action.

"You have a very interesting collection of books here, Mr Carson."

"Yes, yes."

"Must have practically every crime novel that's been published."

"No, of course not. I concentrate on what is known as the golden age of detective fiction – from the 20's to the 50's and I have large gaps in that category."

"You don't go for the modern crime-writers?"

"There's so much violence . . ."

"It's become messy and sordid, hasn't it?" said Roland, "not the cerebral exercise it was in Agatha Christie's day; but I'm afraid that's what murder is really like. Have you read all these?" He gestured to the book-shelves.

"Of course."

"Must put ideas into your head. Death threats, malicious jokes – could come straight out of the pages of one of these." And hadn't Brasnett suggested just the same thing? thought Roland.

"Now, look here, you've no right to come here making these scandalous statements! They're libellous! You've no evidence . . ."

"If it's evidence you want, all I can say is that your name keeps cropping up at every turn and now I learn that you were on the scene in the early hours of Sunday morning at about the time that Captain Todd was killed."

"What the hell do you mean?"

"Sergeant Mansfield?"

"You rang the police at 2.0am to report a disturb-ance at Holgate Park." Mansfield pretended to read from his notes.

"This is a fact?" asked Roland pleasantly.

"Yes" said Carson shortly, "but I wasn't THERE. I was over the other side of the village and I happened to notice these flashing lights and strange noise."

"Whilst walking your dog?"

"Yes."

"At 2 am?"

"Look, I'm a poor sleeper, especially in this heat, and Trixie's always game for a walk. There's no law that says you mustn't walk your dog in the night, is there!"

"No, I just find it somewhat strange and coincidental. Did you notice anything in the course of your walk?"

"I've told you – these odd lights and a sort of throbbing noise, nothing else. Look here, inspector, you don't really think I'm The Joker, do you?"

"I'm keeping an open mind, but in my place, wouldn't you be suspicious?"

"But why should I have played these tricks? What reasons am I supposed to have for wanting to scare these people? Poor Alison Barnard . . ."

"I have yet to find a motive for that one but it's well known that you had a grudge against Mervyn Souster and an upset with Charles Todd." This last was a shot in the dark but it payed off.

"I don't know who told you that but I can assure you that I wasn't the only one. If you're looking for people who were at odds with Todd you'd better arrest the entire village!"

"I'll bear that in mind. Is there anything else that we need to ask Mr Carson, sergeant?"

"What were you doing on Saturday evening from six oclock onwards?"

"That would be before your midnight perambulations" added Roland, managing to extricate himself from his chair without too much loss of dignity.

"I was here, reading and watching the television."

"Alone?"

"Yes."

"That's a pity.

"But . . ." As the two detectives prepared to leave, Carson hurriedly ushered them down the hall and opened the front door. ". . . you surely can't imagine I had anything to do with Charlie Todd's murder!"

"I don't imagine anything. I collect facts and facts add up to evidence."

"One badly rattled man" said Mansfield as they walked back past the church, "do you reckon we've achieved anything?"

"If he's entirely innocent it was a wasted visit but if he HAS got something to hide it may jolt him into an indiscretion."

"From what we've heard so far it doesn't look as if anyone is going to mourn Todd, does it?"

"No, what a sad indictment of someone's life. Still, it doesn't make any difference to our task. Liked or not, his killer is going to be brought to justice."

"Maybe it's a conspiracy. A plot involving a group of local residents who decided to get rid of him."

"Is that intended to encourage me? Come on, now we're in the village we'll call at the antiques shop and have a few words with Mark Copley. He should be there now and I also want to meet Eileen Dexter."

"She's probably got the wind up if she believes what she reads in the local rag."

"I want to know if she's received any anonymous communications like Alison Barnard and how well she knew Todd. They're both lived here a long time and she may be able to give us some background facts that will help."

Eileen Dexter was fixing a poster advertising an antiques fair to the door of her shop when the two detectives arrived. She looked worried and alarmed when she saw them standing outside and was no more at ease after they had introduced themselves.

"Oh dear, the police . . . has anything else happened?"

"Could we come in please, Miss Dexter?"

It was cool and dim inside the shop and a cornucopia of

treasures cluttered every available surface. Roland suddenly remembered that he had been here with Ginny a couple of years before when they had been looking for a pine chest, but he couldn't recall Eileen Dexter. She was a small, grey-haired woman in her sixties with an anxious expression on her face and primly dressed in a navy skirt and blouse. His eyes were drawn to the black brooch pinned at her neck. The mourning brooch, he supposed; she must have had it repaired. He explained the reasons for their visit and asked if she had been a friend of Captain Todd.

"A friend? Oh no! I knew him of course, but I wouldn't have called him a friend. I don't mean that I disliked him . . ." She was becoming flustered, ". . . but we weren't close, he was just an acquaintance . . ."

"Quite. You're being very circumspect, Miss Dexter, but I've already been given to understand that he was not a popular man."

"Well, yes, that's true. Our circles obviously overlapped from time to time . . . various local activities . . . but I tried not to get involved."

"Can you think of anyone who may have hated him enough to have killed him?"

"Oh, goodness no. I mean, it's one thing to dislike someone but you don't go around killing everybody you don't agree with, do you?"

"Someone had a reason for wanting him dead."

"Yes, I suppose so. What about this . . . this Joker? Was he killed by the person who's been carrying out these cruel hoaxes? I had one played on me you know."

"Yes, we know about that, Miss Dexter. I think someone was just pulling your leg. Nothing further has happened, has it?"

"What do you mean?"

"No anonymous letters or anything like that?"

"Anonymous letters? No . . . Have . . .?"

"Not to worry, just a routine check. Now, we want to see your assistant, Mr Copley. Is he about?"

"Mark? I don't think he'll be able to help you, inspector, he was less acquainted with Captain Todd than myself."

"Is he here?"

"He's out in the yard tinkering with the car. He thought the radiator had a slight leak."

"Right, we'll go and find him. Through this way?"

"Yes, through the conservatory and the door in the wall."

All they could see of Mark Copley was a pair of feet in scruffy trainers sticking out from under the Volvo, which stood black and hearse-like in the middle of the yard that ran behind the building.

"Mr Copley?"

He scrambled out from under the car and stood up, alarm spreading across his face as he recognised Roland and Mansfield.

"Alison? Something's happened to Alison . . .?"

"Not that I'm aware of, Mr Copley. Were you expecting something to happen?"

"Christ no, I hope not! You took me unawares, just for a minute I was afraid . . ." He wiped his hands on a greasy rag and eyed them uneasily. "There's some mischief afoot in this village. I'm afraid for Alison and Eileen is like a cat on hot bricks."

"I should use a stronger word than mischief to describe murder. I am investigating Charles Todd's murder and I believe you were at the Rave party that was held in the grounds of Holgate Park School on Saturday night."

"Yes, I was, and I was also manhandled by the police that same night!"

"Manhandled? Did you hear that sergeant?" Roland asked Mansfield in exaggerated surprise.

"Are you making an official complaint, sir?"

"No. I suppose you were within your rights, though I don't know why you are pestering me again."

"A man has been killed and his body was found within a few yards of this gathering. We're questioning everybody who was there in the hope that someone may have noticed something that may help us in our enquiries."

"No, I know nothing about it."

"His body was left there at some time during the course of the night. I find it hard to believe that over a hundred and fifty people were milling around nearby and nobody noticed anything."

"Well I'm afraid I didn't. Perhaps you'll strike lucky with someone else."

"Perhaps. Why did you go to this Rave?"

"I don't understand, why shouldn't I? What's the harm in it?"

Roland began to feel he was re-playing the scene with Simon.

"Leaving aside the little matter of drugs and associated problems, how did you get to hear about the Rave? These things aren't advertised. Who invited you?"

"Tina."

"Tina?"

"Tina Fairbrother."

The two detectives exchanged a quick glance. Both were sure this was a name that hadn't come up before. There had been no Tina Fairbrother on the list of people questioned by the police that night.

"And how would she have known about it?"

"She was one of the organisers, wasn't she?" Aware that he had said too much, Mark Copley tried to cover up by a display of righteous anger. "Look, I can't see what this has to do with you, with a Murder investigation!"

"I'm sorry, I was under the impression that you were engaged to Miss Barnard, forgive me for the mistake."

"I AM engaged to Alison Barnard."

"And Tina Fairbrother?"

"Is an ex-girlfriend" he replied sulkily.

"EX?"

"Yes, EX! Look, what IS this? A witch hunt?"

"I'm just trying to get things sorted out in my mind. Your fiancée is seriously ill and you decide to go off to a party with an ex-girlfriend? That is hardly likely to aid her recovery if she gets to hear about it."

"I don't see that it's any of your business! Anyway, she doesn't know and I didn't go WITH Tina."

"Oh no, I forgot, you said she was one of the organisers?"

"No, you misunderstood me. She knows the organiser and was helping to publicise the Rave for him."

"A certain Rod Lewis?"

"I wouldn't know. I happened to bump into her and she suggested I go along and I thought why not? I didn't even enjoy it, it was a bore!"

"And yet you stayed there all night and didn't leave until it was broken up by the police?"

"What's the good of talking to you? You're just twisting everything I say. I went to the bloody Rave on the spur of the moment. I couldn't get into the spirit of the thing. I kept thinking of Alison and comparing her with all the fit, able-bodied girls abusing themselves with drugs and I felt angry. Angry and depressed on her behalf. I got more and more miserable – and you couldn't even get a damned drink – but I determined to stick it out to the bitter end."

"I'm not quite sure why. Perhaps you were hoping to make it with Tina Fairbrother again?"

"That's a ridiculous idea! I'm not interested in Tina."

"Well, that's between you and your conscience, but I need to have her address. You may have seen nothing of the murder scenario but perhaps she did. Does she live here in Saxton?"

"Yes," said Copley sulkily, tugging at his earring with a greasy finger and thumb, "but she won't be at home now, she works in the Music Rite record shop in Felstone."

"Right, we'll have her home address as well."

Mansfield wrote down the address reluctantly given and as they took their leave Copley said urgently:

"Look, you don't have to tell Alison, do you – about me being at the Rave?"

"I've got better things to do with my time" said Roland coldly. "Meanwhile, if you remember anything that might help us please let us know immediately."

"Don't you think you were rather hard on him?" said Mansfield as they drove to Felstone. "A night on the tiles with a large group of people is not really two-timing his fiancée and he wasn't into drugs."

"Young people nowadays have such a loose idea about what constitutes an engagement. Alison Barnard deserves better." Which was good coming from him, who had played fast and loose with many women, including several married ones, before he had met Ginny, thought Mansfield. He said out loud:

"I think you fancy her."

"Don't be ridiculous, Pat, I feel desperately sorry for her, that's all. But I tell you what; I think she HAS made a conquest – our William couldn't keep his eyes off her."

"Don't encourage him. Evans recovering from a broken romance was bad enough; Evans in love with a dying woman would be more than any man on the Force could take – he'd drive us up the wall."

"How come we missed out on this Tina Fairbrother?"

"She must have avoided the road blocks. Copley really dropped her in it, didn't he?"

"He didn't realise we hadn't already got a line on her. If she's an associate of Rod Lewis she was probably peddling drugs alongside him that night."

"She'll be clean now though, won't she? We won't be able to pin anything on her after the time lapse."

"No, more's the pity, but I shall be interested to hear what she has to say for herself. We'll leave the car at the Station and go on foot.

There was a man in his early thirties behind the counter in the record shop and a younger man unpacking boxes nearby. A slim, dark young woman of Indian origin was talking to a customer near the door and over on the other side of the shop a well-developed girl with dyed platinum hair was lethargically dusting the shelves. Roland wondered which of them was Tina Fairbrother. He and Mansfield approached the counter and produced their ID cards.

"I'd like to speak with Miss Tina Fairbrother." said Roland and the manager looked wary.

"Tina? There's nothing wrong is there? She . . .?"

"We're investigating the murder of a man in Saxton and questioning all the local residents."

"Yes, of course. She's over there, tidying the shelves.

Tina, the police want to talk to you" he called, and the blond girl looked startled and hurried towards them.

"Go into the office, it's more private."

She led the way through a doorway behind the counter into a small room cluttered with cupboards, filing cabinets and a large table and desk. Roland introduced himself and Mansfield and she perched herself on the table and swung her legs.

"You're the policeman in charge of that murder case, aren't you?" She gave Roland the eye. "They said you were interviewing all the people who live in Saxton. Have you spoken to my mum and dad yet?"

"Were they at the Rave too?"

"Rave? What Rave?"

"Miss Fairbrother, you were at the Rave party in Saxton the other evening . . ."

"No, I wasn't! I don't know what you're talking about!" she interrupted him.

"We know that you were. In fact, I understand that you helped to organise it with Rod Lewis – who is now facing charges of drug pushing, amongst other things."

"Who told you that? It's not true – I had nothing to do with it!" She was frightened and angry.

"Perhaps you'd like to tell us your version of the Rave?"

"Look, I *do* know Rod, I admit it, but he's only a casual friend. I knew he'd set up this Rave and I just passed the word around amongst my friends. That's all there was to it, I swear!"

"How did you manage to avoid the police road blocks?"

"I wasn't in a car, was I? I just walked home."

Roland had a sudden vision of her scampering home, dodging the police presence, her bleached head bobbing amongst the undergrowth. There had been too many people abroad that night.

"Did you go near the shed on the other side of the barn?"

"That's where Charlie Todd's body was found, wasn't it?"

"Yes. Now answer truthfully; I'm not trying to catch you out but you may have seen something."

"You mean the murderer?"

"Did you see or hear anything in that vicinity?"

"No, I went the other way" She said it defiantly, then a puzzled look settled on her face as she appeared to think.

"You've remembered something?"

"No. At least . . . it wasn't near the shed . . ."

"Go on."

"It was earlier in the evening. I'd gone outside to get a breather and I heard a car driving away through the school grounds."

"Surely there were plenty of cars coming and going all the time?"

"No. The Ravers were all there by then and they'd been directed round the other side of the park and their vehicles left near the sports pavilion . . . It must have been someone leaving early and they must have thought it would be a short cut to go that way . . ."

"What time was this?"

"I can't remember."

"Please try and think, Tina, it could be important." She screwed up her face in concentration, then shook her head.

"It's no good, I really can't remember."

"Before midnight or after?"

"It didn't get going until nearly midnight so it must have been after . . ." she shrugged.

Bombed out of her mind, supposed Roland. He wondered if she really had heard a car at all.

"Are you sure there's nothing else you can tell us?"

"No." She ran a hand laden with silver rings through her platinum spkkes. "I don't know why you're pestering me – what about all the other people who were there?"

"Don't worry, we're working through them. Are there many more like you who we didn't pick up?"

"How should I know? I don't tell tales – but I'd like to know who grassed on me! I've got a right to know!"

"Your name was mentioned to us by a Mr Mark Copley."

"I might have known!"

Roland said nothing and she continued angrily:

"He's just trying to make trouble for me!"

"Why should he do that?"

"He's probably still sore because I gave him the push. We used to knock around together but I decided he's not my type." Roland could well believe that. Chalk and cheese, as the Super would say and they were wasting their time; Tina Fairbrother knew nothing of importance.

By the end of the week Roland was no nearer finding out who had killed Charles Todd. Everybody known to have been at the Rave had been interviewed and a house-to-house in Saxton had produced no leads whatsoever. The murderer had moved Todd's body under cover of darkness from his house to the shed in Holgate Park School grounds without anyone noticing anything. Forensics had come up with nothing useful either. The ground had been so hard and dry that no tyre marks were visible and the amount of fingerprints all over the barn and on the debris left behind made it an impossible task for identification. They had confirmed that the plastic sheet had been used to enwrap the body – scales of skin tissue and a few hairs belonging to the dead man had been found – but the murderer had left nothing of himself behind.

Roland tried to concentrate on motive but there again he was stymied. Of those who had known him in the village, most had fallen out with him at some time or other, so he was faced with the daunting task of checking the alibis of a large proportion of the locals and that could take weeks. He was mulling it over with Mansfield after a particularly sticky meeting with Bob Lacey who demanded results and was not at all happy with the lack of progress.

"You know, Patrick, Saxton is a village divided into two domains and ne'er the twain shall meet."

"The old and the new?"

"Yes. You've got the dormitory dwellers: the people who've moved into new properties or tarted-up old ones. The men commute to offices in Felstone and Woodford or further afield; the wives have their own cars and visit ditto for shopping and socializing and their kids are ferried to private schools outside the area. They take no part in the life of the place; they are IN the village but not OF it. Then you've got the other half; the people who were born in the village and have lived there all their lives and the folks who moved in years ago and have been integrated into the community and are now part of a tightly-knit society. There's almost an incestuous feel about it."

"You mean too much inter-marrying."

"I'm sure there's been plenty of that but I was speaking figuratively. Everybody knows everybody's business. As Lacey would say, they live in each other's pockets and there's an unhealthy feel about it."

"I know what you mean. We live in a village but Wallingford is different; the old and the new are all mixed up and there's not the sense of an enclosed community like there is in Saxton."

"Yes, it's almost as if it were still under the yoke of a local squire."

"And wasn't Charles Todd supposed to fancy himself in that role?"

"Yes, and it didn't go down too well. It sounds absurd, but you can sense undercurrents – resentment, malice, spite – hovering below the surface. I wonder if we'll ever bring Todd's killer to justice."

"You're not harking back to my theory of conspiracy, are you?"

"No, I'm sure there was no conspiracy to kill him but it's almost as if there is a conspiracy of silence now. If people are not exactly withholding evidence they're certainly not coming forward and volunteering any. I feel there is some sort of cover-up going on."

"Well, let's hope we get a break before anything else happens."

Afterwards, Anthea Campbell-Haigh, the curator of the Holgate Lodge Museum, couldn't think why she had happened to look out of the window at just that point. She had been hard at work since seven oclock on the word processor, transposing her late husband's cryptic notes onto disk and had felt the need for a break. She had fished an apple out of her basket and gone over to the window, consuming her snack with her elbows propped on the sill.

This window overlooked the parkland in front of the Lodge. Immediately below her was a gravelled courtyard enclosed on two sides by a low box hedge. The driveway led from this courtyard, skirting the lake and disappearing into an avenue of trees. The lake glimmered dully under the hazy sun; it looked opaque, like a giant globule of mercury spilled onto the surface of the earth and many of the reed clumps surrounding it had been left high and dry by the evaporating water. In the loop of lake bordered by the drive the water was deeper, lapping a reinforced embankment, and here a group of mallard was worrying at something below the surface.

She could make out a bulky outline in the water and her first thought was that it was a fallen treetrunk. She immediately told herself this couldn't be so, there were no trees within a hundred yards of the lake at that point and there had been no wind to fell one. She stared in puzzlement and as she watched, whatever it was broke surface for a few seconds and she caught a glimpse of something black before it rolled back into the water. The feeling of unease that had gnawed at her turned to dread. It looked like . . .!

She slammed her glass down on the table and hurried out of the room and down the stairs, nearly measuring her length as she tripped at the bottom. The heavy front door was locked and bolted and she wasted seconds getting it undone. The heat struck her like an fist as she plunged outside and crossed the courtyard and she screwed up her eyes and squinted in the direction of the lake. From ground level she could see nothing but she noticed a figure approaching through the avenue of trees and felt a surge of relief. If the object in the water was what she feared it was she had need of reinforcements.

She slowed down as she neared the lake and stared fearfully at the protesting ducks. The object resolved itself into a human shape; a body floating face downwards in the water. She fought to conquer the scream of hysteria that was rising in her throat and glanced wildly at the person who had left the shelter of the trees and was walking towards her. It was Alison Barnard. Immediately another surge of panic shot through her. Alison mustn't see this!

With uncontrolled gait she stumbled along the driveway.

"Alison, you shouldn't be here! It's far too hot for you today. I don't need you this morning."

"What's the matter? You look as if you've seen a ghost."

"Do . . . Do I? Look, why don't you turn round and go home. I'll phone you later . . ."

"Anthea, that's got into you? Has something happened? What were you looking at in the lake?"

"Nothing! Nothing . . . The ducks are just making a commotion . . ."

"There's something in the water . . ."

Alison shook off the other woman's hand and ran down to the water's edge. She checked in horror.

"Oh my God!"

CHAPTER 7

The body had been removed from the lake and laid on the bank. As soon as it had been lifted from the water blood had started to run from a blunt laceration on the back of the head, mingling garishly with the sodden, gunmetal grey hair plastered to the skull. Roland stared down, a grim expression on his face, noting the missing shoe and the green slimy weed clasped tightly in the hands.

"It's Eileen Dexter, isn't it?" said Mansfield.

"Yes, and she didn't trip and fall in unaided by the look of it. That's a nasty blow on the back of her head."

"You think she was killed and then tipped into the lake?"

"Can't tell at his stage but Brasnett should be able to give us a better idea; where the hell is he anyway? He should be here by now."

"I think that's his car just coming through the trees."

George Brasnett, the pathologist, drove a silver Rover Vitesse. He pulled off the drive and parked it on the verge and walked bouncily towards them, the sun glinting off his bifocals. He nodded at Roland and Mansfield and the other policemen gathered at the lakeside and turned his attention to the corpse.

"Are you going to tell me what I think you are?" he asked Roland.

"Yes. It's Eileen Dexter, the woman who had the hoax played on her."

Brasnett's eyebrows climbed towards his receding hairline and he pursed his lips but said nothing. He dropped down beside the body and started his examination.

"I want to know whether she was pushed in the water and left to drown or whether she was killed elsewhere and dumped in the lake."

"She's been in the water some time but at this stage I wouldn't have thought that blow on the back of the head killed her. It's a nasty ragged laceration and there appears to be bruising of the surrounding scalp but it's fairly superficial."

"What sort of weapon are we looking for?"

"Something with a rough surface – could be a lump of wood, say a branch."

"Can you give me any indication how long she's been dead?"

"Help me with her clothes."

A short while later Brasnett shook his rectal thermometer and returned it to its case. "A temperature of 24C and there's some rigor mortis in the jaws but nowhere else. Say six to twelve hours ago."

"Can't you get nearer than that?"

"Don't provoke me, James. You know how difficult deaths from drowning are to establish."

"You'll be telling me next that it will be impossible to tell whether she died from drowning or not."

"You're learning. There is always the possibility that a victim may have died from dry drowning – that is, shock on entering the water, but I don't think so in this case. Look at the top of her shoulders . . ." Roland bent closer to the area indicated. ". . . there's discoloration there, pressure marks."

"So, if I'm reading this right, she was bashed over the head – from behind – and toppled into the water and then her attacker held her under the water until she died."

"That's a possibility."

"And I don't think she was unconscious when she went into the water. I think she struggled a little – look at her hands – they're clutching pieces of water-weed as if she'd threshed about a bit in the water and that's probably how she lost a shoe. If we can find that shoe we'll know where she went into the water, always supposing it wasn't here where she was found."

"Who found her and how?"

"Mrs Campbell-Haigh, the curator of the museum, noticed something in the water when she looked out of

113

a window. She came out to investigate and arrived here at the same time as Alison Barnard who was walking through the park on her way to the Lodge."

"Alison Barnard? Isn't she another of The Joker's potential victims?"

"Don't say it. This has turned all my theories on the head and you can imagine how it affected her. They could see enough to recognise who it was in the water and Mrs Campbell-Haigh got her to the Lodge and rang us. Evans is taking their statements now and taking a hell of a long while about it."

"Have we any idea who her next-of-kin is?" asked Mansfield who had been examining the turf verging the lake. The ducks had long since departed and could be heard quacking over on the far side of the water.

"She may not have any, she certainly wasn't married. Mark Copley, her assistant, will probably know and can put us in the picture about her background. Go and pick him up – he can officially identify the body and spare the two women the task. When the team arrive I want every inch of the verges round the lake searched and I want the frogmen too. Hopefully they'll find the shoe somewhere in the lake and it's quite likely the killer chucked the weapon he used to hit her with in the water afterwards." Roland turned back to Brasnett who was gazing at the much embellished Lodge.

"Impressive, isn't it?"

"They forgot the gargoyles. Have you finished with me here?"

"Yes. I'll arrange' for the body to be taken to the mortuary. Thanks Doc."

"Here comes young Evans. How *can* he wear that colour shirt with that hair?"

William Evans was wearing a stone-washed coral denim shirt with his jeans. It was a couple of shades lighter than his complexion and fought a glorious battle with his carroty mop of hair. He was hurrying towards them.

"Sir, do you think Miss Barnard could be taken home? She can't do much good hanging about here."

"Have you taken their statements?"

"She's very distressed, I think it would be better to speak to her again later. Mrs Campbell-Haigh has given me the gist of what happened."

"Okay, Evans, I expect you're right; we don't want another tragedy on our hands. I presume you're offering to act as chauffeur? Take her home and get back here FAST. Her sister will probably need to get her doctor to her."

Evans departed with the shocked Alison Barnard and Roland went back into the Lodge to question Anthea Campbell-Haigh again. She was sitting huddled on an oak chest near the foot of the grand staircase smoking a cigarette. Her hair was escaping from its chignon and straggling down her back but she was oblivious to it. She stared at Roland through a haze of smoke with haunted eyes and waited for him to speak.

"Mrs Campbell-Haigh, I know this has been a great shock to you but I've just a few more questions to ask."

"I've just *told* your constable how I . . . we . . . found her . . ."

"Yes, I know. We'll have to have an official signed statement from you later but bear with me for now. I know you live in the gate-house over on the other side of the park – did you walk past the lake on your way here this morning?"

"No, I came along the path at the back of the house, it's quicker. I never went near the lake and the first time I saw it today was when I looked out of the window."

"What time did you get here?"

"About sevenish."

"As early as that? Do you normally start work at that hour?"

"Look, I don't work office hours." She wearily stubbed out her cigarette in the ashtray beside her. "I'm in charge here, how I carry out my duties is up to me. I couldn't sleep last night and I got up early and decided to put in some work on my husband's notes before Alison arrived."

"You were expecting her?"

"Yes, she phoned yesterday evening to say she was coming in this morning – more's the pity!"

"What time did you leave here yesterday?"

"I locked up about six and went home."

"So you wouldn't have known if anyone was in the area after that? It is possible to see or hear anything going on in this part of the park from the gate-house?"

"No, it's too far away."

"Were you at home all the evening or did you go out at all?"

"I was entertaining a friend. We didn't go out."

From the way she spoke Roland guessed it was a male friend.

"What time did your friend leave?"

"I think you are exceeding your terms of reference, Inspector." Her eyes snapped at him.

"Mrs Campbell-Haigh, I am only interested in your private life in so far as it affects my inquiry. I am investigating a very nasty murder and I need to establish whether your friend might have noticed any activity in the park on the way home."

"I doubt it. He left about half-past eleven and drove the other way, by the back road to Felstone."

"I see." Roland regarded her closely. She was obviously deeply shocked, but was it shock at having a murder on her doorstep or was she genuinely upset because a friend had died? "How well did you know Eileen Dexter? Was she a friend of yours?"

"Not a close friend but I liked her well enough. She was a typical spinster but she had her moments. I got to know her soon after I came here through the antiques business. If she picked up something that she thought should grace the museum she gave me first refusal and I haggled on behalf of the trustees. In the same way, if any of our visitors showed an interest in collecting stuff from the Pre-Raphaelite period I would suggest they visited her shop; she had quite a few books on the subject in her collection."

"Well, thank you Mrs Campbell-Haigh. I'm afraid the museum can't open today. I'm sealing off the park and there will be a large police presence here."

"You have your duty to do. For God's sake find out who killed her before he strikes again . . ."

"I intend to. Do you know if she had any enemies?"

"Eileen? Who would want to kill Eileen? It's absurd, horrible, like something on television . . ." She scrabbled in her pocket and produced a battered packet of cigarettes. She shook one out and lit it with trembling fingers and inhaled deeply, leaning back against the panelling with closed eyes.

"Just one more question, Mrs Campbell-Haigh. Why were you so certain she had been murdered?"

"She *was* murdered, wasn't she?"

"Yes, but I don't see how you could have known that from seeing her body in the water. You didn't touch or examine it, did you?"

"No." She shuddered.

"I'm wondering why you didn't assume that she had slipped in and drowned or even committed suicide."

"Well, I knew that was impossible . . ."

"Why?"

"Because she was terrified of water, that's why. It petrified her. I believe she'd had an accident as a kid – fallen in some pond and was fished out half-drowned. She never learnt to swim because of that, wouldn't go near the sea or the river. I knew she'd never go close enough to the lake to fall in. I tell you what, Inspector . . ." her troubled hazel eyes held his, ". . . someone must have really hated her to kill her like that."

Where the hell was Eileen? Mark Copley banged down the phone and frowned at his watch. It was nearly ten o'clock; where could she have got to? They were supposed to be checking through some trunk loads of old clothes prior to a visit from a London dealer who was arriving at midday. He'd been at the shop since before nine but Eileen hadn't turned up and there had been no reply each time he had tried to phone her house. Surely she hadn't forgotten the arrangements and gone off somewhere else? But where? The car was in the yard and as far as he knew there were no auctions or viewing anywhere that day.

Perhaps she'd been taken ill? But surely she would have phoned – unless she had collapsed and was lying

117

unconscious in her home? There were no customers about at that moment and he decided to close shop and go over to her house. He locked the front door and propped up a notice that read "Back in Five Minutes" and let himself out of the back door. He decided not to bother with the car, there was an old bicycle propped up in the shed and he took this and pedalled through the village.

He had often queried why she didn't live on the premises, there were adequate living quarters above the shop; but Eileen had always been afraid that their stock would attract thieves and she said that she didn't want to be around when they called. He would have liked to live there himself – it was an interesting old building and the rent would surely be cheaper than what he was paying now – but she said the same thing applied. She didn't want him being mugged by any would-be burglar, and anyway, every room and inch of space was used as storage and crammed with goods. This was true and he hadn't pressed her, so he still lived in the top flat of the converted manse and she lived in her little house beyond the post office.

There was no sign of life when he arrived outside the gate. He propped the bike up against the hedge and walked up the path and knocked on the door. There was no reply so he walked round the side of the house to the back door. Eileen's cat, a large, black, neutered tom, sprang out from behind a carved, pedestal bird-bath and wound itself around his legs, mewing plaintively.

"Where's your mistress, Sammy? You look as if you haven't been fed today."

Sammy agreed and butted him with his head and Mark banged on the back door and tried the handle. As he had expected it was locked so he peered in the kitchen window. All he could see was a small pile of crockery that had been left to drain near the sink and a corner of the kitchen table which was empty. He moved round to the next window which belonged to the sitting room. As far as he could see it was neat and tidy and there was no sign of Eileen. He heard somebody in the next door garden and went over to the hedge. Eileen's neighbour, a man in his sixties, was watering his roses with a watering-can and Mark called to him.

118

"Have you seen Eileen?"

"No, can't say I have. Shouldn't she be at the shop?"

"She hasn't turned up and I'm rather worried."

The man put down the watering-can and moved over to the hedge.

"You're Mark, her assistant, aren't you?"

"Yes, I've been trying to ring her ever since I got to the shop but there's been no reply so I thought I'd better come round."

"You don't think she's had a heart attack or collapsed or something, do you?"

"That's what I'm afraid of. I can't see any sign of life through the downstairs' windows but she may be upstairs."

"I've got an extending ladder. Come round and help me carry it and we'll see if we can prop it up against the bedroom windows and inside."

Mark went into the next door garden and the two men manhandled the ladder into position.

"When did you see her last?"

"I heard her go out yesterday evening. At least, I heard the door slam and gate click so I presumed she was going out."

"What time did she get back?"

"I didn't hear her come back. I'd got the telly on loud and I went to bed early."

Mark climbed the ladder and squinted through the window.

"Can you see anything?" called the elderly man from below.

"No. The bed is made and she's certainly not lying on the floor."

"What about the bathroom?"

"It's frosted glass, you can't see in. Wait a minute, I'll come down and we'll move the ladder along to the other bedroom window."

At that moment there was the sound of a car door slamming and an authorative voice called out:

"What's going on here?"

"Hell! Someone thinks we're burglars" said Mark

Copley, scrambling down the ladder and coming face to face with Patrick Mansfield.

Mansfield had already called at the antiques shop and, finding it closed, was driving through the village towards the old manse where he knew that Copley lived. He had been astonished, on passing Eileen Dexter's house, to see what looked like two men breaking into an upstairs window. He now recognised the man who had been up the ladder.

"Mr Copley? I'm looking for you, sir."

"Not again! I told you all I know about the Rave the other day!"

"May I ask what you were doing up that ladder?"

"Looking to see if Eileen – Miss Dexter – is lying ill in there. She didn't turn up at the shop this morning and I'm worried about her."

"Oh yes, that is why I'm here, sir; Miss Dexter has had an accident."

"An accident?" said the neighbour looking shocked. "Oh dear, I hope she's not badly hurt?"

Mansfield ignored him and addressed Copley. "If you would just come with me, sir; Inspector Roland asked me to fetch you."

Copley shrugged at the neighbour and let himself me led out to the car.

"How badly is she hurt?"

"I'm afraid she's been killed."

"You mean she's DEAD?"

"Yes, sir."

"But . . . but I don't understand how she could have been knocked down in the village and killed without me . . . without anyone knowing about it. When did it happen?"

"It wasn't a road accident. She was found dead in the lake at Holgate Park and we have reason to believe she was murdered."

"Oh my God! Is this true?" He stumbled against the car and put out a hand to steady himself.

"I'm afraid so. We'd like you to identify the body."

"Oh . . . Do I have to?"

"It's just a formality, sir. You knew her as well as

anyone in the village and I understand she had no close relations?"

"No, she always used to say she was alone in the world. She was engaged once, years ago, but he was killed . . ."

Mark Copley got into the car and fumbled with the seat belt. His olive skin looked sallow and he leaned back in a daze as if he hadn't really taken in what he had just been told. Mansfield reversed the car and drove back towards the park and Copley spoke haltingly, as if to himself, his eyes fixed unseeingly on the windscreen:

"It's like a nightmare . . . like that horrible hoax that was played on her . . . it's come true, hasn't it?" he appealed to Mansfield. Mansfield ignored this outburst.

"Do you happen to know Miss Dexter's movements yesterday evening?"

"I presume she went straight home from the shop and spent the evening there; she certainly didn't mention going out anywhere."

"Or that she was expecting any visitors?"

"No. Wait a minute though . . ." he tugged fretfully at his bottom lip. ". . . she received a phone call yesterday afternoon. I don't know who it was from but it sounded as if she was making arrangements to meet someone. I don't know where – she never mentioned the call after she had rung off – but I suppose it could have been for yesterday evening." If that was so, thought Mansfield, she definitely knew her killer and had been lured to a rendez-vous which ended in her death.

"She hated the water you know" continued Copley, "it's horrible to think of her being drowned . . ."

"Did I say she drowned?"

"Oh . . . I took it for granted as you said she'd been found in the lake. How . . . how did she die?"

"We mustn't speculate at this point, sir."

That shut Mark Copley up and he stared apprehensively at the large amount of policemen swarming over the park as the car swung through the gates and was driven towards the Lodge. Mansfield parked in the courtyard and the two men walked down towards the lake. Roland saw them coming and went to meet them.

121

"Mr Copley, I'm glad you've arrived. They are waiting to take the body away but I thought it would be easier for you to see it here rather than having to go to the mortuary."

"I . . . I can't believe it . . ." The younger man looked sick but followed docilely in the detective's wake. The body was already in a body bag lying on a stretcher. Roland unzipped it part way revealing the dead woman's head and shoulders. She was on her back so the head wound was not visible. The mourning brooch nestled like a nugget of anthracite in the sodden folds of her blouse.

"Well?"

"Yes, it's her" mumbled Copley.

"Are you sure?"

"Yes, it's Eileen Dexter. How did she die?"

"We must await the autopsy results but somebody made very sure she was dead."

"Oh Christ!" He gulped. "Who found her?"

"Your girlfriend and Mrs Campbell-Haigh."

"Alison? You don't mean Alison? But how . . .?"

"Miss Barnard was walking through the park on her way to the Lodge. She saw Mrs Campbell-Haigh looking agitated by the edge of the lake and went to join her."

"But this is terrible! Where is she now?"

"She has been taken home."

"I must go to her!" He started to blunder away but Roland's voice recalled him.

"All in good time, Mr Copley, but first I have some questions that need answers. Who is Miss Dexter's next-of-kin?"

"I don't know." He looked blank. "She hadn't got any living relations as far as I know."

"Do you know who was her solicitor?"

"She used Merrin and Glaister in Felstone for any legal business involving the shop."

"She may have lodged a will with them. Have you any idea who will inherit her estate?"

"Knowing Eileen, she's probably left it to a cat's home. Oh my God!" he continued, as a thought struck him, "I'm probably out of a job!"

"How long have you been working for Miss Dexter?"

"About seven years."

"That would take us back to your school days surely?"

"I started work in the shop as soon as I left school."

"I always thought the antiques trade was a very knowledgeable affair and a minefield for the initiated. Are you telling me she employed a school-leaver without any experience to help her in her business?"

"Look, I don't really see that it's any business of yours or what it's got to do with Eileen's death, but there was a reason for it."

"And what was that?" Mark Copley shrugged and decided to humour the detective.

"My Grandmother was Eileen's best friend. My parents were killed in a car crash when I was very young and my grandmother brought me up until her own death. Eileen had always run her business on her own without any outside help but as she got older she decided she needed an assistant and she thought of me. She trained me in every aspect of the trade and I'm a quick learner. I got as hooked on it as she was and she came to trust my judgement as well as her own. It worked fine, Inspector, we both had our own special interests and . . . and now it's *ruined!*" He glared at Roland and the detective could see that he was drumming up his anger to disguise the tears that were threatening to un-man him. "Why the hell aren't you finding this bloody maniac instead of wasting time asking me these useless questions?.."

"They're not useless, Mr Copley. I'm trying to build up a picture of Miss Dexter's background and habits. Do you know what she was doing yesterday evening?"

"I've already told your sergeant all that!"

"Fine. Did you also tell him how you spent the evening?"

"Not with Eileen" he retorted. "Alison and I were going to the cinema in Felstone but she didn't feel up to it so we stayed in talking and then she decided to go to bed early so I went back to my flat and spent the rest of the evening watching the box and reading. Look, can I go after her now? You don't want me anymore, do you?"

"Not for now. We shall certainly want to speak to you again later. Do you have your own keys to the shop?"

"Yes."

"Who else has keys?"

"Just myself and Eileen."

"Where did she keep hers?"

"In her handbag, always."

"Her handbag is missing. May we have yours please?"

"But . . ."

"You don't intend opening up and carrying on business today, do you?"

Hell, no . . .!"

"You shall have a receipt for them and they'll be returned to you as soon as possible."

Copley handed over the keys and looked askance at the mortuary van that was backing towards them.

"Have you finished with me?"

"Yes, Mr Copley. Just one more thing: you're going to get pestered by the Press and the media. I think it will be in everyone's interests, and especially Miss Barnard's, if you leave it to the Police to make an official statement. Don't gossip to any reporters."

"They're ghouls! I certainly shan't say anything and I'll stop them pestering Alison."

And just how you're going to do that I don't know, thought Roland watching him walk away, but good luck to you.

"Sir, we think we've found the weapon that was used."

One of the men searching the area ran up to Roland.

"Where?"

"In those reeds over the other side. We haven't touched it."

"Is it under water?"

"No. It looks as if he tried to chuck it in the lake and it got caught up in the reeds."

"Right, let me see."

Roland and Mansfield walked round to the other side of the lake and Roland stepped across the dried mud fringe into the forest of reeds whose clumped roots were half out of the water. Normally they would have been submerged and inaccessible from land.

"It's here, sir," The man who had fetched him parted a handful of reeds, "and there are marks on one end that could be blood stains."

Roland donned thin plastic gloves and carefully picked up the branch. It was about half a metre long with rough corrugated bark. He thought it was oak.

"Good. I think this may well be the weapon and as you say there is staining one end. Get it over to the lab as quick as possible. I don't think we'll have any joy with fingerprints on that surface but they may find something."

The branch was sealed up in a polythene bag and taken away and Roland went over to give instructions to the diving team who had now arrived,

"You're looking for a shoe and a handbag. The body was found just over there where the lawn slopes down to the water but the weapon we think was used was in those reeds over by the bank near the trees, so she probably went in there. Good hunting."

"Are you alright, Miss . . . er . . . Alison?" Evans squinted sideways at his passenger who lay back with closed eyes. She looked so pale and lifeless that he was afraid she had fainted. With an effort she opened her eyes and murmured ironically:

"Would you be alright if you'd just discovered a body?"

"It's an occupational hazard."

She considered this. "Yes, I suppose it is. Do you ever get used to it, immune to the horror . . .?"

"No, never, and any policeman who tries to tell you different is kidding himself; but I suppose we learn ways of coping with it so that we can function properly and carry out our job."

"You're not doing very well so far, are you?"

William Evans started to reply indignantly, then realized that he had overshot her cottage. He jammed on the brakes and reversed until the car was outside the front gate. He killed the engine and turned to her.

"We'll get him. I promise you that. You mustn't worry."

"Worry? That's the understatement of the year!"

125

"Listen, he's not going to harm you, whoever he is." He reached over and enclosed one of her slender hands in his massive ones. "We're going to find him and bring him to justice."

"You are sticking your neck out, Constable . . ."

"Evans. *William.* Come on, lets get you in."

He got out of the car and walked round to her door. He felt strangely protective towards her and also incredibly gauche. His last girlfriend had been a nurse. She had been a robust, competent, down-to-earth person, quite capable of looking after herself and him too, if he had let her. Alison Barnard was so different; so fragile and vulnerable, like a delicate piece of porcelain that needed careful handling; and against her he felt so clumsy and awkward. He wanted to lift her in his arms and carry her into the house. He knew better than to try it. She might be crushed by illness and events but he recognised a thread of steel beneath her seeming helplessness. He opened the door and helped her out and escorted her up the path.

"Is your sister in? Have you got a key?"

"The back door is open. Lindsey is probably in her studio. Thank you for bringing me home."

He ignored this dismissal and walked round the side of the cottage with her to the back door which he opened and stepped through after her into a large, old-fashioned kitchen. There was an aga in the big recess that had once held an open spit fire and beside this were two windsor chairs. She sank into one of these and fanned herself with a hand.

"I shall be okay now."

"Don't be in such a hurry to get rid of me. You need a drink – hot, strong . . ."

". . . sweet tea" she finished for him with a grimace. I don't take sugar and I'd much prefer a coffee."

"Coffee it shall be." He filled the kettle at the sink and plugged it in, lifted mugs off hooks on the dresser and found the coffee and milk. "Now, where is this sister of yours?"

"She's in the studio, on the other side of the terrace. I can hear her working."

William Evans listened. He could hear a loud thudding

126

noise as if something was being bashed against a hard surface.

"What on earth is she doing?"

"Wedging clay."

At his look of mystification she explained:

"Before you start work with a lump of clay you have to wedge it – that means banging it about to make sure you've got all the air bubbles out, otherwise it can crack or shatter when you get to the firing stage."

"Sounds complicated. I'll go and root her out. Keep an eye on that kettle, can you?"

"I'm not completely helpless" she retorted. "I think this drink is more for your benefit than mine!"

"How did you guess?" He grinned at her and went across the sunbowl of a terrace to the studio. The door was wide open and he stood undetected in the doorway for a couple of minutes watching Lindsey Barnard at work. Her brown, powerful hands lifted the clay and slammed it down on the bench top, then she pushed it away with the ball of her hands, folded it back, turned it round 25 degrees, pushed and pulled it again, then lifted it up and started the process again. There was something hypnotic in the fluid movements and the regular rhythm of the thud of the clay. She made it look so easy and effortless yet he was sure it must be hard work, especially in the heat. She sensed someone was watching her and looked up, recognising him instantly. She ran her hands down the front of the old shirt she wore as a smock, leaving further smears of earthenware clay and said sharply:

"What's up now?"

He told her what had happened and she gaped at him.

"I don't believe it! Eileen Dexter's been killed and Alison found her?"

"I'm afraid so. I've brought her home."

"She must be in a terrible state!" She tugged at the shirt, pulled it over her head and threw it on the bench and rushed towards the door.

"She's bearing up well but she may suffer from delayed shock. Perhaps her doctor should be sent for."

127

"She'll need more than that if you lot don't do something soon!"

Lindsey paused in the doorway and darted back inside the studio. She picked up the lump of clay she had been working and jerked open a door at the back of the room. To Evans inexperienced eye it looked like a walk-in cupboard; the interior was dark and a damp, foisty smell oozed out.

"What's that?"

"My damp cupboard." She slapped the clay down on a shelf and closed the door. "If I leave the clay lying around it will dry out too quickly, especially in this heat."

Alison had made the coffee and was cradling a mug in her hands as if she were cold and trying to derive some warmth from it. Her features looked more pinched than when Evans had left her and she stared at her sister despondently.

"Oh Allie! You look awful!"

"Don't fuss. Have a coffee."

"You should be in bed. I'm going to ring Dr Firbank."

"What's the point. I'm next on the list."

"You mustn't talk like that! It's nonsense!"

"Is it? *you* don't think so, do you?" she suddenly shot at Evans. "There's a maniac out there bumping people off and it will be my turn soon!"

"You mustn't think like that, Alison," said Evans firmly, "you're just giving in to this Joker."

"But why me? Who is it who wants me dead so badly they can't wait for me to die!" Her voice rose in hysteria and a sudden question flashed into Evans' mind – what manner of death had The Joker predicted for Alison Barnard? He stowed it away for further consideration later and tried to comfort her.

"Look, we've no idea yet why Eileen Dexter was killed, or Charles Todd, but their deaths may be totally unconnected. Just because they both had hoaxes played on them doesn't mean they were killed by the same person. Their deaths probably have nothing to do with this sick person who's been playing nasty tricks."

"And is that supposed to be a comfort?" demanded

Lindsey. "The fact that there may be more than one homicidal maniac on the loose in the village?"

I'm not handling this very well, thought Evans, running a hand through his hair. I should be asking questions about their relationship with Eileen Dexter and their movements last night, but now is not the right time. He gulped down his coffee.

"Try and not brood on it. I'm afraid we shall have to have a signed statement from you, Alison, but it will do later when you're feeling better. Thanks for the drink."

He left by the back door and Lindsey walked round the side of the cottage with him.

"What will happen to Mark? Mark Copley – he worked for Eileen."

"Why don't you ask him; isn't that him coming down the road?"

Lindsey followed his gaze and he happened to glance back at her as her eyes alighted on Copley who was loping towards them. For a split second he saw the longing and delight in her face before she dropped her lids and turned away, the colour mounting in her cheeks.

"He's probably come to see how Alison is. Goodbye, constable."

"Goodbye, Miss Barnard."

He got into the car and watched Mark Copley turn into the gateway and pound up the path after Lindsey. So that was the way the land lay? Lucky fellow; it looked as if not one, but two Barnard sisters had the hots for him.

CHAPTER 8

"Are you still trying to tell me there's no connection between these deaths?" Superintendent Lacey leaned forward on his elbows and scowled at Roland. "You insist that Todd was killed by someone with a grudge against him who was using this Joker as a cover? Well, what about this Eileen Dexter?"

"I've discovered no motive so far."

"But you surely don't think the same applies to HER death? It just won't do, James – people settling old scores and knocking off their enemies and The Joker getting the blame – it's bloody ridiculous! Too far-fetched!"

"I'm keeping an open mind about it."

"Try telling that to the Chief Constable. Yes, I've had him on my back this morning. He doesn't want vague theories, he wants answers! He wants to know just how this investigation is progressing and whether we are getting anywhere. If I tell him my officer-in-charge has got an open mind about the situation he is going to blow his top – he's already talking about calling in the Yard!"

"I can't see how they could do any better than us, sir. Londoners who know nothing of village life and its ramifications would be at a disadvantage from the start. We're following up all the usual lines of detection – forensic evidence, house-to-house enquiries etc. – but the break-through is going to come with some snippet of information that one of the locals lets drop, and my men are more likely to pick up something like that than strangers from the City. If these murders are the work of this so-called Joker we are not dealing with your normal killing – for gain, for fear or a domestic – we're dealing with a mentally deranged person."

"A bloody maniac! I agree with you there, which is why I've got Dr McNalty coming in to see us. Do you remember him?"

"He was that psychiatrist who helped on the Randall case a couple of years ago; did some psychological profiling for us."

"That's the bloke. We'll chew it over with him and see if he can throw any light on the situation."

Roland tried not to show his surprise. Normally the superintendent looked on all branches of psychiatry as so much mumbo-jumbo. He had no time for what he called cranky theories and psycho-babble excuses.

"Mind you, I think half of these shrinks are round the twist themselves," continued Lacey, unaware of Roland's reaction, "but it takes one to know one, eh?" He pressed the button on his intercom and barked into it:

"Has McNalty arrived yet? Just coming in? Well, send him straight up and bring us some tea. PROPER tea, not that cat's piss with lemon you served up yesterday." He turned back to Roland and said in disgust: "It will be iced coffee next! Don't they understand that hot, strong tea is the best thing to drink in a heatwave? Makes you sweat and cools you down – like the wogs eating curry in India."

Roland managed to keep silent. How Lacey had avoided being hauled before the Race Relations Boards years ago he didn't know.

"What have you got scheduled for the rest of the morning?"

"It's Jason Ball's funeral."

"The lad who got himself drowned?!"

"Yes."

"Well, at least we know HE wasn't the victim of The Joker. I've been going through the list of all his fellow ravers . . ."

Wait for it, thought Roland with a sigh. ". . . have they all been dealt with?"

"Yes, sir" he said firmly.

"Are you taking young Simon with you to the funeral?"

"Yes, I think he should go."

"Good thinking, James; it will bring it home to him. By

131

the way, I've got something that may interest you." He got to his feet and lumbered over to his filing cabinet where he rummaged through the papers piled on top whilst Roland couldn't believe his luck. He had been expecting a long lecture on parental authority, embarrassment to the Force and out-of-control teenagers. "Here we are . . ." he handed a leaflet to his inspector. ". . . it's not a proper Outward Bound course but it's a similar thing. Send him on that and get him out of the way for a few weeks. There's nothing like physical exhaustion to keep them in line."

Roland looked at the leaflet. It appeared to be about residential courses which were held in a converted castle in the Highlands of Scotland and involved walking and rock climbing and sailing and canoeing amongst other things.

"Where did you get this from?"

"Someone in Probation passed it on to me a while ago. Trying to soften me up. These young thugs who knock old ladies on the head and terrorize the neighbourhood need a spell in the pen, not a bleeding holiday! But we're not talking about a real offender here, are we James?"

"No, sir" he replied faintly.

There was a knock on the door and a WPC entered carrying a steaming tray and followed by Austin McNalty. McNalty was a tall, well-built man in his forties. He topped most of the men on the Force by a couple of inches and he played up to his contours by wearing ostentatious clothes. He favoured loud checks and velvet bow ties and that day was wearing lilac tweeds, complete with waistcoat despite the heat. He had long, shaggy curls and wore glasses with lenses like bottle bottoms through which he peered like a discerning owl.

"Ah, McNalty, glad you could make it. You know Detective Inspector Roland, don't you?"

"Yes, we've met." He acknowledged Roland with a nod. "I can guess why you're consulting me. You want my opinion on this so-called Joker?"

"I want to know what I'm dealing with" growled Lacey.

"Is he behind these murders?" Lacey left Roland to field that one,

"It's beginning to look like it." Roland was not sure how

132

much of the facts the psychiatrist knew or how much Lacey wanted him told. The superintendent waded in.

"Is he loony?"

McNalty looked pained. "There are degrees of madness as I'm sure you know. The line between madness and sanity is very tenuous. As you know I believe no-one is totally sane, we are all a little mad . . ."

"Yes, yes" said Lacey tetchily, already beginning to regret his decision to bring in the psychiatrist, "but we're talking about the person who carried out these hoaxes."

"However," continued McNalty, ignoring Lacey, "if you're asking me if a murderer is mad, then I should have to say that in a layman's conception of the term the answer is probably yes. To put it in words you would understand, someone who kills has a vital part of his personality missing. He has no compassion, no feeling for his fellow men. Murder is the ultimate crime but he has no compunction about robbing someone of their life. Of course, you realize here that I am talking about cold-blooded, premeditated murder, not your crime of passion or heat-of-the moment killing."

"If this Joker has been carrying out these murders, they're premeditated all right" said Lacey grimly.

"You're looking for someone who appears perfectly normal . . ."

"I was afraid you were going to say that!"

"Someone who has a grudge against life and delights in seeing people suffer and squirm but who has managed to curb these traits until now. He sees slights in quite innocent actions and in his imagination he devises situations in which he gets his back on these people who he thinks have humiliated or be-littled him. He thinks up bizarre scenarios which would frighten and hurt the recipients and gets great enjoyment out of these flights of fantasy, but eventually that is not enough. He decides to put one of his hypothetical schemes into action. He could have spent months working it out in minute detail and he now carries it out for real and sits back to enjoy the results. And they would be highly satisfactory to him. The victim reacts predictably, the publicity is all he could have wished for and

133

it feeds his sense of being superior to everyone else. It gives him a feeling of being in power, of being in charge."

"Okay, I may buy that; but it's a big step from committing imaginary crimes to actually carrying them out" interrupted Lacey.

"No, not for the sort of psyche we're talking about. Our man finds it increasingly difficult to differentiate between his make-believe world and the real thing. Inevitably something happens to tip him over the edge and he really does kill his victim in the way he has predicted through a hoax. Do you follow me?"

"It sounds plausible to me" said Roland, "but how do you explain the first death? Mervyn Souster, our Morris dancer, had a death hoax played on him and then he was killed, but his death was nothing to do with the Joker – it was definitely the result of a brawl that got out of hand."

"But don't you see – that was just the trigger to set our man off. He has set up these elaborate tricks and is enjoying the ensuing drama and then one of his victims is really murdered and in the manner he had devised for him. He is affronted and enraged. This was HIS game and now someone else has moved in on it and is getting all the glory."

"Glory?" snorted Lacey in disgust.

"That's how he sees it. He now has to prove that HE is the mastermind, the one in control, so he starts killing and it escalates from there."

"Are you saying he will go on killing?"

"I can't see him stopping now, he's developed a taste for it. The police appear powerless and it's gone to his head. How many more victims has he got lined up?"

"One that we know of."

"A round-the-clock bodyguard? That won't stop him. He'll be content to bide his time and wait, even if it takes months or years."

"We're going to catch him" said Lacey grimly. "We're looking for someone with a grudge against all the people concerned, dead or alive?"

"It's not as simple as that. It's not a case of having it in for someone because they're run off with your wife or suchlike. These grudges are probably slights or insults that he's blown up out of all proportion with his unbalanced reasoning and the victims probably would have had no memory of them or no idea of their significance. They could have happened years ago and they've been festering at the back of his mind ever since."

"You keep saying *him*," said Roland, "does that mean you think it is definitely a man and we can rule out the possibility of it being a woman?"

"Not at all. After all, a large percentage of poison pen letters are written by women – as you know very well – and this state of mind could equally belong to a man or a woman. You know whether a woman was capable of carrying out these hoaxes and murders."

"It certainly can't be ruled out on physical grounds."

"Well, it's been interesting to hear how *your* mind has interpreted the situation but I'm not saying I agree with you" said Lacey bringing the meeting to an end. "Thanks, doctor, anyway, for coming in and giving us your opinion."

"Don't worry, I shall send in my bill." Mcnalty's eyes twinkled behind his pebble lenses as he got up to leave. Roland opened the door for him and the psychiatrist paused in the doorway and looked back at Lacey.

"Don't play into his hands. All this coverage and speculation in the Press."

"That's below the belt!" roared the superintendent when McNalty was out of earshot.

Ginny darted out of the house when she heard the car draw up outside and looked disappointed when she saw it was her husband.

"I thought you were the doctor."

"Doctor? Is she worse?" Katherine had been fretful in the night and hadn't wanted any breakfast. Ginny had thought she was teething.

"She's feverish and coughing so I rang up Dr Firbank and he promised to drop in this morning. Have you got time for a coffee?"

"No, I can't really spare the time to go to this funeral. Is Simon ready?"

"He's upstairs – screwing his courage to the sticking point I think. I suppose I really ought to go; after all, I used to teach him."

"You can't leave Katherine, especially now she's ill. Don't worry, the family will be well represented."

"But are you representing us or the Police?"

"Both. Don't quibble."

He gave her a quick kiss and bounded up the stairs, calling out to Simon, before going to look at his daughter. She was lying listlessly in her cot and when she saw her father she started to grizzle.

"How's my Kate?" He held out his hand but instead of grabbing it and pulling herself up as she usually did she jerked her head away and started to cry in earnest, choking and coughing at the same time.

"She's certainly not very happy, is she?" he said to Ginny who had followed him upstairs. "What do you think is wrong?"

"Probably just a feverish chill; I expect I'm making a fuss about nothing but I thought it best to take no chances."

"Quite right." He knew that the same dreaded word "meningitis" was hovering unspoken between them. There had been a minor epidemic in the county last winter and it was always there, lurking in the back of the mind, whenever Katherine or Simon were off-colour.

"Simon, are you ready?"

Simon emerged from his bedroom and Roland did a double-take. He was so used to seeing the youth in scruffy jeans and trainers that he hardly recognised him in collar and tie and school blazer with his black, unruly hair plastered smooth.

"Do I look alright?"

"Very respectable. Come on, we'll be late."

Simon was silent in the car and Roland could feel the tension emanating from him. He remembered the leaflet Lacey had given him and dug it out of his pocket and handed it over.

"I thought this might interest you."

Simon glanced through it as Roland drove out of the village and headed for Felstone. "Well?"

136

"Is it trick or treat?"

Roland's lips twitched. "I'M not going to get a holiday this summer but I thought you might like to get away for a few weeks; have a complete change of scene, do something different."

Simon read the leaflet in greater detail. "This sailing sounds good; I've always wanted to learn to sail properly."

"So do you want me to try and book you in?"

"Is this for my benefit or yours?"

"For God's sake Simon, don't always try to read ulterior motives into my actions. I thought it would help you to have a break from all this; put it behind you and have something new to think about. We're not talking about me – I've got damn sight worse things occupying my attention at the moment than a teenager experimenting at a Rave party!"

"Heck, I'm sorry James! These murders – are you getting anywhere?"

"Do you want the official or the unofficial position? Officially, we're following up several lines of inquiry and are hopeful of making an early arrest; unofficially, we've drawn a blank so far – zilch, nix, sweet F.A."

"So what happens now?"

"We slog on, asking questions, checking out statements, hoping for a breakthrough."

"Before he strikes again?"

"Don't say it! And remember, this conversation is for your ears only."

"Of course, my lips are sealed. Is it a psychopath? A serial killer?"

"Simon, we don't know yet if these murders were committed by the same person! If they were – well, a serial killer has an Mo – modus operandi – that never varies, which certainly isn't the case here. As to being a psychopath; who knows what motivates him, but to you and me and the man in the street he would appear perfectly normal. Now, discuss those courses with your mother and have a good think about them."

"Can we afford it?"

"I expect we can scrape together enough" said Roland drily.

The funeral was being held in the parish church of St Thomas; there would be a private cremation afterwards. As Roland drew near the streets were clogged with traffic, all seemingly homing in on the church. It looked as if half the population of Felstone was attending the ceremony. He managed to park in a back street and the two of them joined the throng converging on the church porch and sat in a pew near the back of the nave. The school was well represented with a sea of pupils, both male and female, clad in black blazers like Simon's. Roland recognised many of the teachers present and knew that several of their charges had been at Saxton on the night of Jason Ball's death and Charles Todd's murder. Had any of them witnessed anything of the latter event? So far nobody interviewed had come up with anything useful but he was still hopeful that memories might be jogged. At the moment they were far more concerned with the death of their contemporary and friend than that of an elderly stranger, which was to be expected.

By the time the service was drawing to a close and "The Lord is My Shepherd" was being sung many of the congregation were in tears and beside him, Simon was blowing his nose. What a cruel waste of a young life, he thought as the coffin, ablaze with summer blooms, was carried back down the aisle. Simon had told him that Jason had taken a year off prior to taking up a university place at Durham and had been doing charity work after six months back-packing round Europe. How could the parents cope with a loss like this? It was a question he always asked himself when he had to deal with the violent death of a child or young person and now that he was a father – for real and by proxy – it was brought home to him all the more intensely. And it wasn't just violent death; infants could be snatched away by illness even in this day and age. How was Katherine? Had the doctor been yet?

"Do you want to stay around with your mates?" He asked Simon as they filed out of the church.

"No" said Simon hurriedly, "but I can make my own way back if you're busy."

"No problem. I'll drop you off at home and check whether the doctor has been in to see Katherine yet."

"She's not seriously ill, is she?"

"No, I don't think so. Come on, let's get back."

Neville Firbank, the doctor, was just taking his leave of Ginny at the front door when they drew up outside. He was nearing retirement age and Roland would be sorry when he finally called it a day. As well as a doctor, they looked on him as a friend. He was one of the old school of general practitioners and hid a caring, devoted attitude to his work and patients beneath a brisk, gruff exterior.

"How is she?" asked Roland, bounding up the path.

"She'll live – to plague you as she grows older" said the doctor drily. "Chickenpox."

"Chickenpox?"

"Yes, she's come out in a beautiful rash. I presume you've had it?" he asked Simon who looked blank.

"Yes, when he was about four" said Ginny. "Thanks for coming, it's set my mind at rest."

"Can you spare a minute, Neville?" asked Roland as the doctor walked back to his car.

"Not really, and I shouldn't think you can either."

"It won't take long. I want to pick your brains."

"You'd better get in." Neville Firbank unlocked his car and Roland folded himself into the front passenger seat. "Now, what's all this about? You're not still worried about Ginny, are you? She's doing fine and I just wished all my patients got over depression so well."

"No, this is about work."

"These murders? Nasty business, how can I help?"

"Alison Barnard," said Roland slowly, "she's one of your patients, isn't she?"

"I've been her GP for many years but of course she's under Bletchdale, the haematologist at the hospital now."

"You know she's been the victim of a hoax by this Joker?"

"I can and do read the papers and I presume that what they print is basically true even if it's a highly embellished and lurid version of the truth. You're afraid she's going to be next in the firing line?"

"Yes. Just how ill is she?"

"You're not expecting me to divulge her medical records to you, are you James?"

"I just want to know her real diagnosis and what her chances are. You can surely tell me that without breaking your hypocratic oath?"

"This is most unethical."

"I need to know. It may be a case of some sort of protection for her."

"Well, this is all most irregular but I suppose I can tell you. She's suffering from Acute Myeloid Leukaemia."

"And the prognosis?"

"About a 30–40% chance of a cure."

"As low as that?" Roland was dismayed.

"She's holding her own at the moment, though this business isn't helping, and she starts her last course of chemotherapy soon."

"And if that isn't effective?"

"Then her only chance, if the chemotherapy fails to halt the advance of the disease, is a bone marrow transplant if one could find a matched donar. Now please remember, this is in strict confidence; it's not to go in any police file."

"Of course not. Thanks, Neville."

"Now please get out of my car and let me get on."

Roland went back to his own car and drove to the office of Merrin and Galister, Eileen Dewhurst's solicitors that was situated in Felstone High Street.

Mansfield was sprawled at his desk whistling between his teeth and playing with his matches and tobacco pouch when Roland arrived back.

"You look mighty pleased with yourself; like a dog with two tails."

"That's the buzz word – dog." Mansfield leaned back and grinned at his colleague.

"I presume you're going to tell me what you're on about?"

"Two reports in – the PM on Eileen Dexter and something from Forensics that will really interest you. That lump of wood was definitely the one used to bash her

140

over the head; the bloodstains match up and also the hairs."

"You're not telling me they actually got the murderer's dabs off it?"

"No, but they found tooth marks."

"Tooth marks?"

"Identified as those of a dog."

"I can't see how that helps us."

"I should have thought that was obvious. That piece of wood has been played with and chewed by a dog so it looks as if our murderer owns a dog. If we can match up those tooth marks with a dog then we're home and dry."

"It won't wash, Pat. That branch was probably just lying around and our killer grabbed it on the spur of the moment as a suitable weapon. There are probably masses of pieces of wood in Holgate Park that have been used as playthings for local dogs. I know the park is supposed to be private property but that doesn't seem to deter the villagers. I've gathered they all use it as a sort of recreation ground – walk dogs, do their courting etc. Besides, he's hardly likely to have had a dog in attendance when he did the job."

"We had a dog once," said Mansfield, seemingly going off at a tangent, "it had a favourite stick – part of an old fencing stake – and everytime we took it for a walk that stick had to come too and be thrown for him to retrieve, over and over again. This one could be significant."

"So we pursue dental proofs of every dog in Saxton."

"Well, there's an obvious one to start with – Stewart Carson's dog."

"Y..es. But suppose we did match them up, it wouldn't be any sort of proof. He could just say he picked up branches he found in the park for his dog to play with."

"Yes, but if you can definitely say to him that the murder weapon used to attack Eileen Dexter has YOUR dog's teeth marks on it – well, if he's guilty he could get badly rattled; make a slip and give himself away."

"I suppose it's worth a try. We're so short of suspects that anyone we can fit into the frame, however loosely, must be investigated."

141

"How do we go about it? Try and find something else the dog has chewed?"

"That couldn't be used as evidence; no, I think we'll press him openly. Get Evans to go and see him and ask for his cooperation. He can tell him what we're checking out and ask for a stick or toy that the dog's chewed so that we can match it or eliminate it as the case may be. If he refuses it's going to look mighty suspicious."

"He can always say he hasn't got anything chewed for us to take away."

"Then make sure that Evans takes a bar of soap or lump of cheese with him so that we can get a mould.

"How did you get on at the solicitor's?"

"Interesting. He didn't want to discuss Eileen Dexter's will but when I pressed him he coughed up. She had no relations and she was comfortably off. She owned the house she lived in and the shop was leasehold and the terms of the will are quite simple. The house and contents are to be sold and income derived to be divided equally between The National Trust, The Wildlife Trust and her local church. The leasehold of the shop she has left to Mark Copley, plus the contents.

"So he receives a nice little inheritance."

"Not as generous as it once would have been."

"Oh?"

"Business has been going down of late. With the shut down of the American Bases she had lost half her clientele. She was just about ticking over but whether Copley will be able to keep going is another matter. Of course, the stock of antiques will be quite valuable but there was a proviso in the will. It was left to him on condition that he carries on the antiques business and doesn't sell out or change the nature of the enterprise for five years.

"I see; so this legacy could be rather a millstone round his neck?"

"Possibly. Anyway, he told me something else. She had been thinking of changing her will. She's had a couple of good offers for the shop and she was toying with the idea of selling up completely and retiring."

"Did Copley know this? It could give him a good motive for getting rid of her before she acted."

"It's not as simple as that. Apparently she was worried about what affect this would have on him and was thinking along the lines of a lump sum to compensate him. Glaister said she had discussed this with him but she hadn't made up her mind so the original will stands."

"So actually if she had revoked the old will he might stand to gain?"

"It's difficult to say. Glaister didn't mention the actual sums involved but he did say that she had felt partly responsible for him – he was the grandson of an old friend."

At that point Evans poked his head round the door. "Do you want me?"

"Yes. I've got another job for you. How good are you with dogs?"

He explained what he wanted done and Evans looked resigned,

"Have I got to do *all* the dogs in Saxton?"

"It may come to that but try Stewart Carson first and note his reactions carefully."

"Okay. By the way, we haven't got a signed statement from Alison Barnard yet – do you think I ought to follow that up whilst I'm in the village?"

"That will do later. What's the matter now?"

"I've just remembered – something that struck me yesterday – how *is* Alison Barnard supposed to die?"

"What the devil do you mean!"

"Well, with Mervyn Souster it was stabbing, with Charles Todd it was hanging, for Eileen Dexter it was drowning . . . the hoax that was set up for Alison – how was she supposed to have died?"

Roland and Mansfield exchanged glances.

"You've got a point there. Maybe the Joker is predicting that her illness will catch up with her and she'll die from that."

After Evans had departed on his errand Roland read through the rest of the report from Forensics. Eileen Dexter's missing shoe and handbag had been found by the frogmen near to the spot where she had gone in. Nothing of significance had been extracted from them. The handbag had been sodden inside as well as outside and the only prints found were very smudged ones of Eileen Dexter's on some of the articles it contained. These included the usual objects to be found in a woman's handbag: a wallet purse with cash, credit cards and library ticket, an address book, a hankie, a tube of pastilles and also a keyring with the keys to the shop and her house. There was no diary.

"What about the autopsy report?" asked Roland, looking up.

"Nothing new from what Brasnett told us on the spot." Mansfield handed it over. "A blow on the back of the head which knocked her into the water. Death by drowning and the bruise marks on her shoulders consistent with her being held under until she died."

"She would have thrashed about a bit, her assailant must have got soaked; though of course in this weather he'd have dried off quickly."

"Unless the blow rendered her unconscious?"

"Either way she didn't stand much chance. I hope she WAS unconscious, poor woman. Imagine being terrified of water and being deliberately forced beneath the surface."

Roland put the reports to one side. "It's funny we haven't found a diary. There was definitely no sign of one in the house. I think I'm going to go and have another poke around in the shop; we may have overlooked something."

Roland let himself into the shop and sat down behind the table that did duty as counter and cash desk. With the lighting off it was dim and eerie and claustrophobic. Eileen Dexter had certainly utilized every inch of space. The shelves were loaded with porcelain and glassware; the walls, where they weren't lined with shelves, were covered in pictures; and pieces of furniture, including a very nice drum table, crowded the floor and provided obstacles for the unwary. A clock ticked loudly from the top of a tallboy and a whirring clatter startled him until he traced it to a grandfather clock in the corner whose chime had been muffled. It would not be the place for a nervous person after dark, he decided, aware of a row of glass eyes boring into his back. They belonged to her collection of antique dolls and he turned round to look at them, wondering if the one that had been used to perpetrate the hoax on her was amongst them.

Blue eyes, brown eyes, violet eyes, under arched brows stared at him from above pink, bisque cheeks. An eyelid on one doll was partially closed, a half moon of rigid, spiky lashes stuck over a slit of aquamarine giving the doll a droll, saucy look. He was reminded of the waxwork sporting Alison Barnard's wig that had lain in Holgate Wood, successfully imitating her down to the cornflower blue eyes. That was an astute remark Evans had made, he thought, and one he should have picked up on a long while ago. Just WHAT manner of death had The Joker been predicting for her? Natural death? Suicide? POISON?

How had Elizabeth Siddal, the Pre-Raphaelite model, died? He was sure Anthea Campbell-Haigh had mentioned it but he couldn't remember. Ginny would know. He pulled the telephone towards him and dialled his home number. Ginny answered almost immediately.

"How did Elizabeth Siddal die?"

"What?"

Roland explained what he wanted to know.

"I'm not sure but I think she died young. Probably consumption, it carried off a lot at that time. Do you want me to check?"

"Please."

There was a long pause whilst Ginny consulted her art books, then she was back on the line.

"She died of an overdose of laudanum, self-administrated. Does that answer your question?"

"Yes, thanks."

He asked after his daughter and put the phone down. An overdose. It was an answer that troubled him. Presumably Alison Barnard was on drugs of some sort; it would be easy for her to take an overdose or for someone to administer one to her. He pushed the thought to the back of his mind and got on with the task in hand.

The drawer of the table contained only old catalogues

and an assortment of pens, paperclips, scrap paper and elastic bands. The desk and cupboard in the office had already been examined minutely but he looked through them again in case something had been missed. Her account books were well-kept and there was an order book containing names and addresses against lists of articles. There was certainly no diary to be seen. The nearest thing approaching it was a slim-line calendar on which were pencilled dates of antique fairs and auctions and house sales. He supposed it was possible for an elderly woman, living on her own with very little social life, to have no needs of an engagements diary. It was very sad somehow. He checked that there was nothing on the calendar for the evening she had met her death and then had a quick look around the rest of the shop.

The plants in the conservatory were wilting. They hadn't been watered since she had died and there was already a neglected air about the place. The book department smelt of mould and fustiness. Did people really buy tatty, dog-eared old paperbacks? Presumably there was a market for them; perhaps Stewart Carson bought volumes for his collection from here? It would be worth checking. He strolled back to the main part of the shop. For whatever reason Eileen Dexter had been killed it wasn't to be found here. He let himself out and locked the door behind him convinced of only one thing; the contents must be of considerable value. Even if everything were reproduction and not genuine, it would still add up to a tidy sum.

Tina Fairbrother was walking home through the village when she noticed the Volvo estate that Mark Copley drove parked further down the road outside his home. He lived in the bottom half of the Old Manse that had been converted into two flats when the nearby chapel had been pulled down. The sight of the car reminded her that she had a bone to pick with him. He had sneaked to the police about her being at the Rave; had even hinted that she had been involved in the running of it, and she had intended having it out with him. What better opportunity than now? He was obviously at home;

146

with Eileen Dexter dead she supposed he was out of a job.

She quickened her pace and almost collided with the man and dog who hurried out of a side road in front of her. The dog jumped excitedly around her legs, entangling her in the lead, and she recognised its owner as the old busybody, Stewart Carson, who had complained about her mini-skirts to her boss. He glared at her and Tina was just about to retort that it wasn't her fault and he should keep his dog under control when a shot rang out. It sounded very loud and very close and she instinctively ducked.

"What was that?" she gasped. "Where did it come from?" He ignored her, jerking the dog towards him and talking to that.

"Come along Trixie, there's a good girl. Don't take any notice of her."

He scurried off and she shrugged and resumed walking down the road. The sound had seemed to come from the direction of the Old Manse; what the hell was going on? As she got near the gate it was flung open and Mark Copley rushed out. He grabbed hold of her.

"Did you see anyone?"

He was agitated and breathing heavily and she could see a pulse jumping in his neck.

"Stewart Carson's just gone down the lane with his dog."

"Stewart Carson?" He checked and then shook her roughly. "No one else?"

"Hey, keep your cool!" She twisted away from him. "Anyone would think someone had been taking pot shots at you! Oh my God! They weren't, were they?"

"I . . . You'd better come and see . . ."

"See what?"

She followed him through the gate. It opened onto a paved courtyard that ran down one side of the house. It had been the original stableyard and the remains of the old mounting block still stood over on the far side, now holding pots of geraniums in full bloom. On the other side was a high privet hedge and Mark nodded at the arch cut in it through which could be seen a stretch of grass.

147

"I was in the garden getting in my washing when there was this loud bang like a gunshot. It sounded as if someone was shooting at me. Did you hear it?"

She nodded. "What did you do?"

"Well, I dropped the laundry basket and ducked behind the hedge. Then when nothing more happened I came out here. There was no-one about and then I saw that." He pointed to the area behind the mounting block and she followed him round it. Lying on the ground was what looked like a small shotgun. She stared at it.

"But that's a toy gun, it's not a real one."

"I think it's meant to be symbolic" he said drily.

"How do you mean?"

"Use your eyes."

Then she saw what he meant. Beyond the gun a figure had been drawn in black on the white paving slabs. It was crudely, primitively executed but it was recognisable as a man lying on his side, almost in the foetal position, with outflung arms and long hair depicted, in a few savage strokes, as a ponytail.

"Cripes! That's meant to be YOU . . ."

They stared at each other and despite the heat she suddenly felt cold.

"The Joker! Mark, you don't think it's the work of The Joker, do you?"

"It's not a nice thought is it?"

His dark eyes looked haunted and she suddenly realized how shaken he was although he was trying to appear calm.

"But why you?"

"Why me, why anyone? You tell me!"

"You must tell the police! Now, straight away!"

"Yes, I suppose I must, though what good will it do? This Joker seems to be running circles round them so far!"

"Yes . . . but they must be told."

"Okay, I'll go and ring them. You'd better stay around – you're a witness."

"I suppose I am. Oh damn, I didn't want to tangle with them again – and that reminds me: what I was coming to see you about . . ."

"You were coming to see ME?"

"Yes, Mark Copley, you've got some explaining to do! Why did you tell the police about me being at the Rave?"

"You mean they didn't already know?"

"No."

"Oh hell, Tina, I thought they'd already questioned everyone who was there. How did you manage to avoid the road blocks?"

"I obviously know my way around here better than you!"

Whilst Mark was indoors phoning the police Tina mooched round the courtyard. She viewed the figure drawn on the ground from different angles. There was no doubting it, it was definitely meant to be Mark. How spooky. It was like having the Evil Eye put on you. Who had done it and where was he? She certainly hadn't seen anyone else around apart from Stewart Carson, and whoever it was couldn't have hidden in the garden if Mark was already there. She wandered over to the gap in the hedge and looked around. Something glinting on the ground beneath the hedge caught her eye and she bent down to look closer. It was only a broken piece of glass catching the light, but as she straightened up she saw something else lying nearby. It looked like a thick black crayon and she rolled it over with her foot. It was a charcoal stick, partly encased in a black and white band and the exposed end crumbled a little under the onslaught of her toes. Had this been used to draw the figure? Had Mark noticed it? The police were sure to – and she'd probably get a rocket for interfering with evidence.

She moved back to the mounting block.

Mansfield had decided to pop home for a break. With any luck Jean would have a meal in the oven and if he could just forget about the case for a couple of hours perhaps he'd be able to think more clearly instead of going round and round in circles. He lived in the same village as the Rolands, but at the eastern end where the outlying cottages of Wallingford met the sprawling suburbs of Felstone. He left the car outside his house and let himself in, pleased to hear Jean moving about in the kitchen.

Jean Mansfield was a small, brisk woman in her forties with crisp, greying hair and warm brown eyes. She devoted much of her time to voluntary work, being Brown Owl of the local Brownie pack, a helper on the Felstone CAB team and a committee member of the Wildlife Trust amongst other things. She had been a social worker when she had first met Patrick Mansfield but had relinquished that career, because of a possible clash of interests, and devoted herself to bringing up their family, and latterly, increasing charity work. Mansfield had always felt guilty about this decision but Jean had never admitted any regret and had willingly channelled her considerable energy into other outlets.

She was reading a magazine when he arrived home and seemed somewhat subdued, not her usual bright self. He wondered if he had promised to get back earlier or whether he had forgotten some social date; not that he or any of the team had any hope of socializing when they were involved in an investigation as serious as this one. Jean Mansfield made a pot of tea and set about heating a casserole.

"How is it going? Or don't you want to talk about it?"

"There's not much to say. We're following up all possible leads and getting nowhere fast. The trouble is there's no logic behind these killings. We're dealing with someone who is quietly insane and things like motive and opportunity seem to turn on a whim."

"It's horrible. How is James reacting? It can't be doing his reputation any good."

Although she liked James Roland, was a friend of Ginny and a godmother to their daughter, Jean had always been rather resentful of the fact that Roland had ridden ahead career-wise over her older, more experienced husband. That it bothered Patrick not at all only added to her pique.

"He's buzzing around like a blue-arsed fly. There's talk of bringing in the Yard."

"That won't suit."

"No, and he's got problems at home too. There's this

business of Simon being involved in the Rave party and now Katherine's got chickenpox. Thank God our children are off our hands and we don't have those worries anymore."

"Don't be too sure." Jean eyed her husband warily. "We've had a letter from Jean."

"What's wrong with that? You were only moaning the other day that she never writes or phones."

Jane was the younger of their two children and had just finished her first year at college. She was spending the summer vacation working in an hotel in Scarborough.

"She wants to get married."

"She WHAT!!!"

"To Jeremy – that's a boy in her year at college" said Jean poker-faced,

"I've never heard anything so ridiculous! She can't, she's under age – I shall put my foot down!"

"She's eighteen. You can't stop her."

"How can you sit there so . . . so *calmly*. You're surely not on her side?"

"Of course not, she's far too young, but you're going about it the wrong way entirely."

"What do you mean?"

"If we put up too much opposition we'll drive her straight into his arms, you know how stubborn she's always been."

"So what do you suggest?"

"That we play it down and hope she comes to her senses. After all, he's probably a perfectly nice lad and she has her Dad's good taste."

Mansfield looked at her suspiciously.

"She can only have known him a few months, she ought to have more sense."

"Would you rather they lived together than got married?"

"You know I don't hold with that. I don't approve of all this sleeping together, so casual like, but I'm not sure I wouldn't be happier if that were the case here. At least it wouldn't be such a disaster when they split up."

"Perhaps they won't split up. I mean, she just needs time to get to know him properly, so we mustn't hassle her."

And what is that supposed to mean?"

"We'll invite him here to stay when she finishes at Scarborough and you'll be on your best behaviour and not treat him like an undesirable alien."

"What about her college course? She's surely not going to throw all those years of studying down the drain?"

"It may not come to that; don't over-react Pat."

At that moment Mansfield's pager went and his wife looked resigned as he went to the phone. "I suppose this means you don't get to eat after all?"

She turned down the gas under the vegetables and tried to listen to the conversation going on over the phone. Her husband's contributions seemed to be confined to grunts and monosyllables and when he returned a few minutes later there was a grim look on his face. She raised her eyebrows enquiringly.

"Put it on hold, can you? Something's come up."

"Not another murder?"

"Another hoax."

"A hoax? Or do you mean a death threat?

CHAPTER 9

Roland and Mansfield arrived at the Old Manse almost simultaneously and met beside their parked cars.

"What's happened? You didn't say on the phone."

"Copley's reported an incident with a gun."

"You mean he's been shot at?"

"I think there's been a hoax played on him involving a gun here where he lives. Come on, let's find out."

Mark Copley was waiting for them in the garden and with him, to their surprise, was Tina Fairbrother.

"That was quick of you, inspector, I didn't expect you so soon."

"It sounded like an emergency, perhaps you'll put us in the picture."

Copley explained what had happened and the two detectives examined the toy gun and the drawing.

"It's meant to be me, isn't it?"

"It would appear so." Roland looked at the man beside him. Today his hair was loose and hung in an untidy mane round his face and neck. "From what direction did the sound of the shot come?"

"I'm not sure. It sounded very close and I really thought someone was firing at me."

"You say you were out in the street, Miss Fairbrother – did you see anyone nearby?"

"Only Stewart Carson out walking his dog. He was in a filthy mood and wouldn't even answer when I asked him what had happened."

"Did you notice anything else?" asked Roland, avoiding Mansfield's eye.

"No, there was just the smell of gunpowder." She wrinkled up her nose.

153

"You say you were collecting your linen off the line, Mr Copley? How long had you been in the garden?"

"A few minutes, certainly no longer."

"And you walked across this yard to get to the garden – yet you didn't see this?"

"No, I never noticed it, but it was obscured by the pots. It must have been there though, mustn't it? Whoever did it wouldn't have had time to set that up whilst I was unpegging my shirts."

"That seems a fair assumption."

The linen basket still lay toppled on its side, disgorging its contents on the brown, parched grass.

"You must have been under observation, Mr Copley," said Mansfield, who had been scribbling in his notebook. "What were you doing before you went into the garden?"

"I was in my flat. I'd been there since about four o'clock and I'd made myself a meal and cleared up afterwards."

"You sound highly domesticated."

"Look, I live by myself and I look after myself – what's the big deal about that?"

"No need to get excited, sir. I just wondered if maybe you employed help in the place, a woman who comes in and does for you and who might have noticed something going on out here."

"No, I don't employ any domestic help and I didn't notice anyone hanging around this afternoon. It's a horrible thought – someone watching your movements and moving in . . . Why am I being got at? Why has someone got it in for me?"

"For you?"

Copley stared at him angrily. "It's obvious, isn't it? First my fiancée has a nasty hoax played on her, then my friend and employer is threatened and killed, and now they're turning their attention to me. Wouldn't you feel menaced in my place?"

"Yes, I can understand that" said Roland soothingly, "but there have also been incidents involving other people."

"God I know! I'm sorry, I'm getting paranoid about it, but what the hell is going on? What are you DOING about

154

it? It seems to me as if this Joker is having a big laugh at your expense."

"You're entitled to your opinion, Mr Copley" said Roland, "but I can assure you we're doing our utmost to solve this case and our investigations are well in hand."

"So what am I supposed to do now?"

"Be vigilant. Try not to be on your own in an isolated situation. We'll investigate this episode." Roland carefully picked up the toy gun through the folds of his handkerchief. "We'll check this for fingerprints and I'll send someone along to photograph this little artistic offering. In the meanwhile, don't discuss this with *anyone* – and this aplies to you too, Miss Fairbrother. We don't want the Press getting to hear of it and splashing it all over the front pages."

"My lips are sealed, inspector."

"Stewart Carson AGAIN!" said Mansfield, getting into Roland's car to confer about the latest happening. "That HAS to be significant!"

"Things are certainly looking black against him. If he set this latest hoax up it must have been a shock to him to come face to face with Tina Fairbrother just after he's left the scene of crime, especially if he had been keeping a watch on Copley and thought he had chosen a time when no-one else was around."

"Surely she'd have noticed if he'd been carrying a gun?"

"I'm sure he wasn't toting a shotgun. That sound needn't have been caused by a gun. It could have been a starting pistol or even a firework."

"Are we going to run him in?"

"Not yet. I hope we'll have another piece of evidence against him tomorrow."

"Did Evans get any joy with the dog?"

"That's what I was just going to tell you. Carson was very un-cooperative. He was in his garden with the dog when Evans called and at first refused outright the very idea of a cast being made of his dog's bite. When Evans told him that we would draw the obvious conclusion about this refusal he said the dog was snappy and would bite Evans if he tried to get it to perform. Tell me, is Evans afraid of dogs?

Apparently he gave up after this, but he noticed several pieces of wood lying about the garden that the dog had obviously played with and chewed and he asked for one of these. Carson grudgingly agreed to this and the exhibit is now with Forensics. With any luck they'll be able to tell us yea or nay in the morning."

"Do you think Copley is in danger?"

"If I knew the answer to that we wouldn't be sitting here talking about it. If The Joker set up that hoax and is picking off his victims one by one – then yes, he IS in danger. We'll have to try and set up some sort of surveillance but it's difficult to lay on the sort of protection that would shield him from a sniper's bullet."

"But suppose it *is* Stewart Carson? He could come back tonight and finish him off."

"No, that's not The Joker's style at all. He threatens his victim and leaves him of plenty of time to work up into a morbid state of fear and apprehension before he strikes. Mark Copley will be safe at the moment, I'd stake my life on it."

"How about checking up on gun licences issued locally. There can't be many."

"I shouldn't bet on that. This is a rural community. I reckon quite a high proportion of the population owns a shotgun for potting at pigeons and going after game."

"Yes, you're probably right and anyway, it would have to be an unlicenced and illegally owned gun, wouldn't it, to prevent us from tracing it afterwards. Anyway, it's let Copley off the hook. He can hardly be the villain if he himself has received a death threat."

"He could have set it up himself, it would have been easy enough."

"To put us off the scent you mean? But how can you tie him in with the other two victims?"

"Everyone in the village knew Charles Todd but we haven't picked up any hints that he got across Copley anymore than anyone else and there seems to be no connection with Mervyn Souster at all."

"What about Alison Barnard? You can't believe anyone would do this to her let alone someone who's supposed to love her. Though of course he could be getting fed up with being tied to an invalid and wants his freedom."

"You mean he may want out and rather than hurt her by breaking the engagement he devises a scheme to frighten her to death or is actually planning to bump her off? It won't wash."

"No, it doesn't make sense, does it? And he certainly seems devoted to her even if he DID go to the Rave because his exgirlfriend asked him."

"Yes. Tina Fairbrother . . . I wonder what she was doing round here?"

"She's got it in for Alison Barnard because she stole her boyfriend; ditto Copley because he ditched her . . ."

"And what about the others?"

"Yes, it falls down there, doesn't it? But she was on the scene the night Charlie Todd was topped. She's also capable physically of carrying out the attacks, wouldn't you say?"

"Oh yes, we can't rule her out on that account; she's a big, strong, wench."

Roland rolled his window down further and propped his elbow on the sill.

"We're not getting anywhere. Go home, Pat, we can't do anymore this evening. Tomorrow morning we'll tackle Stewart Carson."

"First the good news," said Roland to Mansfield the next morning, "I've been on to the Lab and they've definitely matched up teeth marks on that piece of wood with the ones on the branch used to clobber Eileen Dexter."

"That's good – so Carson's implicated through his dog."

"I haven't told you the bad news yet. There were tooth marks from other dogs on it too, meaning Carson probably picked it up in Holgate Wood and his dog played with it and brought it home in his mouth. It's useless as evidence – and it would be laughed out of court."

"So we're back to square one?"

"Not quite. We can confront Carson with the fact that the weapon used on Eileen Dexter definitely had his dog's tooth marks on it and put the fear of God into him and see where that gets us."

"But he's only got to say that he's in the habit of picking up stray branches in the wood for the dog to retrieve and we haven't got a leg to stand on and he'll know that."

"Then we'll insist that he allows us to take another cast of the dog's bite then and there – via a nice chunk of cheese – and see how he reacts to that."

"So, back to Saxton?"

Roland looked at his watch. "Give me an hour, I've got to check through that evidence for the Burleigh case, it comes up in court at the end of this week. We should find Carson back from his morning's walkies if we leave it until after eleven. In the meanwhile, sift through the reports from the door-to-door and see if there's anything we've overlooked, especially in connection with Carson."

Rain had swept though the area overnight, a violent thunderstorm in the small hours that had temporarily flooded rock-hard gardens and fields; but by daybreak the clouds had rolled on across the North Sea and the sun rose with renewed vigour. The sultriness had gone but it was still very hot and the hedge tops steamed as the two men drove through the village.

Stewart Carson looked as if he had spent a bad night. His eyes were bloodshot and there was a haggard air about him; he appeared to have visibly shrunk. When he saw who was on his doorstep he all but shut the door in their faces. Mansfield propped it open with his shoulder whilst Roland addressed him.

"Can we come in Mr Carson?"

"What for? I've got nothing more to say to you."

"But I've got a great deal to say to you."

"It's not convenient."

"Carson, I'm being very kind to you. I could have had you brought into Felstone HQ for questioning, but instead I've come here so what is it to be? An interview room at the Station or the comfort of your own home?"

Carson stepped back reluctantly and allowed them into the house. There was no sign of the dog.

"I don't know what this is all about," he grumbled as they went into the sitting room. "You're persecuting me, it shouldn't be allowed. I shall complain to my MP."

"Your MP will be of no help to you, Stop playing games and tell me why you killed Eileen Dexter."

Carson's mouth actually fell open, then his face turned a mottled red.

"What the hell do you mean? I've never heard such rubbish . . . This is outrageous . . .!"

"Cut the bluster, this is no idle accusation. We have proof."

"You can't have! This is insane!"

"Are you denying that you were visited by Detective Constable Evans yesterday afternoon and he removed a certain piece of wood from your garden with your permission?"

No, but . . ."

"This piece of wood contained teeth marks made by your dog. The Forensic Laboratory has found an exact match of these teeth marks with the ones on the branch used as a weapon to attack Miss Dexter. What have you to say to that?"

"It doesn't prove anything! Look, I go through the wood to the park every day to exercise Trixie and I pick up bits of branch and twigs that are lying around and she plays with them, then they get chucked away or she hangs on to them. That's what happened yesterday morning. We went into the park and I was throwing sticks for her and she brought one home in her mouth."

"Yesterday morning?" queried Roland poker-faced whilst Mansfield's note taking was temporarily suspended.

"Yes. And I never saw Eileen Dexter. I didn't go near the lake! I thought she had been drowned but if you say she was killed by being hit with a branch – well, you can't pin it on me! Anyone could have picked up a lump of wood that had been discarded by Trixie or any other dog and bashed her over the head . . .!"

"Bashed over the head? How did you know that?"

"You're putting words in my mouth!" he snarled.

"Where were you the evening before Eileen Dewhurst's body was found in the lake?"

"At a meeting."

"Whereabouts?"

"In Woodford. It was a meeting of the local History Society."

"I see. How long did this meeting last?"

"From seven oclock until about ten fifteen and then some of us committee members stayed on to watch a video made by one of our members on the Sutton Hoo excavations."

Hell! thought Roland. If he was really there then he couldn't have been in Holgate Park arranging the demise of Eileen Dewhurst.

"I presume there are witnesses to to your presence at this meeting?"

"Your Chief Constable is our chairman" he replied triumphantly. "Anyway, what is this? Why do you want to know about that evening? Eileen Dewhurst was killed yesterday morning, wasn't she?"

Roland ignored these questions. "Where were you yesterday evening?"

"Walking Trixie. I've told you that's my normal procedure."

"Where did you go?"

"Around the village, I don't really remember."

"Did you go near the Old Manse where Mr Copley lives?"

"I don't think so."

"We have a witness who says she saw you in the vicinity just after the shot was fired."

"Shot? What shot? You're not saying Mark has been shot?" Roland ignored this.

"This same witness says she asked you if you'd heard a shot. Don't you remember the episode?"

"Look, I remember vaguely bumping into someone but it didn't really register."

"And you didn't hear the shot? I find that hard to believe."

"It didn't make any impression. If I heard it at all I probably thought it was someone potting pheasants."

160

"This is the close season, Carson."

"Look, I don't know what this is all about – has Mark been hurt?"

"As far as I know he's alive and well, which is more than can be said for some of The Joker's victims."

"You mean he's had a hoax played on him?"

"I didn't say that, Carson. I'd advice you not to speculate; and we don't want anymore titbits appearing in the Press, do we? Anything along that line will lead directly back to you, I'm warning you."

"I don't know what you're talking about . . . I've already told you I had nothing to do with anything the papers got hold of. I've got nothing to hide!"

"Really. I'm not sure I believe that." Roland moved towards the door and Mansfield snapped shut his notebook and followed him.

"You're going?" Carson sounded as if he couldn't believe his luck.

"Yes, but we'll be back. Stay around, Carson."

As soon as they were back in the car Mansfield burst out:

"Do you really believe he thinks that Eileen Dewhurst was done in yesterday morning?"

"Whether that's a ploy to throw us off the scent or not, he appears to have an alibi for the evening."

"Could he have done it before he went to this meeting?"

"To get to Woodford by seven he must have left here by six-thirty and according to Brasnett the time of death was later than that. I'll have another word with him to see if it is possible she was killed earlier."

"Perhaps he popped out of the meeting for a short while, rushed back here, did the deed and then went back to Woodford and put in an appearance again."

"It would have taken too long. I just don't think it's on but we'll have to check his alibi. Are you offering to interview the CC. Pat?"

"She'll be alright, Lindsey. You heard what the doctor said, it's just a temporary hiccup."

Mark Copley put his arm round Lindsey Barnard and she snuggled up to him and rested her head against his chest.

"I know it's par for the course but I still worry. I'm afraid they'll discover the disease is rampant again and they'll keep her in and . . . and I feel so guilty . . ."

"Guilty? what for?"

"You know why." Her voice was muffled against his chest. For a long moment he held her, his heart thudding against her chest, then, at the sound of a car door slamming, he quickly disengaged himself and glanced out of the window.

"Someone's coming, you've got a visitor."

With ragged breath and flushed cheeks Lindsey pulled herself together.

"It's that policeman . . . one of the detectives. I didn't hear his car."

Unbeknown to William Evans who had just driven up outside, Tina Fairbrother, deep in thought, was also approaching the Saxton Pottery from the other direction. Ever since the malicious jokes and murders had started she had taken a ghoulish interest in them, and with her friend Karen had speculated wildly about who The Joker could be and his motive. But what had started out as a rather flippant exercise, trying to match up victim and motive, was now taking on sinister undertones. She could now see a cogent thread running through all the incidents linking one to the other and leading to . . . No, it wasn't possible . . . it couldn't be . . . and yet?

It was the hoax that had been played on Mark that had really made it all start to hang together . . . the first real evidence . . . the stick of charcoal she had seen under the hedge . . .

When she had finally got away from his place and the police grilling yesterday evening, something had been nagging at the back of her mind. It wasn't until this morning that the significance of what she had seen had hit her with force. That stick of charcoal – that must have been used to draw the caricature of Mark – was the same as the ones she had once trampled underfoot in the Barnards' studio. From there it had been a short step to deciding it must have come from their studio . . . She had mulled this over and, as it was her morning off and she wasn't due in Felstone until after lunch, she had found herself walking through the village, drawn towards the pottery like a magnet. Now she was actually here she didn't know what she was going to do, what her course of action should be . . . There was a gap in the hedge and whilst she hesitated she peeked through it towards the house. What she saw made her check.

Mark Copley was standing in the Barnard's sitting room. She could see his black hair in its familiar ponytail through the window. Well, she didn't want to bump into him again. As she hesitated Lindsey Barnard came into view and under her speculative gaze the two appeared to go into a clinch. Well, what do you know? she thought to herself. Just who was cheating on who and where was Alison? This was just further evidence . . . At that moment Lindsey came out of the embrace and looked out of the window. For a few seconds their eyes locked and then Tina ducked and moved backwards feeling as if she'd been caught doing something shameful. This needed more thought. Thank goodness she hadn't blundered in shouting her mouth off . . . She must discuss this with Karen . . . talk it through and decide what to do . . . She was suddenly aware of William Evans approaching the gate. So the Barnards had another visitor anyway. She turned and walked back the way she had come as he went through into the front garden.

"Look, I don't want to meet him" said Copley hurriedly, seeing the red-haired Welshman walking up the path. "I've had enough of the police poking and prying. I'll go out the back way and avoid him. What time did you say she'd be ready to come home?"

"About five o'clock."

"I'll pick her up then and bring her home."

Mark Copley slipped out of the back door as Lindsey Barnard answered the knock on the front door.

"Alison hasn't yet given us a signed statement about her discovery of Miss Dexter's body in the lake at Holgate Park," said Evans, disappointed that it was Lindsey and not Alison on the doorstep. "I've come to take her to the Station, it won't take long."

"You won't be taking her anywhere today I'm afraid – she's in hospital."

"In hospital? Is she ill? I mean, has she had a relapse?"

"She's having a blood transfusion."

"And is that good or bad? It sounds pretty desperate!"

"It's necessary, shall we say. She has regular bloodtests to monitor her blood count and her haemoglobin is low so she's having a blood transfusion."

"Oh, I see. Will she be in hospital long?"

"They do it as an outpatient. She'll be home later today. I'll tell her you called and she'll probably drive herself in to the Police Station tomorrow."

"She's . . . er . . . able to drive?"

"Of course. She leads as normal a life as possible and she always feels much better after a transfusion. Was there anything else you wanted, constable?"

"Nothing *you* can help me with, Miss Barnard."

Feeling frustrated, Evans turned on his heel and started to walk back down the path but Lindsey followed him.

"Are you getting anywhere? Are the police any nearer to finding out who The Joker is?"

"Our investigations are proceeding satisfactorily."

"You sound just like Mr Plod. How can they be satisfactory when people are being bumped off?"

"I AM Mr Plod," Evans was stung to reply, "and we are close to making an arrest. No-one else is going to get killed, I promise you."

"I wish I could believe you. I just keep thinking about these horrible hoaxes . . . death threats . . . and wondering who is going to get picked off next – Alison or Mark."

"Who told you about Mark Copley?" He snapped to attention.

"He did, earlier this morning, but we didn't mention what had happened to Alison."

"He was told to keep it to himself. If the Press get hold of it everyone will know, including your sister."

"It won't go any further. Mark only told me because . . . well, because of Alison. Don't you think . . . don't you think she should have a bodyguard?"

"What do you think I am?" Her eyes widened in surprise. "I didn't realize . . .?"

"Unofficial" said Evans, tapping his finger against his nose, "but I shall be around and she's got you. Between us we should be able to protect her."

"Y..es. Inspector Roland didn't mention this . . ."

"He wouldn't have discussed this with you" said Evans hurriedly, "it's an undercover job . . . alright."

By late morning Stewart Carson's alibi had been checked out. The secretary of the History Society, who had been minuting the meeting vouched for his presence during the entire proceedings and Brasnett had confirmed that Eileen Dewhurst had been killed later in the evening, certainly after nine o'clock.

"He could have done it after he got back" said Mansfield.

"That wasn't until after half past eleven. How could he have lured her out there at that time of night?" said Roland.

"Yes, I supppose you're right." Mansfield stuffed tobacco into his pipe with vicious jabs of his thumb. "So that let's him off the hook."

"He can't be the murderer but he could still be The Joker, if we can believe they are two separate people."

"Do you really think that's likely?"

"No, it's too far-fetched, but we're right back to square one again now, aren't we?"

"Well, if it wasn't him who set up the latest hoax on Copley and it wasn't Tina Fairbrother, there must have been someone else in the vicinity, mustn't there?"

"We'll have to question the neighbours and all the other households in that part of the village."

"More hard work and man-power."

"Yes, but maybe it *was* Tina Fairbrother."

"You're not seriously trying to put her in the frame as the murderer, are you? What possible motive could she have?"

"Not the murderer. I'm thinking that maybe she's just seized the chance to get her own back on Copley. In the same way that we once thought that Charles Todd's murder was carried out by someone cashing in on the publicity over The Joker, perhaps she was paying him back for ditching her in favour of Alison Barnard."

"Maybe. Everything so far is speculation. If only we could come up with one little piece of hard evidence to point us in the right direction."

"We need some luck, don't we? What do they say – detection work is 90% hard slog and 10% inspiration? They left out the bit about luck – but you can't get far without it."

Mansfield tapped out his pipe and got to his feet. "I'll go and set up the check on Copley's neighbourhood. By the way, where is Evans?"

"You may well ask. I haven't seen him all morning, have you?"

Tina Fairbrother sat beneath the pine tree eating her sandwiches and feeling annoyed and frustrated. She had been expecting to meet Karen; they usually spent their lunch hour together, when they would eat their packed lunches and discuss their love lives or lack of them, but today Karen had gone off with that nerd Gary without one thought for her friend. Ever since she'd had this new boyfried she'd been so wrapped up in him she'd got no time for her old friends.

It was very hot even in the shade. Left on her own, she had strolled down to the gardens that flanked the promenade hoping it would be cooler along the sea front; but the canopy of branches hung motionless above her head and not a breath of air stirred the serried ranks of pine needles. When she looked out to sea the glitter off the water was blinding. There were sparrows having dust baths in a nearby flowerbed and she threw them the remains of her sandwich. As she watched them chirping and fluttering she felt as if her thoughts were echoing their disorderly movements. What should she DO?

She knew what Karen would say if she were here. She'd tell her to go to the police and lay her suspicions before them but she was reluctant to get involved with the Old Bill again, have them breathing down her neck. Besides, she had no real proof, just this gut feeling that wouldn't go away but she couldn't ignore it. She sighed. She supposed she had better go and talk to that policeman, the tall, dark one who'd pitched into her over the Rave. He'd been sarcastic and disdainful but she wouldn't mind chewing the rag with him; he was really quite dishy even if he was ancient.

She got up and brushed the pine needles and dust off her skirt and checked her watch. She was due in the shop in fifteen minutes but Steven couldn't bawl her out over this, she was helping the police in their enquiries. She screwed up the sandwich wrapping into a tight ball and dropped it into the litter bin and slogged back up the cliff path.

The town was crowded. It was market day and it seemed as if the entire population of Felstone was spending its lunch hour on the busy streets. She pushed through the thronging people and turned up High Street. The Police Headquarters were situated on the other side of the road at the far end beside the council offices. She might as well cross now at the zebra crossing. She felt hot and sticky as she waited on the kerb for the lights to change; jostling masses at her back, the traffic thundering past in front of her. Someone was pushing through from behind, she could feel the pressure on her shoulders. Christ, some people just couldn't wait! She tried to turn round to complain but the pressure increased; it was an iron fist in the middle of her back edging her forwards. She struggled to resist and keep her balance but she was driven relentlessly towards the road until her legs gave way. As she hurtled onto the road she last thing she was aware of was the red bus bearing inexorably down on her and the sound of screaming.

CHAPTER 10

William Evans wondered if he could prolong his absence for longer and visit Alison Barnard in hospital but decided Roland wouldn't wear it. He must get back to HQ and pretend he had been on legitimate police business for the last couple of hours. In any case, he wasn't sure that he wanted to see her wired up to bottles of plasma and wouldn't know what to say. Drips and needles gave him the willies and even the smell of hospitals – that invidious mixture of disinfectant, antiseptics and polish – made him feel ill. He drove back through the town centre toying with the idea of calling at a florist and ordering flowers for her but hadn't got the courage to carry it through.

As he manoeuvred through the congested roads he was almost scraped by an ambulance that roared out of High Street with siren blaring and flashing lights and went the wrong direction down a one-way street. Fire, illness or accident he wondered, thanking his lucky stars he wasn't having to deal with it. He stopped at a snack bar for a coffee and doughnut and detoured to a garage to pick up a new brake cable for his car.

Back at the Station he chatted to the Duty Sergeant who was an old sparring partner.

"Is my Gov back yet?"

"Yes, and out for your blood. Where have you been, laddie?"

"On official CID business."

"Oh yer? Pull the other one."

"So what's new?"

"There's been a nasty accident in High Street."

"It's about time they pedestrianised it, they've been talking about it for ever."

"This was a pedestrian; got run over by a bus."

"Some doddering old lady who shouldn't have been out on her own I suppose."

"Wrong again, it was a young woman – worked in the record shop next door to Boots." Evans stared at him, feeling a prickle starting at the base of his spine.

"What's her name?"

The Duty Sergeant consulted his records.

"Tina Fairbrother. She was rushed to hospital but pronounced dead on arrival."

"Bloody hell! Does Roland know?"

"What should I know?" Roland strode into the reception area followed by Mansfield.

"It's nice some of us have time to gossip."

"Wait till you hear this. Tina Fairbrother has been killed in a road accident."

"Is this your idea of a joke, Evans?"

"It's the truth, sir – ask Tom."

Tom Black, the Duty Sergeant gave Roland the facts as he knew them.

"Who dealt with it?"

"The traffic police. Excuse me, sir, but is this Tina Fairbrother involved in your case?"

"That's the billion dollar question" said Roland grimly. "There must have been witnesses to the accident – who saw what happened?

"The bus driver was treated for shock by the doctor and sent home. There were a lot of people waiting at the zebra crossing with her but you know what it's like. There's always a crowd to gawp at an accident but when you actually want witnesses they melt away. Anyway, several onlookers were questioned but nobody seems to know what actually happened."

"Get those names and addresses" said Roland to Evans, "we may need them."

Back in his officer, Roland sent out for sandwiches and coffee and the three men discussed the situation.

"You don't really think there's any connection between her death and The Joker's activities, do you?" Mansfield asked Roland, helping himself to a limp, plastic ham sandwich.

"On the face of it it's a straightforward traffic accident –
BUT it's a hell of a coincidence, isn't it?"

"But she didn't have a hoax played on her, did she?" said
Evans, "so why should she suddenly become the target of
The Joker?"

"No reason, except that she's popped up several times
in this case. I don't suppose there IS any connection but
I'm not happy about it. I think we'll have to interview
the witnesses ourselves." Roland consulted the names on
the list. "This Mrs Goodwin who was standing next to her
seems to be our best bet. You go and speak to her Evans,
and find out what she thinks happened. We've also got
a Mr Jones and a Miss Sinclair down here who were
near her at the zebra crossing. I'll leave them to you,
Pat, whilst I interview the bus driver. Now, remember
to keep this very low key. I don't want any connection
made with this incident and The Joker and the other
deaths."

The bus driver lived on a small estate not far from the bus
station. The door was answered by a middle-aged woman
who looked harassed and wary.

"Mrs Fletcher? I should like to have a few words with
your husband."

Roland introduced himself and she looked even more
nervous.

"It wasn't his fault . . . she went right in front of him . . .
he didn't stand a chance."

"I'm not here to cast blame, Mrs Fletcher. I just need to
hear from him exactly what happened."

"He told the other policemen, he doesn't want to be
pestered again. He's in a terrible state and the doctor said
he was to rest and try and not dwell on it."

"I'm sorry, but I really must see him. It's probably
better for him in the long run to face up to it and not
push it to the back of his mind and brood. Is he in
bed?"

"He won't go to bed. The doctor gave him some pills
to take and he won't take them either. He's sitting in the
lounge shivering. Shivering! In this weather! You'd better
come in."

Frank Fletcher was huddled in an armchair staring into space, an untouched cup of tea covered with a skin on the low table beside him.

"Frank? This is another policeman, he wants to ask you some more questions. I told him you didn't want to be disturbed . . ."

"I am disturbed, Mary. I can't get it out of my head. I keep going over and over it again like an action replay . . ."

"I'm sorry to bother you, Mr Fletcher" said Roland, sitting himself on the armchair opposite, "I know this has been a terrible shock for you, but I'm trying to establish whether Miss Fairbrother fell or was pushed."

"Pushed? Who would have pushed her!" exclaimed Mary Fletcher clasping her hands together.

"Your husband's tea has got cold. Do you think you could make another pot? Tea is good for shock and I should appreciate a cup."

Mary Fletcher took herself off to the kitchen and Roland leaned towards her husband.

"I know it all happened in a few seconds but what impression did you get?"

Frank Fletcher spoke in a daze: "I wasn't going fast. I could see by the amount of people waiting at the crossing that the lights were due to change. Just as I crossed the white line she fell right under my wheels. I stood on the brakes but there was no way I could avoid her . . ."

"I'm sure you did all you could, nobody is blaming you, Mr Fletcher, but in your opinion did she accidentally trip or was she forced into the road?"

"She didn't trip – she was flung in front of me. I saw her face . . ."

"Yes?"

"I shall never forget the look on her face, not as long as I live . . ."

The man seemed to go off in a trance and Roland prompted him.

"Mr Fletcher?"

He lifted haggard eyes to the detective. "I can't describe it, but I can tell you one thing: it was no accident – she knew she'd been pushed!"

"And have you any idea who could have done it? Did you see anyone running away?"

The bus driver looked at Roland as if he were mad.

"Give me a break! It was chaos . . . all those people screaming and her lying in the road all smashed up . . ."

He covered his face with his hands and shuddered. After a few minutes, whilst Roland watched him sympathetically, he pulled himself together.

"I've been driving over thirty-five years and this is the first time I've been involved in an accident. I'm due to retire in a couple of years . . . why did it have to happen to me?"

Mrs Fletcher came back into the room bearing a laden tray and after Roland had drunk the proffered tea he had a few more words with the distraught man and left to drive back to the Station, wondering how Mansfield and Evans had got on with their enquiries.

"I've got their comments, for what they're worth." Mansfield collapsed on a chair in Roland's office and ran a finger round the inside of his collar and consulted his notebook. "Both of them are very shocked and not making much sense. Jones is a man in his seventies. He'd just been to collect his pension and was waiting to cross the road. He noticed Tina – remarked on her blond hair – and seemed to think she was shouldering her way through the crowd to be the first over when the lights changed. As to what actually happened – he hadn't got a clue. In his own words: 'One minute she were beside me, the next she were in the road under the bus.' Quote, unquote."

"What about the other one?"

"Miss Sinclair is about the same age as Tina. She goes to the College – is studying art – and she was carrying a portfolio and some pictures. She says she was jammed up in this crush and all she was aware of was the corners of the frames being rammed into her ribs. Suddenly the pressure eased and the girl who had been standing next to her was in the road."

"Hmm. That's not much to go on. What about you, Evans?"

"Mrs Goodwin. She was almost enjoying herself in a ghoulish sort of way when I questioned her. She reckons someone behind them was shoving hard to get through and she thinks she was lucky not to be the one flung in front of the bus."

"So, it's inconclusive. Nobody's saying that they think she was deliberately pushed."

"What about the bus driver?"

"Oh he thought so but it could still have been an accident; someone getting impatient and trying to get to the front. They're not going to own up, are they, after what's happened?"

"No way. Well at least Stewart Carson wasn't involved in this incident. At the time Tina Fairbrother was falling under the bus we were with him in his own home."

"Yes, I'd worked that out." Roland took a gulp of his coffee and pulled a wry face. "I'm keeping an open mind about the whole thing. Right now we're going through every piece of evidence on this case to see if we've overlooked anything."

Karen Green hadn't slept. Ever since she had heard about the dreadful accident that had befallen her friend the day before she had been in a state of shock. She couldn't believe that Tina was dead; that she wouldn't come trundling along in her old banger to offer a lift, that there would be no more long phonecalls, cut short by irate parents, no more giggling discussions after a night out, that she would never set eyes again on her spikey, platinum hair and cheerful face.

She had thrashed and groaned all night long under the twisted sheet, seeing in her mind's eye the broken body of Tina lying under the bus. Why had it happened to her? How could someone as fit and strong as Tina let herself be accidentally pushed under a bus? Supposing it hadn't been an accident, a little voice niggled at the back of her mind; supposing it had been deliberate? Oh, this was ridiculous, she had scolded herself turning over and thumping the pillow, why should anyone want to harm Tina? Because she knew too much insisted the voice. Suddenly she was wide awake. Sitting up the bed she run a hand through her damp hair and tried desparately to remember what Tina had tried to tell her the day before. She had been talking about The Joker and had hinted that she had worked out his identity, but what had she actually *said*?

Karen moaned and squinted at the grey light that was starting to filter through the gap in the curtains. Oh God! Why hadn't she listened to Tina? Why hadn't she taken her seriously? Why had she been so taken up with Gary that she had cut short her friend's intimations and dismissed them? Hadn't really registered what she had said at all? She strained to remember and disjointed pieces of conversation floated back from her sub-conscience. Tina had talked of going to the police and laying her suspicions before them. If only she could recall more of what Tina had tried to tell her . . . Had she enough information to go to them herself?

She finally decided that she owed it to Tina to deliver to the Dicks what scraps she could scrape up from her memory. They'd probably laugh at her, but at least it would ease her conscience. On the other hand, perhaps Tina HAD gone to see them yesterday. Perhaps she had been killed after leaving the Police Station. Either way she wouldn't be happy until she had checked. She would go this morning. She couldn't face going to work; the building society that employed her would have to do without her services today. She couldn't face breakfast either, only a cup of black coffee, and when her sympathetic family tried to chat she snarled at them until they left her alone. Two hours later she was at the enquiry desk of Felstone Police asking for Detective Inspector Roland.

When Roland appeared she went straight to the point.

"You *are* the policeman who is in charge of The Joker investigation, aren't you?"

Roland agreed and wondered who was the distraught young woman facing him. She was very pale with haunted eyes and a mass of unnaturally black hair.

"Who are you?"

"I'm Karen Green. I'm . . . I was a friend of Tina Fairbrother."

"The young woman who was run over yesterday."

"Yes. It's . . . it's terrible her being killed like that . . ." Tears well in her eyes and she produced a hankie from a pocket and blew her nose vigorously.

"It's very tragic but I don't quite see why you are here, Miss Green, or why you want to see me."

"Did Tina come and see you yesterday?"

"No, was she intending to?"

"Yes, I think so . . . It . . . it must have happened on her way here . . ."

"You'd better come into my office."

Once seated in Roland's office she seemed to regret her visit and perched uneasily on the edge of the seat, twisting her hands in her lap.

"Miss Green, if you know anything about Miss Fairbrother's death, please tell me."

"I don't know if it has got anything to do with her death but I think she may have worked out who . . . who The Joker could be . . ."

"Go on."

"Well, that's all really." Karen Green shrugged her shoulders helplessly.

"She told you this?"

"She tried to but I wasn't really listening." Roland leaned forward and said carefully:

"Miss Green, did she share her knowledge with you?"

"She wanted to but I couldn't be bothered to listen . . . If only I hadn't been so off-hand . . . it was the last time I saw her . ."

"What did she actually say?"

"That's just the point – I wouldn't let her tell me. Look, I'd better explain . . . I've got this new boyfriend and . . . well, I suppose I was more taken with him. I was miffed because she wasn't at all interested in hearing about him, I . . . I cut her short . . ."

"So she didn't tell you who she thought The Joker was?"

"No."

"Did she tell you how she had reached her conclusion?"

"Not really, it was something about working out the connection between the different victims . . ."

"This is very important, please think carefully: Have you any idea who she was talking about? Did she mention any names?" Karen Green wrinkled up her brows as she searched desperately through her memory.

"There was something about the Barnard twins . . ."

"The Barnard twins? In what connection?"

"I don't know . . ." She was almost sobbing in frustration.

"Did Tina know the Barnard twins?"

"Everyone knows the Barnard twins, especially since Alison was taken ill."

"Was she a close friend?" asked Roland, thinking that if this were so they had missed out on it.

"Hardly. She used to go around with Mark Copley who's now engaged to Alison. Besides, she ran over their cat . . ."

"Oh?"

"They were very upset about it, especially Lindsey. Tina definitely wasn't flavour of the month with them."

I see."

"I've just remembered something she DID say . . ." Karen spoke eagerly. " . . . something about Mark and Lindsey having it off."

"What made her think that?" asked Roland sharply.

"She'd seen them together I think. I remember now what she actually said – something about Mark Copley having his cake and eating it too . . . I think maybe she was just guessing."

"Is there anything else you can remember?"

"No. I'm sorry this has all been a bit vague; I've probably wasted your time . . ."

"Not at all, thanking you for coming forward."

"I felt she'd have wanted you to know, except that I can't remember what it was she was talking about! I can't believe she's dead . . ."

"I'm very sorry, Miss Green, about your friend. You did the right thing in coming to see me. There's no need to worry about it anymore, we'll deal with it now but don't mention it to anyone else."

"I certainly won't, all I want to do is forget!"

After she had left Roland talked it over with Mansfield and Evans.

"Do you really believe that Tina Fairbrother knew something that we don't?" Mansfield was sceptical.

"Her friend seems to think so. Pity she couldn't have been more explicit. I've thought all along that if only we could make a connection between the victims we'd be half way there."

"But what?"

"Quite. On the face of it there's nothing that connects them. What have we got?" Roland marked them off on his fingers "One; a local teacher who was popular with everyone who knew him. Two; a retired service man who nobody has a good word for. Three; an elderly spinster who was well-known and accepted in the community. Four; a young woman who got her kicks from the Rave scene. Five; a young man who seems to be honest and sincere and six; another young woman who is chronically ill."

"There's a connection between the last three, isn't there?" said Evans, "and Copley worked for Eileen Dewhurst."

"Yes, but there's no common denominator between the six as far as I can see."

"But Tina thought she had latched on to one," said Mansfield. "Are you working on the theory that she was knocked off to silence her?"

"I don't see how that can be, unless she was shouting off her mouth to all and sundry. And even then, it's too much to accept that she was scrubbed just as she happened to be on her way to spill the beans to us."

"Your old coincidence again."

"Don't say it. This case is plagued with them; coincidences that look contrived but could just be genuine."

"I think she was right about Copley carrying on with Lindsey Barnard" Evans wasn't sure if he was outraged or delighted with this news. "I told you before – I saw the way Lindsey Barnard was looking at him when she thought no-one would see her. I'm sure she's got a thing going for him but whether he feels the same . . ."

Who knows? But if it's true I suppose you can under-stand it. His girlfriend is ill but her sister is available and apparently willing."

"I could understand it better if they looked alike. I mean if they were identical twins. I've never seen two sisters, let alone twins, look so different. If they were so alike you couldn't tell them apart I suppose he could substitute one for the other."

"I shouldn't let it worry you, Evans" said Roland dryly.

"She's in hospital. Alison." Seeing his superior's raised brows Evans continued: "She should be out again now but she was in yesterday – for a blood transfusion."

"Well, SHE didn't push Tina Fairbrother under a bus then, did she?" said Mansfield flippantly.

Evans glared at him. "She should have protection . . . both of them should."

"Yes, we must press for it. Even if man-power is very stretched at the moment Lacey will have to sanction it. Just how we go about it is another matter. It should be easy enough to provide protection for Alison Barnard; she doesn't go far and her sister's on hand to look after her most of the time, but it's more difficult with Copley. I don't think he'd take kindly to having a minder."

"Pity they're not co-habiting" said Mansfield, "then we could kill two birds with one stone."

"You wouldn't care to re-phrase that? Perhaps that's what The Joker is leading up to – a grand finale in which he finishes off his last two victims together!"

Later, Roland sat at his desk and tried to plot a graph showing the connections between the people targeted by The Joker, but although there were obvious relationships between some people and others could be tied in with eachother there was no overall link-up between then as far as he could see. The sheet of paper in front of him became a maze of inter-connecting arrows and crossed lines. He screwed it up in disgust and flung it into the wastepaper basket. It was hopeless. The only common denominator was the obvious one – they all lived in Saxton. Could you take this a step further and assume that The Joker was also definitely a Saxton resident? Not really. It seemed likely but he could equally well live in Felstone or even in his own village of Wallingford. It could be someone who hadn't yet cropped up in their investigation, an entirely unknown quantity.

He flung himself back in his chair and stared out of the window. On a parapet opposite a pair of pigeons did their crabbed, sideways walk; scaly claws shuffling, heads bobbing. They were absurdly alike; identical; a pigeon pair. No, that was not right. A pigeon pair meant one of each sex, identical twins were always the same sex. Identical twins . . . He suddenly remembered what it was that had been niggling at the back of his mind; a snatch of conversation that he had known was significant if only he could remember it. Each time he had tried to concentrate on bringing it to mind it had elusively vanished amongst the jumble of his thoughts. Now it surfaced as he remembered Evans' remark. This was something he *could* check out.

He looked at his watch; with any luck he'd catch Firbank before the start of afternoon surgery. He left a message for Mansfield and collected his car.

Dr Firbank was getting out of his car when Roland drew up alongside.

"Good, I've caught you. Can I have words?"

"I'm just about to start my afternoon session and my receptionist has a list of patients as long as my arm. You should have rung and made an appointment."

"This is not about me, I don't want a consultation."

"It's not Ginny is it? I thought she was doing fine."

"No, this is not a health matter I want to talk to you about. At least, not a personal one."

"I suppose you'd better come into the surgery. Whatever it is you'll have to be quick. I'm late as it is."

There were half a dozen patients already in the waiting room. Neville Firbank had a few words with his reception-ist, checked his phone messages and took Roland into his surgery. The eyes which had lit up at the arrival of the doctor turned to disappointment and followed Roland with suspicion as he went through the door.

179

"What's all this about?" Firbank sat down behind his desk and waved Roland to a chair.

"You know I spoke to you before about Alison Barnard, the young woman with leukaemia?"

"Now, James, you know I won't discuss my patients with you."

"This is important or I shouldn't ask. You told me that if her current treatment didn't work her only hope was a bone marrow transplant if a suitable donor could be found?"

"Yes."

"Well surely you've got a suitable donor – her twin sister. They must be compatible?"

Firbank looked troubled.

"No."

"You mean it's been tried? It hasn't worked?"

"I mean they don't match."

"But I thought . . . being twins . . . ?"

"Is this really relevant to your case?"

"That's what I'm trying to find out!"

Firbank got up and paced around the floor. Whilst Roland waited he adjusted the weights on his scales and paused deep in thought before his sight testing chart. Then he seemed to reach a decision and swung round to face the detective.

"They're not twins."

"Not?"

"They're not even sisters."

"What do you mean?"

"There's only three or four days between then but Lindsey was adopted at birth."

"You can't leave it there, Neville, how did it come about?" The doctor sat down again, propped his elbows on the desk and rested his chin on his hands.

"They were born in Kenya. Alison's mother and father were both doctors in a hospital on the outskirts of Nairobi where Lindsey's mother was a nurse. Both were due to give birth at the same time and they were close friends."

"What about Lindsey's father?"

"He wasn't married to her mother. He was a French lawyer who was working out there temporarily. They had an affair that only lasted a few months and he'd left Africa before the pregnancy was even confirmed. Anyway, Alison was born and a few days later Lindsey's mother also gave birth but she didn't recover from the confinement. She'd picked up some virus whilst working with the natives which had lain dormant and was triggered off by childbirth. She died within a week and John and Meg Barnard took over her baby – she had no relatives you see and they thought that was best."

"How the devil do you know all this?"

"Because I was there too. Not actually in Nairobi. At the time I was travelling round the country setting up local clinics but I was based at the same hospital and the Barnards were great friends of mine. Whilst the girls were still babies they decided to come back to England permanently and they settled here with what everyone thought were their twin daughters."

"Do they know about this – that they are not related?"

"They do now."

"What do you mean?"

"I suppose now I've told you so much I shall have to give you all the facts. Remember, only I, the twins and a solicitor up in Norfolk know this: I came back to live and work in England and although I was here in Felstone and the Barnards in Norfolk, we kept in touch and were still very good friends. I agreed to act as executor for them in the unlikely event of them dying first – I was considerably older than them. Well, about eight years ago they were killed in a plane crash. I had to sort out their estate."

"But surely that was straightforward enough if they'd left a will?"

"On the face of it, yes. They left everything to their daughters."

Neville Firbank paused and shook his head.

"What are you trying to say?"

"It turned out they'd never adopted Lindsey officially. Legally she didn't exist."

"But they must have had papers for her when they came back to this country?"

"There had been some bending of the rules after

Lindsey's mother died. Things like that were not so strictly monitored in those days and as I said, there were no other relatives to claim the baby and look after her so the hospital authorities were happy to turn a blind eye when John and Meg accepted responsibility."

"And you connived at this?"

"I wasn't around at the time but I took it for granted that they had gone through the proper channels back here in England and officially adopted her, but it turned out they just hadn't bothered. They looked on her as their own child and everyone else thought she was their daughter."

"So, what you're saying is: Alison inherited everything and Lindsey was left out in the cold?"

"In a nutshell. But it hasn't made any difference to them. Alison has shared everything with Lindsey and as soon as she was old enough she made a will and made sure that Lindsey was named as the beneficiary."

"You say they shared everything – do you mean this was done legally or does Alison still hold the purse strings with Lindsey beholden on her generosity?"

"I think that's rather a crude way of putting it. I believe the house is owned by Alison and she provides the money for its upkeep etc."

"What size inheritance are we talking about?"

"A considerable one. They don't need to work but obviously Lindsey likes to feel independent and they are both quite accomplished artists in their own fields."

"So if Alison dies Lindsey will inherit everything."

"Which she would do if they were real sisters."

"Aren't you forgetting that Alison is engaged and if she marries presumably her husband will become the legatee, not Lindsey."

"James, I don't like the direction your thoughts are taking; those sisters are devoted to eachother."

"I can't help being a suspicious policeman."

"I should never have told you all this. It mustn't go any further – I want your assurance on this."

"I can't give it to you, you must see that, but I promise you I shall only use this knowledge if it becomes necessary to my enquiry."

182

"Why this sudden interest in a bone marrow transplant?"

"It suddenly struck me as odd that as she was a twin it hadn't been tried. Hasn't anyone else queried this?"

"She is being treated with chemotherapy at the moment, Hopefully this will be successful."

"I understand she had to have a blood transfusion yesterday?"

"That's a fairly routine practice but she may have to go back in for a few days for further treatment. Lindsey phoned me this morning – she thinks Alison is feverish."

"You mean she is having a relapse?"

"Melodrama has no place in medical diagnosis. I suspect she has developed a neutropenic fever."

"What in God's name is that?"

"You must remember that the chemotherapy doesn't just kill off the cancerous cells – it knocks out the white cells as well which means she is very vulnerable to infection. She's liable to pick up anything that's going and that's probably what's happened here. She'll need a strong dose of antibiotics and this is best administered in hospital directly into her bloodstream through her Hickman Line."

"I'm not going to ask you what that is – you're just trying to blind me with science, but if you can get her into hospital and keep her there for as long as possible I shall feel much happier. At least in hospital she will be under supervision and we can keep an eye on her."

"James, you don't really believe she is in danger . . .? That Lindsey . . . ?"

"This case has had so many twists and turns that I'm prepared for anything. What you have just told me this afternoon has opened up another whole new area to be investigated. I don't have to tell you to keep this to yourself and please don't let it colour your attitude to the Barnard twins. Act normally, but get Alison into hospital if you possibly can."

"You really think this Lindsey Barnard could be The Joker

– the person behind the hoaxes and killings." Superintendent Lacey was openly sceptical. "You think a woman could fit the frame?"

"I've never ruled out the possibility that it could be a woman" said Roland, "and certainly Lindsey Barnard is strong and powerful enough to have carried them out."

"Yes, you should see her slamming that clay about" put in Evans, and got a glare from Lacey for his pains.

"But her own twin sister? It's unnatural!"

"But she isn't Alison's twin sister, that's the whole point and we know we're dealing with a weirdo, someone who's completely off their trolley beneath a seemingly sane exterior."

"Yes, it's beginning to make horrible sense" said Mansfield, "two people who have been brought up as sisters but one has scooped the jackpot, got all the money *and* the man. You can understand the other one harbouring a grudge. It could have been going on for years, resentment smouldering beneath the surface and then something happens to bring it into the open."

"Her sister walks off with the boy she's keen on? Is it a fact that Lindsey Barnard is also sweet on Mark Copley?"

"That's what we've been given to understand."

"It's certainly the impression I got" said Evans.

"But the girl's ill, probably dying anyway. Why doesn't she just wait?"

"Alison may well recover and even if she doesn't, if she marries Mark first he'll get the money. Also we've got to remember we're dealing with someone evil and malevolent here. This is not just for gain – she's taking a delight in causing the utmost suffering to her sister."

"Okay, maybe I'll buy that but how do you account for the other victims? How do they tie in with Lindsey Barnard? Take Mark Copley: presumably she's hoping to go off with him if Alison is out of the way, but he's received a death threat. It doesn't make sense!"

"I think that death threat could be a red herring. She may have been afraid that suspicion was falling on him and that was a way of diverting it; and it will also be a way of causing her sister further anguish – if Alison is living under the fear that her fiancée could be murdered at any moment."

"Mmm." Lacey pouted his fleshy lips and tapped his pen against them. "What about the others?"

"Who can tell? She could be harbouring a grudge for imagined slights that took place years ago. Mervyn Souster may have actually taught her – she finished her education locally. If she hadn't fallen out with Charles Todd she'd be about the only one from what we've gathered. Then there's Eileen Dewhurst; maybe she'd heard that she was thinking of selling up and thought Copley was going to lose out or maybe Miss Dewhurst refused to sell her pottery in her shop.

"Even if you're right – and don't think for one minute that you've convinced me – what proof have you got?"

"Nothing" admitted Roland, "but we've just got to dig around and come up with something."

"And in the meantime suppose she bumps off her sister?"

"Hopefully Alison is going into hospital for treatment. I'll check that with the doctor and then we must set up round the clock surveillance at the hospital; unobtrusive but an eye must be kept on all her visitors, especially Lindsey. I'll fix that up with the hospital authorities."

"What about Mark Copley – do you think he's safe?"

"We can't take the risk. She may have it in for him too if she thinks he prefers her sister to her. We'll have to provide protection for him too; keep watch on his flat and the antiques shop when he's there. He'll probably spend a lot of his time at the hospital with Alison which will make it easier to safeguard him."

"Okay, so we provide protection for them" said Lacey, "but for how long? This can't go on indefinitely. You think Lindsey Barnard is the culprit? Right, find me proof and I'm behind you one hundred percent, otherwise you're out on a limb."

"So where do we go from here? asked Mansfield a little later after Lacey had left.

"We're going to go to the Barnard's place and have a poke around."

"How are you going to do that – try and get a search warrant?"

"Christ no! I don't want to alert Lindsey to our suspicions. Until we've got some proof she mustn't know we suspect her. I'm sure we can think up some excuse for checking the premises – let her believe we're doing the same for all the households in Saxton."

"But what are we looking for?"

"Anything that could tie her in with any of the hoaxes. The Joker must have had a supply of stage blood and rope and then there's the typewriter that was used for those anonymous letters. Keep your eyes skinned and hope we strike lucky." "Do you want me in on this?" asked Evans.

"Perhaps we'll give you first spell at the hospital. Firbank confirmed when I rang him just now that Alison has been taken in."

Lindsey Barnard answered the door with a worried expression on her face.

"May we come in, Miss Barnard? I understand your sister is in hospital?"

"Yes . . . how did you know?"

"It is my business to know things like that. This is just a routine visit."

They followed her into the sitting room and she looked at them with a frown.

"What do you want?"

"We're checking out all the households in Saxton."

"What for?"

"Trying to find traces The Joker may have left behind. Obviously we're concentrating first on those people who have had a hoax played on them."

"But that wasn't here."

"I know, but the person behind the hoax came here – Alison's wig was stolen."

"Yes, I suppose so; but after all this time . . ."

"That's true, but as I said this is just a routine search. My Super won't be happy until I can assure him we've visited every house in the village."

"Where do you want to look?"

186

"We'll go round the house first and then check your outbuildings."

"Help yourself." She spoke in an off-hand manner but Roland noted the agitated tattoo she beat on the back of a chair with a nervous finger. He and Mansfield looked round the downstairs rooms, trying to make it look as casual as possible whilst not missing anything.

"Do you have to look in all the cupboards?" she asked as doors were opened and shut.

"You object?"

She shrugged. "Um . . . no, it's just that some of them are very untidy."

"That doesn't bother us. Perhaps you would rather not watch? I know it can be upsetting to see a stranger going through your belongings but I promise you we won't disarrange anything."

After that she hovered in doorways and waited on the stairs trying to look unperturbed but unable to conceal her anxiety. They found nothing of interest. The kitchen was well stocked with food and utensils and many of the cupboards in other rooms held pottery and painting gear and books and magazines. The only surprise were the two bedrooms occupied by the twins. One was very feminine, decorated in blue and pink, with flowery curtains and frills and flounces everywhere; the other had stark white walls with geometric design curtains, a black carpet and abstracts prints. Contrary to their expectations, the latter was Alison's room and the pastel boudoir Lindsey's. Both contained the clothes and toiletries and personal belongings they expected to see. There was nothing untoward in Lindsey's room but Roland was prepared for this. If she were The Joker she would hardly be likely to keep the props used in setting up the hoaxes and murders in her bedroom. They were more likely to strike lucky in a shed or garage. He remembered the anonymous letters that had been sent to Alison.

"Do you own a typewriter?"

"No. We keep thinking we ought to invest in a word processor and learn how to use it but I still do all my accounts and commercial correspondence by hand."

That was not conclusive one way or the others, thought Roland; it wouldn't be difficult to type out a couple of envelopes on someone else's machine. Aloud he said:

"Well, we've finished in here, we'll just have a look at your outbuildings."

The studio looked as if it had been unused for several days. The kiln was cold and the damp cupboard empty. There was shelving round two sides of the room containing pottery that had been biscuit fired, and pails of slip and glaze stood in a neat row on the floor. On another row of shelves behind the wheel were screw-top jars containing coloured powders. Roland bent closer to look.

"They're my oxides. I use them to get different colours," she explained seeing Roland's interest.

Colours? Dyes? Could a mixture like stage blood be made from these he wondered?

The Barnards' car was in the garage. It was a Ford Granada 2.01 Ghia, a powerful car for two young women and with a boot large enough to accommodate a body. It filled the space and it must have been a tight squeeze manoeuvring it in and out. The garden shed looked more promising. Besides the usual tools and implements there were piles of boxes and cartons lying about and tins of paint and cartons of fertilizer on the shelf that ran the length of one wall. On the wall opposite a couple of coils of rope hung from nails projecting from the planks. Roland caught Mansfield's eye and nodded imperceptibly at these.

Back in the house Roland explained to Lindsey the security arrangements that had been set-up in the hospital to safeguard Alison and she stared at him perplexed.

"Is it really necessary?"

"Better to be safe than sorry as my Super would say. What is the matter, sergeant?"

Mansfield was patting his pockets. "I've lost my pen, I think I must have dropped it in your shed, Miss – I'll just go and have a look."

Whilst he was gone Lindsey turned to his colleague.

"Inspector Roland, surely no-one could be so . . . so cruel as to do these horrible things."

"Someone has, Miss Barnard, and I intend finding out

who. Whoever it is has to be stopped and I am going to bring their macabre game to an end."

She shrunk back and gazed at him with haunted eyes. The expression of a guilty woman or one sickened by events? He didn't know.

Mansfield came back flourishing a pen.

"Here we are. Just as I thought – it was on the shed floor."

"Good. Well, we'll leave you in peace now, Miss Barnard, and move on to the next place."

"It's going to take you forever" she said, opening the front door.

"This is a murder enquiry. I have a large team of men at my disposal, we'll get through."

Back in the car Roland asked:

"Did you get it?"

"Yes." As the car turned the corner Mansfield produced a plastic bag from his pocket containing a short piece of rope. "It looks very similar to the one used to string up Charlie Todd."

"Excellent, we'll get it straight to the Lab. If if matches up we've got enough proof to pull her in."

CHAPTER 11

Alison Barnard stared up at the ceiling above her head. A crack ran diagonally across it from the corner to a point over her bed where it splintered into a myriad of tiny fissures like a dried up river bed. Yesterday, when she had been in the grip of a high fever this pattern of cracks had taken on a sinister dimension. It had looked like a spider's web and as she had tossed and twisted, drenched in sweat she had been afraid she was going to get caught up in it, be trapped and bound by sticky threads until she couldn't move and then the spider would come and pounce on her . . .

She shook her head, she had been delirious. Today the jagged line looked just what it was, a crack in the ceiling that told its own tale of a health service starved of funds and unable to keep up with running repairs in its own institutions. She still felt bound and immobile. It was because of the drip. She looked at the tube running from her chest up to the bag clamped to a stand beside the bed and sighed . . . She had felt so ill yesterday, her throat so sore that she couldn't bear to swallow so they had set up this drip pinning her to the bed.

She was glad she was in a room on her own and not in the general ward. It was quiet here and she didn't feel so much under the public gaze although there was someone sitting in the little ante-room. A policeman. That's right, she remembered now, that was why she had been moved into this private room. She had heard people talking round her yesterday; odd phrases had come and gone, something about police protection and surveillance and then she had been wheeled in here and had been dimly aware that everytime she looked through the glass panel in the door

190

someone was in attendance the other side. There was a man in there now. Not the red-haired young policeman who had been there before . . . he was rather nice . . . No, today it was an older, dark-haired man. . . . She dozed.

Footsteps echoing down the corridor awoke her. Mark came through the door carrying an enormous bunch of carnations. He smiled at her but she could tell instantly that something was wrong.

"How are you feeling?" He bent over the bed and kissed her and the smell of his after-shave enveloped her.

"Much better today. What lovely flowers."

"I'll put them on here for now and look for a vase later." He laid them on her bedside locker and sat on the bed, picking up one of her hands and cradling it in his.

"You certainly look better today, you were really grotty yesterday."

"I know." She studied him carefully. "What is the matter?"

"What do you mean?"

"Something's wrong. It's no good pretending otherwise, Mark. I know you too well."

He signed and flicked his ponytail back over his shoulder.

"Have you seen the paper today? Has the WRVS trolley been round yet?"

"No. Why?"

"I hoped I'd get here first and be able to break it to you before you read it for yourself."

"Read what? What's happened? Mark, what is it – you're frightening me."

"I suppose you'll have to know . . ."

"Know what?" She was thoroughly alarmed.

"I've had a hoax played on me and the Gazette has got hold of it and splashed it all over the front page."

"No! When? What was it?"

"Last week . . ."

"Why didn't you tell me?"

"I didn't want to worry you."

"What happened?"

He explained and she grasped his arm in distress.

191

"But you could be killed, shot at any moment! Some-one's picking us off one by one . . .! I'll be the next and then you! No – I'm to be last, aren't I? That's what that anonymous note said!"

"Shush, Allie, don't upset yourself. Nobody's going to get us – the police are guarding us now."

"The police – they're useless! Surely they could find out who has been giving the facts to the Press – then they'd know who did it."

"You'd think so, wouldn't you" he said bitterly.

"Does Lindsey know about the death threat to you?"

"Yes."

"You're ganging up on me!"

"No we're not. We didn't want to worry you unneces-sarily . . ."

"Unnecessarily? Do you think it would be easier if someone came up to me out of the blue and said 'your fiancée has been shot'?"

"Keep your voice down or you'll have that policeman in here. He'll think I'm doing for you . . ."

"Oh Mark . . ."

He put his arm round her and caressed her, staring defiantly at the policeman who had got to his feet and was watching with interest the scene that was taking place on the other side of the glass panel.

Lindsey Barnard backed out of the garage and left the car standing in the drive with the engine running whilst she got out and closed and locked the garage doors behind her. She was running on automatic pilot, performing these simple tasks by reflex action whilst her thoughts were engaged elsewhere in a running argument with herself inside her brain. What was she going to do? How much longer would it be before the police moved in? She was aware of their suspicions and knew that time was running out. She should have acted sooner, it was dangerous to have delayed so long, but she hadn't been able to bring herself to that final act of betrayal. She must do something now that Alison was in hospital . . . before she came out . . .

She got back in the car and manoeuvred out of the

192

gate. Those two detectives thought they had been clever yesterday but she had noticed the look they had exchanged then they had seen the coil of rope and she knew why the elder one had returned to the shed. After they had left she had gone back to the shed herself and looked at the rope hanging on the wall. She knew that it had been moved – it was suspended at a slightly different angle – and when she had looked closer she had seen where the end had been freshly cut. As she drove towards Felstone and the hospital she wondered how she was going to face Alison. It couldn't be today, could it? She did still have time?

Alison was lying on her back with her eyes closed when she reached her room at the hospital. At first she thought she was asleep but as she tiptoed to the bed her sister opened her eyes and stared at her accusingly.

"Why didn't you tell me?"

"Tell you *what?*"

"About Mark having a death threat!"

"How do you know that?" Lindsey sat down on the edge of the bed and dumped the bag of fruit she had brought on the counterpane.

"He told me."

"Mark's been here already this morning?"

"Yes, and he told me all about it."

"Why on earth did he do that? We agreed it would be best for you not to know."

"You agreed! I'm fed up with being treated like a child just because I'm ill! I had every right to know. I want to get out of here – I'm just a sitting duck!"

"Allie, you mustn't upset yourself – your temperature will soar again. You're safe in here, there's a policeman just outside the door."

"Do you really think that will stop The Joker? There could be poison in my food . . ."

"Are you managing to eat again? Good."

"Not yet, but maybe that's been tampered with." Alison indicated her drip. "Maybe there's poison seeping into my veins at this very minute . . ."

"You're being hysterical, please calm down, you mustn't dwell on it."

"There's someone else out there now!" She gestured to the ante-room from where they could hear voices murmuring in an undertone. Lindsey got up to have a better look.

"'They're changing the guard at Buckingham Palace.' Your copper-knob is taking over duty."

William Evans closed the door behind his colleague and walked over to the other door leading into Alison's room. For a few seconds he and Lindsey faced each other through the glass, then she moved aside and he raised his hand in greeting to the girl in the bed and went back to the chair. He searched through his pockets and produced a Waggon-Wheel which he unwrapped and devoured eagerly, wishing he had a paper to read to pass the time.

"Has the doctor been in to see you today?" said Alison, turning her attention back to her sister.

"Not yet, but the nurse said my temperature was almost back to normal."

"That's good. Look, I've got to go now. I'll pop back later – is there anything you want? Something to read?"

"I've got a book but I haven't felt like reading, I can't concentrate."

"Try and relax and have a good rest. Don't brood."

"What else is there to do?" asked Alison to the door closing behind her sister.

Outside, Lindsey tackled Evans.

"What exactly are you doing?"

"Doing, Miss?" Evans stuffed the biscuit wrapper back in his pocket and tried to look important. "I'm keeping an eye on your sister and vetting everyone who comes near her."

"Everyone?"

"Yes, everyone. She's in safe hands, don't worry."

"That's not what's worrying me, constable."

Back in the hospital car park Lindsey unlocked the car door, threw her handbag onto the back seat and subsided behind the wheel. As she fumbled for the ignition she noticed that her hands were trembling and she gripped them together tightly and fought to control her panic. Why in Heaven's name had Mark shot his mouth off to

Alison? Especially now when she was so poorly? Her first thought was to drive straight round to Mark's place and have it out with him but she quickly decided against this. She didn't trust herself face to face with him, she might give the game away. No, she'd go home and phone him from there. She turned the key in the ignition, put the car in gear and drove back through the hospital grounds. As soon as she was outside the gates she put her foot down and accelerated along the road leading to Saxton.

The sun had gone in and there was an almost greenish tinge to the sky ahead. To her left, where the river lay, the clouds were piling up; tumescent coils of gunmetal edged with copper, and above the roar of the engine she thought she heard the rumble of thunder. A storm was coming up with the tide. When she reached the house she left the car out in the road and as she hurried up the path she heard the phone ringing inside in the hall. She jabbed the key in the lock, flung open the door and snatched up the receiver. The caller was Mark.

"Hi, I've just rung to find out if you're going up to the hospital this morning?"

"I've already been, I've just come from there and I was about to ring you."

"Is something wrong?"

"Wrong! WHY did you tell her about the hoax played on you? I thought we had agreed she shouldn't be told?"

"Keep your rag. I rushed over there as soon as I saw the paper – I thought it would be better coming from me."

"What paper? What are you talking about?"

"Haven't you seen the Gazette this morning?"

"No, what about it?"

"It's all in there – details about the hoax played on me. The Joker's got front page coverage again."

"Oh no!"

"Oh yes. Was she very upset when you got there?"

"She was angry with me, with both of us, for keeping her in the dark, but underneath I think she was very disturbed. At least the police are keeping an eye on her."

"Yes, she should be safe in there."

"What about you Mark?"

"Me? Oh I've still got my shadow. I can see him parked outside now keeping a watch on my comings and goings. I don't know who's more embarrassed, him or me."

"But he's doing his job, you should feel grateful."

"That the police are seen to be doing their job? It's cosmetic, Lindsey. If someone intends taking me out with a gun, a solitary policeman idling in his car is not going to stop them."

There was a silence from the other end of the line and Mark hurried on: "Oh Christ, now I've upset you!"

"Are you going to visit her again today?"

"I'm going back later this morning."

"This morning?"

"Yes, I've found a book I thought she might like to look at, it's about the Arts and Crafts Movement and there are some very good colour plates."

"She shouldn't have a lot of visitors, she'll get tired . . ."

"Yes, Nanny. I think I'm one visitor she does want to see, don't you?"

After Mark had rung off Lindsey looked for the morning's newspaper. She couldn't find it, in fact she had no recollection of it coming through the letterbox. Perhaps the paperboy had left her out by mistake. She put the door on the latch and hurried back down the path intending to ask her neighbours if she could borrow their copy, but as she reached the gate she saw the paperboy zig-zagging up the road delivering the Gazette from a bulging sack.

"You're late" she accused as he drew nearer, "did you oversleep?"

"'Taint my fault." He skidded to a halt beside her. "They've only just come. You're lucky – this is the first road on my round." He thrust the paper into her hands and wobbled off and Lindsey returned to her house.

"We're in business." Roland collected Mansfield from the CID General Room where he was laboriously using two fingers on a keyboard and squinting suspiciously at the report appearing on the monitor screen. "That sample of rope is the same as that used to string up Todd. The Lab is definite that they are an exact match."

"Lindsey Barnard – well, well, well. The loving sister!"

"It's not proof that she *is* The Joker but it's enough to pull her in for questioning."

"She'll have a job to talk herself out of that."

"We've got to put the pressure on and hope we can trip her up and get a confession. Go and pick her up, Pat, and bring her in. You can put the fear of God into her but don't let on about the evidence of the rope. I want to spring that on her when we're grilling her."

"She may be at the hospital visiting Alison."

"She can't do for her sister in there. Evans and the others have had strict instructions to monitor every visitor closely and to confiscate any chocolates or fruit etc. taken in to her."

"If William Evans is collecting chocies he's going to pig out."

"Not now I've explained he'd be the modern equivalent of the King's taster."

The first drops of rain were falling as Mansfield crossed the yard and collected his car; plump, heavy drops that almost sizzled as they pocked the scorched ground and scattered dust. Out in the streets people were hurrying to reach their destinations, scarcely able to believe that the weather was breaking at last. He was about half way to Saxton when a car shot out of a side road ahead and almost clipped his bumper as it crossed the carriageway and headed back the way he had come. He caught a glimpse of a set white face haloed in dark curls behind the wheel and slammed on the brakes. Surely it was Lindsey Barnard? He checked in the mirror; the car was a blue Ford Granada. Fortunately the road was wide at this spot and he did an illegal U-turn and hurried after it. As soon as he was close enough to read the number plate he knew it was the Barnards' car and it was definitely Lindsey driving. Where was she going? He followed at a discreet distance. Either she was a very bad driver or her mind was elsewhere. She progressed erratically, taking corners dangerously and alternating bursts of speed with periods when she seemed to dither and veer precariously about the road. She was leading him back to Felstone and when she reached the outskirts she turned down the dock road that skirted the centre of the town. She was going to the hospital, he realized, perhaps even intending harm to her sister right now. He shortened the distance between them.

The storm that had been threatening all morning still held off. The preliminary shower had petered out but the clouds still hung low in the sky, pot-bellied with their burden of rain and growling ominously. Instead of taking the road that led past the park to the hospital, Lindsey Barnard turned right, heading back towards the centre, and Mansfield found himself retracing the route he had taken a short while earlier, only going in the opposite direction. He'd be back at HQ soon – where could she be going? To his astonishment she hesitated when she reached the Police Station and then swung into the car park. He followed her. She drew up in one of the allocated spaces and killed the engine, then she got out of the car and stared up at the building uneasily.

Mansfield drew up next to her. It was too bad if Chief Inspector Dickins turned up to claim his parking space. He, Mansfield was apprehending a criminal, that took priority.

"Miss Barnard?" She swung round and a look of relief crossed her face.

"Oh, sergeant, I'm glad it's you; I must see your boss – Inspector Roland."

"He wants to question you. I was coming to collect you."

"Question me? You mean he suspects too and wants to talk it over? Well, I've got proof now, real proof." Mansfield looked at her oddly. "I'm not sure what you mean, Miss, but yes, you've got a lot of talking to do. Come with me."

Once inside the building, Roland was informed of their presence and soon joined them in one of the interview rooms. He nodded curtly to he and when she was seated he activated the tape recorder, detailing the date and time, her name and his and Mansfield's names and ranks as the two police officers conducting the interview.

"Miss Barnard was on her way to see you, sir" said Mansfield woodenly.

"Yes, I don't know why you're treating me like a suspect" said Lindsey Barnard reproachfully.

"Because you are a suspect, and in very serious trouble."

"I don't understand . . .?"

"Don't waste my time, Miss Barnard, I know that you are The Joker and I have proof of that fact."

She gaped at him. "This is crazy! I don't know what you mean!" Roland leaned across the table towards her. "A piece of rope was removed from your garage yesterday by Sergeant Mansfield here. It has been tested by our Forensic experts and proved beyond doubt that it came from the same length of rope that was used to string up Charles Todd in Holgate Park. It's no use trying to deny it."

"Yes . . . No . . . I *knew* you'd seen it and it *was* mine. It's hung in the garage for as long as I can remember but he took it. He thought I hadn't noticed but I had . . ."

"He?"

"Mark . . . Mark Copley . . ." The name was dragged reluctantly from here and she had gone very pale.

"Trying to implicate someone else is not going to help your case. You are . . ." She interrupted him. "I feel as if I'm going mad! You've got it all wrong!" She gripped the edge of the table and spoke despairingly. "You've got to believe me! You've got to do something or it could be too late!" Roland said nothing and she continued with mounting hysteria:

"How do I get through to you? I'm not trying to save my skin! It's horrible . . . I couldn't believe it either . . . I've had my suspicions for some time but I couldn't . . . wouldn't believe it, but now I know it's true . . ."

"What are you trying to say?"

"Mark Copley is The Joker . . ." Her voice had shrunk to a whisper and she grew even paler. The freckles stood out on her white face like a dalmatian's spots and there was dreadful pain lurking at the back of her eyes.

Listening to her, Roland knew that she was speaking the truth as she saw it. Whatever the real facts were Lindsey Barnard truly believed that Mark Copley was The Joker. He changed tactics and asked quietly:

"Have you proof of this?"

"Yes, yes I have. This morning I was forced to stop behaving like an ostrich, hiding my head in cloud cuckoo land . . ." She paused and to Roland the mixed metaphors lent sincerity to what she was struggling to say. She lifted her head and stared straight at him.

"Inspector, have you seen today's Felstone Gazette?"

When does a busy inspector working on a case have time to read the morning papers, he thought.

"No."

"I think you should." She rummaged in her handbag and produced a battered copy of the newspaper. She unfolded it and laid it on his desk so that the front page was facing him. The headlines bored into him and he ran his eyes down the columns that followed after.

"I don't know how the Press got hold of this but I fail to see what it has to do with Mark Copley."

"Mark went to see Alison early this morning. He told her what was in the paper and said he wanted to break it to her before she read it for herself and got upset."

"Well?"

"This was at nine o'clock."

"Yes?"

She leaned forward and spoke earnestly. "The Gazette wasn't published until after ten. After I'd seen Alison in hospital I went home and looked for my copy to read. It hadn't arrived and then the paperboy called and said they'd only just come through. I rang the Gazette offices and they confirmed that there had been a hold-up. There was a complete computer blackout during the night and the presses didn't start rolling until much later than usual."

Roland nodded at Mansfield who got up quietly and went out of the room, then he turned back to the distraught woman opposite him.

"Perhaps Copley got to hear about it from a contact at the Gazette? A great many people there would know what was appearing on the front page; the News Editor, Chief Sub, the reporter who actually wrote it, apart from those on the production side."

"I'm quite sure Mark doesn't know anyone there and

why should he tell her he'd read it if he'd only been told? The only way he could have known what was going to appear . . ." she waved a hand at the newspaper. ". . . is if he had given the information to the Press himself, and if he did that . . . then . . . he must be The Joker, mustn't he?"

She was staring tragically at Roland when Mansfield returned.

"It's a fact" said the sergeant, "A gremlin got in the works last night. Someone fed a dodgy disk into the main frame and the computer was down for several hours. No member of the public saw a copy of the paper until after ten this morning."

"Miss Barnard, you said you had been suspicious of Copley for some time; what did you mean?" asked Roland.

"Little things that were meaningless on their own but when you put them together . . ." she shrugged. "It's hard to explain . . ."

"Please try."

"Well . . . all the people who had hoaxes played on them had angered him at some time. Nothing serious, but I know he remembered and resented things . . . he didn't forget . . . then he always seemed so well-informed on everything that happened." She ran a hand through her hair and fidgeted with her curls. Her voice sunk lower. "It was after Eileen Dexter was killed that I really began to wonder . . . he was so . . . so untouched by it. Oh, he made the right noises, but they didn't ring true. Underneath he didn't care and he should have done – she had taken him on and been very good to him . . . almost like a surrogate grandmother . . ."

"Did your sister know of your suspicions?"

"No, of course not. They weren't really suspicions . . . more feelings. Anyway, I started to check on him. You check alibis, don't you? Did you check Mark's?"

"Miss Barnard, I . . ."

She cut in on him. "I discovered he often hadn't been where he said he was. There were times when he was supposed to be with Alison but I knew she'd been feeling unwell and he'd left early . . . I think he was around, unaccounted for . . . each time someone was murdered . . ."

"Why didn't you come to us with your suspicions before?"

"I wasn't sure . . . it was all so . . . so unbelievable. You wouldn't have believed me . . . you'd have thought I was hysterical . . . round the bend . . ."

"Why should Copley want to harm his fiancée?"

"She refused to marry him. She said it wouldn't be fair . . . that he mustn't be tied to an invalid . . . she thought she was doing the right thing, but . . ."

"He saw his chances of wedding an heiress slipping through his fingers?"

"Yes." Her voice was so low that Roland could hardly hear it.

"So he turned his attentions elsewhere?"

"I . . . I don't know . . ."

"I think you do, Miss Barnard. I don't think you've told me everything."

"Please don't ask me anymore . . . I can't tell you . . ."

"I think you must. Surely you see that?"

She stared at him wretchedly and Mansfield took pity on her.

"You're sweet on him too, aren't you?" he asked.

There was a long pause and then she nodded.

"Are you having an affair with Mark Copley?" asked Roland. She was horrified. "No, of course I'm not! I wouldn't cheat on my sister . . ."

"Then what are we talking about?"

"We're . . . we're just attracted to each other . . ."

"Who made a play for whom?"

"I don't know what you mean . . ."

"Oh, come on, Lindsey, who made the running?"

"Alright, I'll tell you what happened." There was a hint of defiance in her voice and a slight flush tinged her pale cheeks. "I was attracted to Mark. Wouldn't any girl be?" Well, yes, Roland could see her point. There was something louche about Copley, what would once have been called Bohemian, and he could understand two well-brought up young women from a comfortable middle-class background being excited and intrigued by someone of that ilk.

". . . I tried to fight against it" she continued, "and I certainly didn't try and queer Alison's pitch, but gradually I realized that he felt the same about me. We didn't do anything! Just the odd embrace when our feelings got the better of us . . . but there was never any question of Mark splitting up with Allie. He was adamant about that and so was I. We couldn't do it to her. Anyway, I did know that Mark really cared for me and that he was only standing by Alison because he couldn't bring himself to break the engagement – under the circumstances. I convinced myself that if . . . when she got better, we'd be able to sort it out and she would understand . . ."

"So what ended the honeymoon? When did you fall out of love and decide to shop him?"

"Who said I had fallen out of love? Oh God! Is it possible to still love someone even when you know they're evil and have committed murder?" she burst out.

"Oh yes, we come across it frequently in our line of business."

"I've been feeling so guilty and mixed-up and when these hoaxes started it was almost as if my behaviour had activated some dreadful suppressed malignancy in the community . . . like letting the genie out of a bottle . . . do you understand?" Roland nodded.

"Mark didn't feel the same way. He was excited by the incidents. Oh, he made out he was horrified by the one played on Alison but I could tell he was taking a morbid interest in events. Whereas I was horrified by what seemed to be the community falling apart, he was taking a prurient delight in it – although he tried to cover it up. I started to wonder . . . and . . . and I've told you the rest . . ."

There was a sudden violent clap of thunder and the rain descended, drumming against the windows, cascading down the glass. She flinched and snapped back to the present.

"This is wasting time. You've got to stop him – he's going back to the hospital this morning."

"How do you know?"

"He phoned me just before I left. He told me he was

203

taking a book in for her but I think he was really checking on whether I was going to be there or not."

"Your sister is under surveillance, there is a policeman in attendance all the time; Copley is not going to harm her."

"Aren't you going to arrest him after what I've told you?"

"He is certainly going to be investigated." Roland spoke into the tape-recorder officially ending the interview and switched it off. He and Mansfield got up and she sprang to her feet.

"You're going to the hospital? I will come too."

"You will not, Miss Barnard" said Roland firmly. "You will stay here. I'll get a WPC to keep you company and fetch you some coffee."

The two men got drenched as they dashed across the yard.

"Bloody hell!" said Mansfield as they scrambled into the car. "If this keeps up we'll need a boat not a car!"

William Evans shuffled his feet and stared longingly at the door separating him and Alison Barnard. It was ridiculous, his being on one side and she on the other. He was bored out of his mind and she must be too, just lying there with nothing to do. If he was in there with her they could maybe play cards; gin rummy or crib or a board game.

God it was quiet in here! You couldn't believe you were in a busy hospital. As if to contradict his thoughts, lightning flashed through the room and almost simultaneously thunder crashed overhead and the rain started. He got up and looked out of the window but the view outside was obscured by the rain sheeting down. They were in the old original part of the hospital, in what had once been the private wing. The rooms were pokey with high ceilings and out-of-date fittings and were connected to each other by a maze of narrow, twisting corridors. It had made sense, when the authorities were considering closing down wards to economize, to shut down this section of the hospital and it was why Alison had been brought here. She could be kept in seclusion in a room of her own with a guard outside without it exciting attention. To Evans mind, it was too isolated. Surely she'd be safer in the main part of the hospital, although the hustle and bustle of the busy wards was only the other side of the swing doors.

It was almost as if she had been forgotten here; out of sight, out of mind, as Lacey would say. True, nurses came in at regular intervals to check their patient; one had been in a short while ago and taken her pulse and blood pressure.

Phew! It was hot in here and the storm barrage outside made it seem even more claustrophobic and airless. What wouldn't he give for a beer; a pint of Tolly's best and something to eat with it. Fish and chips or a nice steak and kidney pie . . .

He was brought out of his reverie by the sound of footsteps approaching along the corridor. The door opened and Mark Copley stood framed in the doorway. He beckoned to Evans.

"Your boss – the inspector – wants to see you. He sent me to tell you."

Evans scrambled to his feet and fingered the radio in his pocket suspiciously.

"You're out of radio contact." Copley had seen his action. "The storm. He said it was urgent."

"Where is he?"

"In the car park near the gate."

Copley was wearing a navy kagool from which the water streamed, forming a pool on the threshold. His black hair was plastered to his scalp and hanging down his back in a rat's tail.

"I'm not supposed to leave her."

"It's alright, I'll take over." Copley moved into the room and started to unzip his kagool. "It sounded like an emergency, you'd better hurry!"

"Okay, if you're sure. Hell, I haven't got a jacket. You say he's at the main gate?"

"No, he's waiting at the back entrance over by the maintenance buildings."

"What's he doing there? I'm going to get soaked to the skin. I hope it won't take long, if you'll just hang on till I get back?"

"Of course, it's no trouble. I've come to see her anyway."

He was hanging his kagool over the back of the chair as Evans hurried out of the room.

Alison drifted in and out of sleep. She was dimly aware of the storm crackling overhead and the lightning flooding the room at irregular intervals. When it went dark she thought at first it was just the aftermath of a particularly spectacular streak of lightning, then she thought the storm had caused a power cut. She hadn't heard the click as someone reached out and snapped up the switch. She didn't hear the door open either but she suddenly sensed that someone was in the room with her. It must be her policeman come to check that she was alright . . . she smiled to herself as she dozed off . . .

Something alerted her, she didn't know what. She snapped open her eyes. It wasn't as dark as she had thought; a grey light filled the room, filtering through the curtain of rain outside. Someone was bending over her. She looked up and met the eyes boring into hers, and then she knew. It was all written there in that terrible stare that locked with hers: the hatred, the malice, the madness . . .

She tried to get up and a hand pressed her back, a hand that was cold and clammy like a band of steel on her shoulder.

"It's no use struggling Allie, it's a waste of time." The hand released its pressure and reached out to the drip. With a violent movement it was jerked out of her body and the spasm shuddered through her chest.

"What are you going to do?" she gasped, her voice reduced to a croak.

"You're going for a little ride, Allie. It's the last one you'll take."

She felt the brake being released on the bed and then they were trundling out of the door. She was paralysed by fear and panic. The corridor was a black tunnel closing in on her, the walls pulsating to the accompaniment of the peals of thunder. She must do something; try and attract attention. She opened her mouth to call out and the voice said softly and menacingly:

"It's no good screaming. There's no-one to hear you. We are quite alone."

CHAPTER 12

Roland swung the car in through the hospital gates.

"We'll just check here to see if he is visiting Alison; if not we'll go over to Saxton and pick him up."

The rain was still coming down in torrents and sheets of water lay in the car park forming lakes rather than puddles. Few people were about but Mansfield noticed a tall man dodging amongst the parked cars, his ginger hair darkened by the rain.

"Isn't that Evans over there?

"I thought he was on bedside duty this morning?" Roland sounded his horn and the man looked up and ran across to them.

"What are you doing out here?" demanded Roland.

"Sorry, sir, he said the back entrance but I thought he'd got it wrong."

"What are you talking about?" He rolled the window down further and rain sprayed into the car.

"Copley said you wanted to see me – that you were in the car park and it was urgent."

"And you fell for it!" Roland balled his fist and smashed it down on the steering column; then he revved up the engine and flung the car towards the nearest entrance. Evans stumbled along behind and caught up with them as they tumbled out of the car.

"What's happened? What's up?" he demanded.

"You've only left her with The Joker" snarled Roland, racing up the steps.

"What!?"

"Your head's going to roll for this. It's back on the beat for you, sonny" said Mansfield pounding along after Roland with Evans in his wake. As they swept through the building, he put the Welshman in the picture.

"How long ago did you leave them?" snapped Roland, pausing beside the lift and then deciding it was quicker to go up the stairs.

"About seven or eight minutes. I'm sure he wasn't concealing a weapon about his person" he added, and was rewarded with a look from his superior that should have curdled his blood.

By the time they arrived on the corridor that led to Alison's room they had collected a following; several nurses were hard on their heels. Roland reached the room first and flung open the door. The room was empty. Only a bedside locker knocked askew and the drip leaking its contents across the floor remained.

"Where the hell is she? The bed's gone too! Surely you can't move a bed about this place without someone noticing?" He glared at the nearest nurse who was gasping in distress.

"He can't have taken her far – how many more rooms are there along this corridor?"

They rushed through every doorway, snapping on lights to reveal empty cubicles and deserted beds.

"What's through there?" They had reached the end of the corridor and Roland pointed to the door they could see through the swing doors,

"It's the old sluice room" said one of the nurses.
The door was locked but there was the sound of movement from inside.

"Get it open!" ordered Roland, and Mansfield and Evans hurled themselves at it. At the second attempt the wood splintered and they burst into the room. The bed took up nearly the entire room, jammed up against the sinks, and on it lay Alison Barnard, a pillow over her face.

Roland snatched the pillow away and to his horrified eyes she looked exactly like the waxwork that had lain on the bank in Holgate Wood; completely lifeless. The noise they had heard had been made by Mark Copley forcing his way out of the window. At the moment they erupted into the room he slipped through the gap and only his hand, still grasping the sill, could be seen. With one wild look at the girl on the bed, Evans sprang after him.

Whilst a nurse bleeped for the Crash Team, Evans grabbed at Copley's arm and tried to yank him back into the room. Copley had swung sideways and got his feet onto the old fire escape that ran from the next door room. He resisted the detective's pull, gaining purchase on the slippery metal rungs as Evans tugged. Evans snarled in frustration and, still keeping a firm grip on the arm, he squeezed his bulk through the window and crashed down on the other man. For a few seconds both men sprawled on the narrow landing temporarily winded, then the fight began in earnest. They rolled about the confined space locked in furious combat. Mansfield saw what was happening and hurried next door and pushed open the door leading onto the fire escape.

Copley was fighting for his freedom and he fought dirty, kicking and biting his opponent. But Evans was bigger and fired by revenge. After a tense few minutes when they crashed and slammed across the slippery metal plates, Evans gradually got the upper hand. He managed to get a grip on Copley's ponytail and he yanked his head up and dragged him through the door where Mansfield snapped the handcuffs on him. As they rolled him over Copley laughed.

"You're too late! The Joker bows out. My task is completed!" Evans went berserk and started to smash the other man with his fists and Mansfield hauled him off.

"Stop it you fool! Do you want to face a murder charge too?"

The Crash Team had arrived with the resuscitation trolley and Roland watched as a nurse passed an airway into Alison Barnard's mouth. The last thing he saw, as she was wheeled away surrounded by doctors and medics, was the nurse squeezing the ambu bag held above her, forcing the air into the corpse-like figure lying white and still on the bed.

"DC Evans deserted his post? And left her lying there with The Joker? I can't believe I'm hearing this!" Lacey paced up and down the room like a marauding elephant.

"He thought he was leaving her with the one person with

whom she would be safe" said Roland, who was presenting his case to the superintendent. "Our suspicions were centred on Lindsey Barnard; as far as he knew, Copley wasn't in the frame at all."

"How did he manage to wheel her out of her room into another part of the hospital without being caught? It doesn't say much for hospital security."

"He only took her a little further down the same corridor."

"But why bother to do that? He could easily have snuffed her out where she lay, surely?"

"That would have been too tame. He wanted to build up the tension and wring every ounce of drama out of the situation."

"So he trundles her around in her hospital bed – damn clumsy contraptions they are – and nobody saw or heard anything?"

"Events conspired to help him. There had been an emergency in the far end of the nearby ward and the medical staff were all occupied with that and then, of course, the thunder covered any noise he may have made."

The climax of the storm had coincided with the last act of The Joker. There was a phrase to cover this sort of occurence, wasn't there? thought Roland. He searched in his memory and dredged it up . . . pathetic fallacy . . . that was it . . .

"Have you got enough evidence to nail him for the other murders?" said Lacey.

"I don't need evidence, he's confessed – if you can call it a confession. Boasting would be nearer the mark. He couldn't wait to put us in the picture as to how clever he had been. He thinks he's won because he carried out all the threats as planned. The only thing that's likely to puncture his arrogance is if he doesn't get full coverage in the Press or if Alison Barnard recovers!"

"I thought you said they'd saved her?"

"They revived her but this is not going to help her chance of a full recovery – she's a very ill young woman indeed."

Roland was re-living the harrowing time he had spent at the hospital after Mansfield and Evans had been dispatched

211

back to the Station in charge of the prisoner. He had hung around outside the cubicle whilst the Crash Team had gone into action. He could only guess at what was going on on the other side of the curtains, what drama was taking place, as he heard the snapped instructions from the doctors and the unidentified noises. They had brought Alison back from the very verge of death and she was now in Intensive Care. The first thing he had done when he had got back was to send Lindsey up to the hospital in a police car.

"How did he get away with it for so long?"

"With cunning and luck and the audacity to grab any chance that offered."

"The defence will plead insanity" said Lacey in digust, "but he's not mad, is he?"

"Not as you and I understand it; just evil and very wily."

"So what made him tick?"

"It all goes back to his childhood" said Roland and was rewarded by a snort from Lacey.

"Don't give me that Freudian crap!"

Roland shrugged. "His parents were killed when he was very young and he was brought up by his grandmother. I gather she had no love for him and only gave him a home out of a sense of duty. She kept him on a very tight rein and he resented the lack of freedom and affection. When she died he was boarded out with various people whilst he finished his education. Believe it or not, he actually lived with the Souster family for a short time."

"The first victim."

"But not murdered by him, that's definite. However, Copley was jealous of his loving, close-knit family and then, according to him, Souster blocked his ambitions to go to university. I think what probably happened was that Souster didn't think he was suited to further education and tried to dissuade him, but Copley took it wrong and felt he was ill-done by and brooded and blew it up out of all proportion."

"So what about the other victims? How did they get in his bad books?"

"It was a similar thing with Charlie Todd. Copley wanted

to play in the local cricket team but Todd turned him down and Copley took it as a slight and thought he had been passed over because he hadn't a public school background. With Eileen Dexter it was even more unbelievable. She took him on and trained him but he resented the fact that she gave the orders and was upset because she wouldn't let him expand the business into selling craft work. She had hinted to him that she would leave the business to him, but then he heard rumours that she was thinking of retiring and selling up so he really had it in for her.

"Fair enough, but what about Alison Barnard? Surely he must have loved her – as capable as someone like that is of loving anyone – to have got engaged to her?"

Roland shrugged. "Reading between the lines, he latched onto her because she was so very different a sort of person from Tina Fairbrother, the girl he went out with before, but after a while the attraction started to pall. Then she became unwell and he seems to think she became deliberately ill to spite him! He discovered that she had money and when she refused to marry him because of her illness, he turned his attentions to her sister who would inherit. Lindsey made it easy for him – he bowled her over – and he knew when Alison died he would make it with her sister, but Alison refused to die. She was responding to treatment and he could see himself being tied to her for ever and by now any liking he had had for her had turned to loathing."

"And he plots to scrub out all these people he's taken against?" said Lacey. "If it wasn't true it would be unbelievable!"

I'm sure that, originally, he didn't intend killing them. It just appealed to his macabre sense of humour to plot the hoaxes like murder blueprints. There is a large collection of old crime fiction in Eileen Dewhurst's shop – he looked after that side of the business – and I think he read so many and got so hooked on the sort of bizarre scenarios that Agatha Christie and the like used to cook up that he had difficulty in differentiating between fact and fiction. We're talking about a severe personality disorder kept tightly under control for years. Possibly if Mervyn Souster

213

hadn't been killed it would have gone no further, but as McNalty said, his death was the trigger that tipped him over the edge."

"So our shrink got it right for once; I'm glad he's earned his inflated fee!"

"From then on he played it for real" finished Roland, ignoring Lacey's remarks and wondering, as he often did, why it was he found himself talking in clichés whenever he had a session with the superintendent.

"What about Tina Fairbrother's death? Did he have a hand in that?"

"Yes, he's admitted it. He pushed her under the bus because he thought she had rumbled him."

"How come?"

"Well, this is only his side of the story – we shall never know how true it is with her being dead – but apparently he slipped up when he set up the supposed hoax on himself. He used a charcoal stick he had taken from the Barnards's studio to draw the figure on the ground and he threw it under the nearby hedge intending to retrieve it later, but Tina noticed it before he could do so and he thought she recognised where it had come from."

"Didn't you pick up on it?"

"No, it wasn't there when we looked around. He must have palmed it at an opportune moment. Anyway, I don't know why he thought this crayon would lead her to him, but the next day when he was at the Barnards' he saw her coming towards the house and he panicked and thought she was going to blow the whistle on him so he decided she had to be silenced. He dogged her footsteps for the rest of the morning and when she was caught up in the traffic in High Street he saw his opportunity and shoved her in the path of a bus."

"So he snuffed her out just like that."

"She was a marked woman anyway. He had already designated her as another victim – as I said, she had been his girlfriend at one time and after she threw him over he harboured a grudge against her – but he had to get rid of her before he had a chance to plan a hoax and death for her. He is very annoyed about that." Roland spoke drily.

"He shows no compunction at all, only anger that he was stampeded into an impromtu action." He leaned back and tapped his fingers on the arm of his chair. "So there you have it."

"You can't leave it there! How did he manage to carry out three – nearly four murders right under our noses!"

"He took incredible risks and grabbed the opportunities offered. He'd been watching Charlie Todd for some time and he knew about the Rave because he'd got an invitation. He knew Todd was on his own that evening and he killed him just as we surmised. He dumped the body in the hedge at the bottom of Todd's garden and went back later on and picked it up in the Volvo. He drove to Holgate Park, strung it up in the shed, parked the car a long way off and went back and joined the Rave. Nobody saw him and he made sure, when the police raided it, that he was seen and questioned so that he would have an alibi. He'd previously helped himself to a piece of the rope he had seen hanging in the Barnards' shed."

"What about Eileen Dexter?"

"That was easy. He pretended that Anthea Campbell-Haigh had rung up and and asked her to go over that evening to the Lodge to look at some pictures she had picked up. Copley offered to walk over with her. They took the footpath through the park and when they got near the lake he bashed her over the head with a handy branch of wood, pushed her into the lake and held her under until she died."

"But how could he be sure no-one else would be in the park?"

"He was playing it by ear. If there had been other people about he would have aborted his plans and tried again another time."

"And I suppose he set up the hoax on himself to put us off the scent?"

"Yes, he thought if he was marked out as one of The Joker's victims we wouldn't suspect him of being the instigator. Again, he carefully chose his moment. He'd worked out exactly what he was going to do but he needed witnesses and he put his plan into action when he saw Tina

Fairbrother in the lane. It was a bonus when he saw a way of implicating Stewart Carson too, especially as he knew we were suspicious of Carson. When he saw him walking his dog nearby he hurriedly set it in motion; drawing the figure in the courtyard, leaving the toy gun nearby and providing a shot. That, by the way, was a firework!"

"I still don't understand why you didn't get on to him sooner, why you wasted so much time on this Stewart Carson."

"Because he always seemed to be on the spot when something happened and he behaved like a guilty man. We wasted time over that business with his dog, but then things began to look black for Lindsey Barnard. When I discovered she was not Alison's twin sister I realized she had a motive for wanting her out of the way – the oldest motive in the world: greed – and from various snippets people had let drop I believed she had crossed swords with the other victims at some time in the past. I thought she had set up the hoax on Copley to stop us suspecting him, and it would have been easy for her to have sent those anonymous letters to her sister."

"Yes, what was the point of them?"

"Copley was just trying to cause Alison the utmost suffering before he worked up to the great finale. It was quite fiendish, and he shows no remorse at all; and, of course, he's going to get all the publicity he could dream of when he comes up for trial."

"I suppose this craving for publicity is why he leaked his hoax to the Press, but he misjudged the moment, didn't he?"

"Yes said Roland shortly. He didn't want to dwell on what would have happened had the newspaper been published normally. It had been a lucky fluke that printing had been delayed on the one day that Copley had been sure the Gazette would carry headlines about the further exploits of The Joker. If Copley hadn't jumped the gun by telling Alison. If Lindsey hadn't been suspicious and checked and then come to them . . . If they had arrived at the hospital only a few minutes later . . . It was all ifs . . . The case had been solved by sheer chance, not through the investigative skills of him and his team . . .

"You haven't come out of this very well, have you James? said Lacey.

Summer had given way to autumn and whilst Mark Copley awaited trial, the inhabitants of Saxton tried to come to terms with the results of his actions. Roland had seen the proliferation of For Sale boards in the village but had also noted that most of these were on the new development' or on renovated property. The commuter belt had been relatively untouched by events but it was this section of the community that had taken fright and was stampeding to leave the area.

The Saxton Pottery was still open but Lindsey Barnard had confided in him that she would probably move to another part of Suffolk. She hadn't said when but Roland knew that she meant afterwards. After Alison had won or lost her battle against leukaemia and the way things were going it looked horribly as if she were losing it. She had had her final course of chemotheraphy but the disease, which had been on hold, was creeping back, insidiously invading her body. Would this have happened anyway, wondered Roland, or had the trauma and suffering she had undergone lessened her chances of a cure? Her only hope was a bone marrow transplant.

Simon had spent several weeks on the course in Scotland and when he returned he seemed to have matured in mind as well as body. He was now nearly as tall as his step-father and had filled out so that he no longer looked a gawky teenager. He confessed the course had been hard but that he had enjoyed it and was now in his first term in the Lower Sixth.

Patrick Mansfield had met his future son-in-law and hoped he wouldn't be. He was having a moan about it to Roland in the latter's office one wet, early October morning.

"What's wrong with him?" asked Roland, rather enjoying the fact that someone else was having problems with their family.

"He's just a kid" said Mansfield. "Oh, a nice enough lad, but nowhere near ready for marriage. It's ridiculous. I can't think why Jean encourages it."

"She's in favour then?"

"She reckons if we protest it will only make Jane all the more bent upon going through with it."

"She's probably right. Jane has always been a determined young woman, hasn't she?"

"She's an obstinate, pig-headed wench" said her father gloomily. "Who'd have children? Thank God she goes back to University this week. I don't know which is worse: having her moping about at home because she's parted from her precious Jeremy, or having him staying with us and falling over the two of them, all lovey-dovey, at every turn. I don't even get away from it here – there's Evans moping around like a love-sick calf all the time."

"Talk of the devil – he's now coming across the yard" said Roland looking out of the window. "He looks pretty grim, I hope nothing has happened."

William Evans was pale beneath his shock of red hair and there was a set look on his face.

"Alison Barnard? Oh Christ . . .!"

A few minutes later Evans burst into the office without knocking. Roland raised his eyebrows sarcastically but the young constable didn't notice.

"They've found a donor! The Anthony Nolan Trust!" he announced, and as the two men looked blank he continued in excitement: "It's a bone marrow transplant register – they've got someone on their books who is a perfect match with Alison!"

"That's marvellous. Will it do the trick?"

"All sorts of things could still go wrong but it's her only chance."

"Well, let's hope it works. You've got some leave owing, haven't you? Why don't you take it? Things are slack at the moment."

After Evans had rushed out again Mansfield turned to his colleague. "Whose benefit is that for I wonder? His or ours?"

218